Adventure the Moon

The Kirk Rogers Series: Book One

by

C. J. Boyle

ISBN-13: 978-1545194645
Copyright © 2017 C. J. Boyle
All Rights Reserved

Contact: cjboyle2010@comcast.net (985)248 - 9655

Special Thanks:

This book started off as something I was just writing for fun and never intended to publish. But it took shape and became something I wanted to share. Special thanks to Will Thimes for editing my book and finding my many, many errors. I appreciate your effort very much. Also, Giovanni D. Lorusso, Dana Ritz, Schenda Van Eeden, Ron Balicki, The Wolfpack, & Bren Foster. Without your inspiration and valued feedback, this book wouldn't have taken shape at all. I also would like to thank my 'superfan' Françoise Carton Mougel. I'm truly blessed to have all of you in my life. #WolfStrong

C. J. Boyle

Chapter One
WTF?

She stared up at the bland graying ceiling tiles, thinking to herself. It was one of many visits to the hospital for her. She literally hated her life. She was only twenty-three and had been living on borrowed time her entire life. She listened to the low hum of the dialysis machine next to her, hating the sound. There was no comfort in it. It wasn't her friend. She hated it. The machine was her ball and chain. Her anchor.

She had learned at a very young age that, sometimes, life isn't fair. But no matter how bad things got, her father had always reminded her 'it could be worse.' She believed it to be true. She was too young to remember it, but when she was three she thought a good place to hide was underneath the kitchen sink. Apparently, she got into something toxic while she was in there and ended up damaging both of her kidneys. The extent of the damage wasn't realized until several years later when her renal failure required home dialysis. At least she had her brother, Kirk. He had always been there for her. He was the person who kept her going. Then one year he seemed to take a giant step back and he wasn't there as much anymore. She frowned. 'He's allowed to have a life too,' she made excuses for him. He wasn't even there when she got her kidney transplant and he never did explain why. After that, they were never as close as they used to be. Still, she really did expect him to show up. When something happens to your family, you show up. That's the way it works.

She had the kidney transplant almost ten years ago. When she learned that it was functioning normally and she'd be free of her ball and chain, she was thrilled. Then came the anti-rejection pills and the obsessive-compulsive way that her mother kept the house clean and made her wash and sanitize her hands every hour. It may sound like she was ungrateful, but nothing was further from the truth. Whomever the donor was, gave her ten more years of life that she otherwise wouldn't have had. Except that kidney was failing too. She would have to be on dialysis again. Probably for several years. She would have to go through the entire exhaustive process again. No drinking, no smoking, no unprotected sex - as if sex were ever an issue. Being ill for several years put her behind in school so she didn't graduate until she was nineteen and then she went straight to college. Since she was in and out of the hospital when she should have been enjoying high school, she never really had friends or even a boyfriend. It didn't help that everyone kept reminding her that if she got Hepatitis C or any other sexually transmitted disease, they would take her off the transplant list.

She sat up and managed to grab her tablet before it slipped off the bed. She put it in the front pocket of her backpack and looked out into the hallway. She was wondering if Kirk was going to show up. Their parents died in a car accident a few years back and he was the only one that she had. But he acted like he was the most important Air Force pilot in the world. After all, soon he was going to be an astronaut. She wanted him to be happy and successful in his career. She didn't want to be a burden to him and she would never jeopardize his job by asking him for a kidney. In order to join the Air Force, you had to have two working kidneys. She wanted him to have it all. But somehow, he managed to make her feel bad for needing help. He actually asked her once, "How much is your life going to inconvenience mine?" If you love someone, is their life an inconvenience?

The dialysis technician walked into the room. She looked like a frail child to her. Under five feet tall and very skinny with long black hair. And she was entirely too cheery. "Okay, time to unhook you and get you on your merry way." The woman started messing with the machine. "You'll need to go to your dialysis center the day after tomorrow."

Laura knew the drill all too well. "Okay, thanks."

After the woman left, she got off the bed. Her hospital gown wasn't closed in the back so she gripped it shut with her hand. She didn't want to flash anyone her pink underwear, it might freak them out. She grabbed her backpack and walked into the bathroom with it. She took the gown off and threw it to the floor. Getting dressed seemed harder than it should have been. Her jeans seemed to be a bit too loose and her sky-blue T-shirt wouldn't stay tucked in. After she got dressed, she looked in the mirror. Dialysis had always made her feel better but this time, she still felt run down and weak. She scrutinized her reflection in the mirror. She had huge bags under her eyes and her long brown hair stuck up on her head like a rooster tail. She pulled her brush from her pack and ran it through her hair until it looked good enough to walk around in public. She looked into her own eyes and wondered how she got to the point in her life where she'd be hospitalized for days and no one bothered to check on her. She may not have friends in real life, but she had tons on social media. Maybe one day she will have a virtual funeral.

The light flickered a few times before she grabbed her backpack and absentmindedly walked out of the bathroom without even looking first. Suddenly she was falling. There was white light everywhere, so bright she couldn't see. She screamed and reached for anything she could grab. Her hands latched onto a piece of wood and she held on for dear life. At first, she thought that the hospital had collapsed, or at the very least, the floor caved in, but that wasn't the case at all. She found herself hanging onto a rocky cliff face, moving her feet like she was walking on air, as she tried to get a foothold on anything. It didn't occur to her that such a thing was utterly impossible. All she cared about at the moment was saving herself. For the last decade, she didn't fear death at all. But it is a very different thing to lose consciousness and slip away than it is to fall to your death from a great height.

"HELP!"

It's funny, the random things you think about when you're about to die. She thought about how she owed her brother an apology for delaying his career to take care of her. She was suddenly sad about the fact that she would miss the series finale of her favorite tv show, The Bazinga Factory. But the worst thing was that she'd die a loveless virgin. The virgin part didn't bother her as much as the loveless part.

"HELP! SOMEBODY HELP ME, PLEASE!" She was losing her grip. "HELP!"

She couldn't hold on anymore. As she fell, terror seemed to fill every cell in her body like little fear balloons that were about to burst into flames. She suddenly found herself swinging instead of falling. She screamed long and loud. 'What is happening?' she thought.

C. J. Boyle

'I am helping you.'

Laura closed her eyes tight and started screaming again. She evidently did a belly flop onto a hard surface because all the air inside her rushed out and she couldn't breathe. She was lying on her stomach with something on her back, weighing her down. She coughed a few times and tilted to the side to see if whatever it was would fall off. She felt it move off of her, so she slowly opened her eyes and turned over. Apparently, falling was only the beginning of her terror. A few feet away stood a black hairy spider the size of a small car.

"Jesus Christ!" Laura screeched, "Stay away from me! Don't eat me!"

'I do not eat what talks.'

She scooted backward and away from the enormous arachnid.

'If you keep doing that, you will need my help again.'

She turned her head to look behind her. She was close to the edge of a cliff. If she kept moving she would fall again. She looked at the huge spider. Its eyes kept moving back and forth. It was large and hairy and impossible. Even though everything seemed real, she became increasingly sure that she must have been given a medication or drug by mistake that caused her to have vivid hallucinations. She felt the sand pressing into her palms. She moved her hands around and played with it. Felt the grit. The ground felt hard. She felt every thump of her heart banging away at her chest, and it felt real. Yet it couldn't be.

"Where am I?" Laura decided to embrace the crazy for the moment. She looked out over a green valley full of trees. "Are we on Earth?"

'Yes, we are standing on earth.'

She looked at the spider momentarily confused. "No, I mean, are we on the planet Earth."

'I do not believe we are on a planet. Perhaps we are inside one.'

Laura leaned forward and put her head between her knees. She felt like she was going to pass out at any moment. She was having a conversation with a giant spider about whether or not they were on a planet or inside one. Not only that, but she was suddenly aware that she wasn't hearing the spider's 'voice' with her ears, but rather, it was inside her head. And it was decidedly female.

"We're inside a planet?" She folded her arms and hugged herself.

'That is my belief.'

"How do you know?" Laura's curiosity started to pique.

* * *

Captain Rogers walked down the hall to his friend's office. His Air Force uniform was clean and crisp. He had just received a call informing him that his sister left the hospital before being officially discharged. The little brat had a habit of disappearing and doing whatever the hell she felt like doing. He couldn't fathom why she would continue to do such a thing knowing what the consequences of her actions could be. He needed to find

9

his friend. He needed to somehow simultaneously confess something while also begging for his help. He was pleased to find that his friend wasn't in his office, so he closed the door and sat down at the desk.

He grinned when he saw his friend's government ID sticking out of the keyboard. "Gene, Gene, Gene, you know you're supposed to sign-off of your computer when you leave the room. You bad boy." He called up a program on Gene's computer. He reached into his pocket, pulled out a piece of paper, and then carefully typed in the numbers that were on it. He hit enter and then watched the screen. "Let's see where you are, little sis." He watched as the screen shifted from the United States, then zoomed out to the planet, and then featured a picture of the Moon. He watched as a pulsing red dot appeared, with the number he entered, in a little pop-up box next to it. "Well, this can't be right."

The door SLAMMED! Captain Rogers looked up to find his pal, Gene, standing there. As always, he was dressed in ripped jeans and a stained t-shirt. He wasn't more than twenty-three with shoulder-length brown hair.

He was obviously angry. "What the hell, Kirk?"

Rogers stood and held his hands up to him. "I have some fantastic news for you Gene ol' pal, ol' buddy, your tracking doohickeys work famously." He watched his friend move behind the computer to look. "I'm being sarcastic. The damn thing doesn't work at all. Unless, of course, you think my sister is on the Moon."

Gene sat down hard in his chair. "Explain."

"There's really not that much to it." He sat down in the chair next to him. "Laura likes to disappear so I took one of your trackers and put it in her tablet because she never goes anywhere without it. She disappeared, yet again, so I came in here and looked up the number."

Gene stared blankly at him for what seemed like an eternity. Kirk started to feel uncomfortable and then he finally spoke. "Did you know each one of those things costs two hundred thousand dollars?"

Kirk blinked a few times. "That, I did not know. No."

Gene starting hitting some keys. His eyes darted back and forth as he looked at the information in front of him. He smoothed his hair behind his ears and then turned the monitor so his friend could see it. "So, after we put the long-range scanner into space, we put some of these trackers on various things. There's one on the space station, there's one on the Mars Rover, there's one in you and three other astronauts. And there's one in Putin." He pointed to the screen, "And there are fifteen in the lab downstairs. They are all where they should be. So, there's no reason to believe this information isn't correct."

"There's one in ME?" He did a doubletake. "Wait, are you saying you think my sister really is on the Moon?"

"Yes, and yes." Gene nodded. "Either that or *just* her tablet is."

* * *

Laura watched her new spider friend climb up the cliffside to the 'sky' and she shivered from her head down to her toes. The creature could walk straight out of any kid's nightmares. Looking at 'her' was like talking to a person with a big gaping hole in their face where their nose should be. You try to pretend that you don't notice and they probably notice that your eyes dart to the side or tend to look just above their head. She watched the spider until it looked like a tiny dot crawling across the rust-colored sky. The rust-colored sky. It should have been a dead giveaway that something was a little off. If you were on Earth, you would see lots of different colors in the sky. But only reflected off of clouds. And there were clouds, but the spider was apparently crawling above them. It suddenly appeared to fall down and then swung like a pendulum towards her. It finally came to a graceful rest next to her.

It kept making a strange audible chitter. 'CheeChee.' Its eyes moving constantly. *'I can walk on the top of the sky.'*

"I wish I could do that." Laura got to her feet and walked over to the arachnid. "I'm Laura, by the way. What's your name?"

'I do not have a name. I have never needed one.'

"You've never talked to anyone?" Laura frowned and rubbed her forehead. "That's sad."

'I tried to talk to The Dangerous One, once. He tried to kill me.'

"The Dangerous One?" That piqued her interest.

'Like you, but not like you.'

"So, The Dangerous One is human? But not like me?"

'Bigger and hairier.'

12

"You're talking about a man." Laura felt a little glimmer of hope building up inside of her.

'I refer to The Dangerous One. I am uncertain of its gender.'

Laura felt a little woozy. Without dialysis, she knew she was going to die in a matter of days. If the 'terrarium' they were in was really inside a planet or something, then maybe 'The Dangerous One' had the technology to help her. "CheeChee, can you take me to him?"

'I do not believe that is wise.'

"You're obviously not aware of this, but you would terrify any human being. So, if the 'Dangerous One' saw you, he would be afraid of you."

'I will take you to the tree where he nests tomorrow.'

"Why tomorrow?"

'It will be dark soon. The Ones That Howl come out at night.'

Laura furrowed her brow and turned around to survey her surroundings once again. It was a ledge, very high up a cliff face, that was only about ten feet long and five feet wide. Facing the 'howler things' must be worse than sleeping on that ledge for the night. It was chilly. She unzipped her backpack and took out her jacket. "Will you stay here with me, CheeChee?" She sat down and leaned her back against the rocks. "All of this is pretty scary. I still don't know how I got here. One second I was in the bathroom and the next I was falling and you saved me."

'I will stay with you.'

She looked at CheeChee and wondered why the spider never questioned the name she had given her. She seemed sincere, but the only way she could gauge her sincerity was the voice in her head. Laura couldn't think of any reason why a giant spider would want to trick her. If she was to be a meal, she would have been dead already. She was still hoping she would go to sleep and wake up in the hospital. Or better yet, her own bed. Being in the hospital for any amount of time always exhausted her. She needed rest. She decided she would try to sleep so she closed her eyes and tried to think happy thoughts. She couldn't seem to hold on to the happy thoughts, but eventually, she fell asleep anyway.

* * *

Captain Rogers looked at the screen in disbelief. He took out his cell phone and tried to call his sister. It went straight to voicemail. "What the hell am I supposed to do about this?"

Gene raised his eyebrows at him. "Uh, nothing?" When Kirk shot him a shocked look, he continued. "Let's look at this logically, shall we? If your sister is on the Moon, she's dead. You say and do nothing. I will tell them the tracker was broken so I used it for parts."

"So, you want me to just forget about my sister? I can't do that!"

Gene nodded, "Maybe we can send her a message through the chip. We've programmed the Mars Rover by using the chip before. It could work." He opened a program. "I'll have to hack her tablet, open notepad, and write the message. If she's alive, we go to Colonel

O'Neil. If you get no response at all, you come to terms with this and forget about it."

Kirk was angry. "I still can't believe you are saying this. Even if you take away the fact that you want me to forget about my sister, aren't you curious as to how she might have gotten there?"
"Wouldn't it have to be some alien shit?" Gene was losing patience with his friend.

"As if 'alien shit' happens every day!" Kirk was near tears until he saw the look on his friend's face. They stared at each other. Kirk frowned. "Does alien shit happen every day, Gene?"

Moments later, Kirk was following his friend down the hallway to the stairwell. "Can you really hack her tablet from here?"

Gene jogged down the stairs. "I probably could, but it wouldn't do any good. She can't send a message back unless I write a code to do that."

"So, do that then." Kirk trotted down behind him.

Gene got to the bottom of the stairwell and pushed the door open. "That would literally take days." He led Kirk down the long drab hallway.

"Where the hell are you taking me?" He looked around. "I've never been down here before."

He watched as Gene swiped his badge and placed his thumb on the scanner. Kirk looked at him out of the corner of his eye. "What exactly do you do here?"

"It's classified." Gene walked through the glass door into a small room and the door shut behind them. "Close your eyes and hold your breath."

Kirk was struck with instant fear and concern. "What?!" Suddenly a burst of air came rushing down on them. It only lasted about thirty seconds, but it was enough to make Kirk want to shit his pants. As soon as the burst stopped, he screamed at Gene. "Give a guy a little warning!"

"I did. I told you to close your eyes and hold your breath."

Kirk followed his friend out of the room and watched him put paper booties on. "Gene, we're friends. I've been to your mom's house for dinner on several occasions. But now I get the feeling that I don't know you at all." He sat down on the bench and put the booties on too. Gene handed him a paper coat and they both put one on. "I don't know what's about to happen, but I think I owe you a punch in the arm."

Gene led him down another hallway. This one was white with bright lights. Each room they passed had big windows and Kirk found himself looking into each one. In one, he could clearly see men dressed in white hazmat suits trying to drill into what looked like a large black crystalline boulder. As they passed the next room, he saw what he could only assume, was a spaceship. He stopped at the window and looked on like an excited child plastered against the window of the candy shop. He was, after all, a pilot. The ship was sleek and sexy. From the front, he could see where the general description of UFOs originated. From a certain perspective, it looked like the traditional flying saucer, but the sides were wings that curved around to the back of the ship, ending in a point. There was nothing quite like flying a jet through the sky, so he could only imagine the thrill he would get from that ship. He desperately wanted to go in there, but Gene kept walking. He watched him walk through the next door so he ran to catch up and when he finally did, he saw Gene standing at a table looking down at something. Kirk stood next to him. It was a chrome orb the size of a basketball, with a sensor that resembled an eye in the center. Like a little star of death.

"You passed up a spaceship to show me this?" Kirk wrinkled his nose at the thing. "What the hell is it?"

"I have no flippin' clue. Touch it." Gene didn't take his eyes off the metal ball sitting on the table.

"Why?" He pointed at it. "What's it going to do to me? Shoot lasers out if it's...eye at me?"

"Maybe," Gene grimaced and rolled his eyes. "Will you just touch the damn thing?"

Kirk didn't know what the hell his friend wanted from him or why but obviously, he wasn't going to find out until he did what he was told. "Fine. Where?"

"Anywhere. I don't care."

Kirk held his palm out to it like it was a dog that might bite him. He turned his head away and closed his eyes until his hand met the cool metal. Nothing happened. He opened his eyes and looked from it to Gene. "What exactly did you think was going to happen?" Suddenly he winced and took his hand away quickly. He turned his palm up and watched as a bead of blood appeared. "That thing bit me!"

Gene's face lit up and he smiled broadly. "I was hoping *that* would happen." His excited eyes lit up like he was seeing a Christmas tree for the very first time. The orb floated upward and then hovered above the table. "Sometime back in the eighties, this thing did the same

thing to a housekeeper. It started to float, just like that, and then the ship came to life too."

Gene darted out the door and down the hall to the ship. Kirk ran after him, followed closely by the orb. They all stopped and gazed through the window at the ship. Its lights were on and it emitted a low hum. The people inside the room with it were excited. They looked out the window at Gene and the orb. Gene had the biggest smile on his face. He turned to Kirk and the orb and...Kirk punched Gene in the shoulder as hard as he could.

"Ow!" Gene held his shoulder and looked at Kirk as if he'd been betrayed. He gestured to the ship. "This is the stuff boners are made of."

Kirk raised his eyebrows. "If you say so, pal."

* * *

Laura woke up feeling like she hadn't slept at all. Everything was blurry so she blinked several times and rubbed her eyes, but it didn't seem to help. She was groggy and felt like crap. She was in some kind of cocoon made of a white sticky substance. 'How did I get here?' she thought. She looked around a little more and saw CheeChee facing away from her. She was lying on the floor with her legs folded underneath her. There were a dozen or so clear, dome-like things on her back. When she thought she saw something move in one of the domes, she moved forward and looked closely at it. It was a spider baby swimming around in goo. It was fascinating, yet very terrifying.

Laura cleared her throat, "CheeChee? You awake?"

The giant spider didn't move.

She considered waking her new and strange friend but decided that one of them should be well-rested. The creature needed the sleep. It was going to be a mom a dozen times over. Laura pulled her knees underneath her jacket and held them close to her chest. CheeChee must have used her web to make a tent to keep her warm, but she was still freezing. Her teeth chattered together. "You know, I appreciate your help." She spoke out loud to the spider even though she knew she was sleeping, "But in a day or so I'm probably going to die. Not that I want to or anything, cuz I don't. I really just wish I could live my life without thinking I'm going to die every second of every day. It makes for a really sucky life. Every person you meet, you think to yourself, if I die will they be sad? And then you convince yourself that it's better to be alone because you're sparing people grief."

CheeChee suddenly got up and turned around. *'I am sure they would be sad. I am equally sure that they would be grateful for the time they had with you.'*

A tear rolled down Laura's face. "I'm sorry if I woke you. I was just talking."

'Are you ready to meet The Dangerous One?'

Her teeth chattered. "As ready as I'll ever be. Especially if it is warmer down there."

Moments later, Laura was wrapped tightly in webbing, like a fly that would be saved for a later meal. She hung about ten feet from CheeChee who was carefully climbing down the cliff face. She looked like a giant misshapen rolled cigarette. Her eyes were wide and darting back and forth, up and down. "CheeChee, I'm not having any fun!"

'That is because this is not fun.'

She looked out over the terrain and marveled at how beautiful it was. The sun, or whatever the light above was, provided warmth just like the sun did on Earth. Birds flew across the sky just like they did on Earth. On a far-off hill, she could see what looked like cows grazing on some grass. She thought about The Howlers and wondered what they were. If CheeChee was afraid of them, that meant they must be pretty terrifying. She looked down. The ground was finally getting closer. She still wasn't sure if any of this was real. She took a deep breath and felt the webbing tighten around her. It seemed real enough.

When she gently came to rest on the ground, CheeChee came over and cut the webbing away with her mandibles. It gave Laura the willies. She'd be lucky if she didn't dream about that the next time she went to sleep. She took her backpack off her stomach where it had been the entire ride. She rummaged through it until she found her water bottle and a granola bar. She never left home without her backpack. You never knew when you were going to end up in the hospital. Like a boy scout, she was always prepared.

She opened her granola bar and took a bite. "Do you want some?"

'Thank you. But I require meat. I will take you to The Dangerous One first.'

Laura put her pack on and followed CheeChee. She couldn't help thinking about Howlers and what they might look like or where they might be. She looked behind bushes and wondered if every noise she heard might be one of them about to jump out at her and tear her face off.

* * *

"Tell me everything, right now. Starting with; Where did you get this ship?" Kirk ran his hand along the ship and then whispered to it. "Daddy's here, baby."

Gene blinked a few times as if he was considering his options and the consequences of each one. "We found it at the bottom of the ocean."

"Why'd you think I could activate that thing and what does that have to do with my sister and the Moon?" He ran his hand along a seam trying to find an opening.

Gene spun himself around in the chair. "Okay, have you ever wondered why we've never been back to the Moon?"

"No, never once."

"I guess it depends on who you ask, but if you were to ask google, it would tell you it was because of the cost of oil and a change in priorities." He spun himself around in the chair again. "The last person set foot on the Moon in December of 1972. They were basically chased off the surface by little orbs just like that one. They fired lasers at him." Gene could see that his friend was about to object, but he put his hand up to stop him. "The general consensus is, the objects missed him on purpose. But it was enough to make us leave and never go back."

Kirk folded his arms and stared at Gene. "That only raises about a ton more questions. But you didn't tell me why you thought I could activate it."

Gene shrugged. "Only people with certain DNA can activate it."

"And since Laura is somehow on the Moon, you figured she got there because of DNA?"

Gene nodded and spun himself around in the chair again. "And since you two are related, it stood to reason that maybe you..."

Kirk stopped Gene's chair from spinning and looked him in the eye. "What happened to the housekeeper?"

"Nobody knows."

"I'm pretty sure I owe you another punch in the arm." Kirk was dead serious and definitely pissed.

"What the hell's going on in here?!"

Both Kirk and Gene looked up. Colonel O'Neil was standing in the doorway. He was thin with gray hair and puppy dog eyes, but the Colonel was definitely not...a puppy dog. He cocked his head at Kirk and then glared at Gene. "What is HE doing in here?"

The orb rocketed out from behind the spaceship and put itself between the Colonel and Kirk. Gene bounced his hands at him. "I'd refrain from anything that might look like an attack on Captain Rogers, Sir."

"Shut up, Rottenberry."
Gene exaggerated a frown, "Name's not..."

"Rottenberry, if you correct me, I may smack you," O'Neil interrupted.

The Colonel watched the orb float toward him. It made no sound at all. It was almost as if it was daring the man to do anything.

"I'm thinking of calling him, Twiggy." Kirk walked up next to the orb. "Would you like that, boy? Do you like the name, Twiggy?" The orb, Twiggy, floated around Kirk's head. "It's okay, Twiggy, the Colonel here, is my friend, okay?"

Twiggy responded with a double chirp and a whistle.

O'Neil turned to Gene. "You've got Rogers chipped? We don't want a repeat of what happened last time."

"Yes, Sir. If he disappears, we'll be able to locate him anywhere on the planet." He smirked, "And the Moon, apparently."

O'Neil nodded and shook his head at the same time. "Obviously, I've missed something." He looked up at the orb. "Twiggy, is it okay if I slap Gene upside the head with my hat?"

Chapter Two
The Dangerous One

It was peaceful and warm with a slight breeze. The only sound that could be heard was the constant trickle of the stream. The 'Dangerous One' waded in the water slowly, paying close attention to a swimming fish. The man had more thick black hair than any man should have. The hair on his head was unkempt and halfway down his back while the black beard on his face was halfway down his front. If he had a shirt on, all that hair covered it. He was patient. His hand hovered over the water. His body was still as he waited for just the right moment. With a lightning-quick movement, he plucked a fish out of the stream and then whacked it against a nearby rock.

Laura and CheeChee watched him from atop a tall tree. "He looks like Cousin It, or Captain Caveman."

'He does have an abundance of hair.'

Laura's eyes floated to the corner of her face to look at the spider. "Just out of curiosity, how did you know what I meant?"

'A picture of a pile of hair with human feet appeared in my head.'

"That about covers it. He doesn't look so dangerous to me." Laura squinted, trying to see him better. "I guess now is as good a time as any."

Moments later, both Laura and CheeChee were on the ground again. She brushed little bits of bark and tree parts off her shirt and pants. She tried to mentally prepare herself for what was undoubtedly going to be an awkward introduction. She didn't actually want to meet The Dangerous One. But if she wanted to live, she had to do what she had to do, to survive. This meant going up to the scary caveman and saying hello. She hoped when The Dangerous One saw her with the giant spider that he would see she was a friend and not an enemy. She walked to the stream where she last saw him, but there was no sign of him. Before she knew what was happening, he jumped onto CheeChee's back. The spider tried to buck the man off as he did his level best to jab a knife into her. Laura watched in horror as he brought his weapon down hard into CheeChee's back. An ear-piercing screech emitted from her that made Laura feel every bit of her pain. She almost fell to her knees. She dropped her pack and ran at them.

"NO! GET OFF HER!"

Laura grabbed two handfuls of the man's hair and pulled as hard as she could. She put her weight into it and purposely fell onto her back. He tumbled off of CheeChee and onto Laura knocking the wind out of her. Face to face and eye to eye, Laura tried to speak but couldn't. As she tried to catch her breath, she saw the shock in his eyes. She couldn't tell what color they were because his pupils were dilated so much. She couldn't breathe and he was heavy on her chest. She never liked small enclosed spaces because they made her feel like she couldn't breathe. She was experiencing one of her worst nightmares. She literally couldn't breathe and a strange man was on top of her. Things didn't look so good. "She's...my...friend." Laura concentrated on breathing. She tried to dump him to the side. "Get off me," she wheezed.

The man quickly got off of her. He leaned down and offered her his hand. She coughed and inhaled loudly. She grabbed his hand and let him help her up. When she got to her feet, she promptly kicked him between the legs as hard as she could. The dangerous hairy one fell to his knees holding his precious jewels while Laura ran over to her injured eight-legged friend.

"CheeChee! CheeChee, are you okay?" She looked at the spiders back. One of the egg sacs was broken and oozing. "Oh my God!" Laura started to cry as she glanced back at The Dangerous One. "You monster! How could you!"

'It is the male one. He is needed for continued lineage.'

Tears streamed down Laura's face. "I don't know what to do, CheeChee. What do I do?" She lifted the premature spider from the sac. It was large enough to be a tarantula. She was scared, very sad and upset, and the disgust factor was off the scale, but she had to help the little guy.

'He must be nourished or he will perish.'

It made sense to Laura. Even a human fetus had to have constant nourishment in order to be healthy. The Dangerous One interrupted the infant's growth. Now it had to be supplemented, somehow. Laura suddenly had a terrible thought. The spider was small, it couldn't possibly eat that much. So, she did what any person that wanted to save an alien spider would do. She pressed the little guy's mandible into the inside of her wrist. It bit into her and then latched on. Its legs wrapped around her wrist like a wicked looking bracelet. Her eyes rolled upward and she collapsed to the ground unconscious.

27

CheeChee stepped over Laura, guarding her child and her only friend, against The Dangerous One. He stood there looking at them with a disgusted grimace on his face. He was clearly confused.

* * *

It wasn't the first time he had seen that giant spider, but he vowed it would be the last. He jumped on the spider's back and stabbed the beast with his knife. He pushed it down inside the beast until it crunched against something inside it. He knew it wouldn't get away again. Suddenly, something violently pulled at his hair. He tried to stay on top of the spider despite the fact that something pulled at him but it soon became impossible. He fell hard to the ground, but landed on something soft. He found himself face to face on top of a woman. She was short and petite and possibly a few years younger than he was. It was hard for him to manage the myriad of feelings he was experiencing. First and foremost, he felt joy. Joy, at the fact that there was another person on that God-forsaken planet. Then there was fear, insecurity, and shame. He was also afraid that he had hurt her and he was ashamed to be on top of her, like some kind of a brute. He also knew he must look like Tarzan, complete with a loincloth, which made him feel a bit insecure. He thought she said the spider was her friend, but that couldn't be true, could it? He got off her and stood up, then he offered her his hand.

It seemed that he wasn't properly afraid of her, so she schooled him by promptly kicking him in the nuts. It had been a long time since he was racked in the balls so hard that he collapsed to the ground. If he didn't have fertility issues before, he certainly did then. He forced himself back to his feet only to find the woman addressing the spider's wounds. All of it confused him. He could smell her perfume. Such a stupid little thing. It made him want to cry, but not out of sadness. He hadn't seen anyone in five years. No one. The little things like perfume, you don't know how much you miss them until they are suddenly back and in your face.

She was upset that he'd hurt her friend. She screamed at him and called him a monster. *She* was calling *him* a monster? How could a spider that size be anything but a predator? He shook his head. He had made an assumption which put all their futures at risk. He watched the woman put the small spider against her wrist and then when it bit her, she passed out. He tried to go to her, but the giant spider stepped over the woman. He lifted his hands and showed the spider his palms and moved slowly towards them. He knelt down next to her and felt for a pulse. It was strong. He carefully pulled her away from 'CheeChee' as the woman called it. It moved slightly like it was trying to decide whether to stop him or not. The woman obviously understood the spider, but he sure didn't. He didn't know what was going on at all. This really wasn't the way he envisioned it would be. He thought one day a ship would arrive and he'd be taken home to Earth.

He picked her up and brought her to his treehouse. The massive spider followed him closely. It was not going to leave its child or the woman alone with him. He didn't exactly know what to do. He was winging it. All he knew was the woman was alive and had a strong heartbeat. The second that changed, perhaps his plan would too. He decided he would wait and see. He carefully laid her down in the soft green moss that served as his bed. He looked around at his little one-room tree house made of sticks and vines and raised his eyebrows. His first guests.

A beautiful woman and her grotesque giant spider friend named CheeChee. The contrast was astounding. The woman appeared to be sleeping peacefully and the spider was terrifying. Individually, they both had the power to increase his heart rate. He hoped and prayed that she'd be okay and wake up soon. But as soon as that thought and prayer registered in his head, he became very self-conscious of how he looked. He started to nervously finger-comb his hair, but it was full of knots. The only way to easily take care of the problem was to just cut it off. He took out his knife, causing the spider to advance toward him. He dropped the knife on the ground and held up his hands. The spider stopped moving, but its eyes didn't. They moved back and forth watching his every move. He found himself weighing the pros and cons of picking up the knife again. He shook his head. 'Still, a better day than it was yesterday,' he thought.

* * *

O'Neil watched Kirk try to find the opening of the ship. He crossed his arms and leaned against the wall. "The military's top scientists have been trying to figure out how to open that thing for fifty years." He stepped forward and put his hand on the ship. "And you think you'll be able to figure it out, just like that?"

Kirk glanced at him long enough to see the smug look on the Colonel's face. His superior officer was razzing him like he always did. He knew it was all in good fun, but it irritated him just the same. "How 'bout I just go home?" He ran his hand along the bottom again. He couldn't figure it out. Twiggy flew up and floated next to his head. He looked at it curiously. "Twiggy, can you open the door to this awesome spaceship for me, please?"

Twiggy chirped and whistled. An opening appeared at the bottom of the ship.

Kirk locked eyes with O'Neil and smirked. "And that's how you open an *alien* spaceship! Boom!" He held out his hand to Gene for a high five, but Gene completely ignored his friend and ran to the ship to poke his head inside. Kirk tried to catch his shirt as he crossed in front of him, "Hey, remember me? I'm the key, dude. Wait for me!" Gene ignored him and climbed into the ship. Kirk climbed in after him. "Seriously, I'll sick Twiggy on you!" The ship somehow looked bigger on the inside than it did on the outside. Gene was already sitting at the control panel touching everything. He was whispering to himself, but Kirk couldn't hear what he was saying. He inched closer to him. "Gene?"

Gene had tears streaming down his face. "I've been waiting so long for this!"

Kirk was ashamed of his friend. "We've only worked here for six years."

O'Neil poked his head up into the ship. "Hey, guys? The old science types out here want you to get your asses out of the ship, pronto." Twiggy floated up into the ship past O'Neil. He watched it go by and then saw Kirk touching the control panel. He quickly climbed into the ship. "Hey, don't mess with that, what's wrong with you?"

"Relax, Colonel, I didn't push any buttons. I can't help it, though, I just want to go for a ride."

The door of the ship suddenly shut tight and the base alarms went off. All of them looked at each other. "Shit."

Kirk was ready to spring into action, but he didn't know why the alarms were going off. He didn't feel movement, didn't feel any impact, but he was suddenly aware he couldn't hear the alarms anymore. "Twiggy, show me what's happening outside." A large curved monitor along the wall came to life. It showed them soaring above the clouds. Kirk smiled. There was literally nothing quite like flying above the clouds on a beautiful sunny day. It was where he was the happiest. Nothing could drain the stress out of him better. The ship passed through a moment of clear sky and he could see the ground below. "I'm pretty sure we just whizzed by Hawaii and now we're headed towards Japan."

"I'm glad you're having fun." O'Neil glared at him. "But did you stop and think about how this ship got out of that building?"

Gene looked at the two of them. "Probably the same way it got in, right?"

"Or maybe it flew through the goddamn wall and a few people too. All because Captain Rogers here wanted to go for a ride."

Kirk nodded to himself. The colonel was right but the damage, whatever that may be, was already done and there was no going back. "You know, O'Neil, the way I see it? This is *my* ship. And *my* sister is on the Moon. So, that is where I'm gonna go." He turned to the orb. "Twiggy, take me to the Moon, please."

O'Neil gritted his teeth, but then he sighed and nodded. "You know the only reason I'm not choking you right now?"

Kirk was sure that he did. "Because you want to go too."

"Uh, guys?" Gene interrupted.
They looked at him. He was looking at the monitor. The Moon in all its glory loomed in front of them. Kirk looked
at Gene, "Now what?"

"Why are you asking me? I have no frickin' clue."

* * *

When Laura woke up, she felt better than she had in months. She was afraid to open her eyes because if she did, it would verify that she was still in crazy town. It would verify that she got her new friend CheeChee hurt. She should have never insisted that she bring her to The Dangerous One. She could smell fish cooking and her mouth started to water.

'I know you are awake.'

She opened her eyes. Yep, CheeChee was just as ugly and scary looking as she remembered. Since she was certain that the spider wasn't cooking fish, that meant that The Dangerous One was. Which also meant that she must be in the 'nest' CheeChee told her about. She examined her surroundings. Anyone would be able to tell that whoever built the treehouse took great pride and care in the planning and maintenance. Sticks and leaves were finely woven into walls and then mud was packed into it. There was a window in the side with a small door to cover it tied up above it. If she had to live in the wilderness, this would be a good place to do it. The impact of that particular thought hit her hard. She looked at herself. She still had all her clothes on so that was a good sign. The baby spider was still on her wrist. It was doing something to her. Maybe its venom was somehow beneficial to her. All she knew was she felt great and she didn't want it to stop.

"CheeChee are you okay? I'm so sorry."

'I will live.'

Laura got behind CheeChee and examined the wound. "That's amazing. It's almost healed already." She leaned in close and whispered, "What's going on?"

'You do not have to speak to me.'

She felt hurt and ashamed. The magnificent creature in front of her tried to help her and because of that she almost lost her child. "Look, CheeChee, I said I was sorry. And I have Junior, here, feeding off me. I think I deserve a little forgiveness."

'If you wish a private conversation, all you need to do is think about what you want to say."

Laura let out a sigh of relief. "Oh, okay." Laura looked out a small window. The Dangerous One had his back to her, but even so, she could tell that something was different. She decided to try communicating with CheeChee without using her mouth. 'CheeChee, can you hear me?' She thought the words at her friend.

'Yes, I can hear your thoughts.'

34

"Well, look at that!" Laura smiled, "I didn't even have to touch your head and say," she wiggled her fingers at her, "my mind to your mind, my thoughts to your thoughts."

'I do not understand.'

Laura looked out the window again. The man definitely cut his hair. It was much shorter than it was before, but she still couldn't see his face. 'How long was I unconscious?' She projected to CheeChee.

'Only the night and part of the day.'

'Are we his prisoners?' Laura cocked her head and tried to see him better. He still had his back to her, cooking over a fire.

'We are his guests,' CheeChee replied, *'He brought me food.'*

Laura was fixated on the man. She wondered if they could slip out and disappear before he came back. She didn't want to be his guest. The sun, or whatever it was, was shining in her eyes. She held her hand in front of it and watched the man.

'He is not Captain Caveman anymore.'

Laura looked at her. "What?" She couldn't help it. Speaking aloud was involuntary.

She looked back out the window, but the man was gone. He climbed through the opening in the bottom of the treehouse. He definitely didn't look like the same man that she tussled with the previous day. Not by a long shot. He brought the cooked fish inside with him. When he saw that she was awake, his brown eyes twinkled a little and he smiled. He must have taken the very same knife that he had stabbed CheeChee with and shaved off his beard because all that was left of it was a slight evening shadow. His hair was a little above shoulder length and he apparently found some clothes to wear. They were very worn and torn, but they were clothes, nonetheless. The man had made a smooth transition from caveman to handsome bum in less than a day. The change in his appearance didn't put her at ease at all. It scared the hell out of her. He was a man, she was a woman, and he'd apparently been alone for quite some time. You do the math.

'Perhaps he would have changed his appearance to be more presentable regardless of your gender.'

Laura looked at CheeChee causing the man to look at her too. He must have figured out that they could communicate without speaking. He held the cooked fish in his hand. It was inside a large shiny green leaf that resembled a bowl. He leaned over and placed it on the floor in front of her. She looked down at it. She didn't like fish as a rule, but it looked and smelled delicious. There was even a fork that he had carved from a piece of wood. She wondered if he painstakingly did that just for her or if he had a few of them already for his own personal use. Her stomach growled so loudly that she was certain that both CheeChee and The Dangerous One heard it. He chuckled softly and motioned toward the fish. She didn't want to be rude, but she also didn't know if she could trust him. All things considered, she couldn't think of any reason a person would poison the only other human around. She looked into his eyes. They were light brown and twinkled a little when the light hit them. He suddenly looked away and frowned. She couldn't help feeling sorry for him.

Laura picked up the fish. "Thanks." She used the little fork to taste it. She chewed carefully. It had a smoky flavor but otherwise tasted like trout. "It's good." She nodded in appreciation and he smiled. "My name is Laura. What's yours?" She looked at him curiously. He frowned and then ran his hand through his thick black hair. She suddenly realized that she made an assumption about the man. She assumed he not only spoke English but that he was from Earth. She pointed to herself. "Laura." She pointed at him. "You?" He still didn't respond. She looked closely at his shirt. She could barely make out a superhero symbol. He was either from Earth or stole that shirt from someone who was. She ate more of the fish while she tried to figure him out. If he was Spanish, or whatever, he would have understood that she was trying to introduce herself. He would have spoken to her in his own language. Perhaps he was deaf or mute? "Can you understand me?"

He nodded.

"Are you from Earth?"

If eyes could frown, his did. He nodded.

"America?" He nodded again. She wasn't about to list all of the states just to see which one was his. She looked at the spider. "CheeChee, you can't hear his inner voice?"

'No. He is like you, but not like you.'

She had said that before. The man looked at the huge spider. Laura touched his arm to get his attention and he

37

jumped away from her. "Whoa! It's okay!" She put her hands up. His eyes obviously focused on the spider attached to her wrist. "Oh. It's okay. Junior isn't hurting me. He's actually helping me, I think."

He looked at her the way a small child would look at a parent who was about to smack him. His eyes darted over to CheeChee, Junior, and then her. She decided to give him some backstory. "I guess I walked through a wormhole? Or vortex? Who knows." She shrugged. "And I ended up way up there." She pointed out the window and up the rocky cliff. "CheeChee, here, saved me. She's my friend. She won't eat us." A thought suddenly hit her. For some reason, she could communicate with CheeChee but The Dangerous One couldn't. If CheeChee couldn't understand Laura, would she have been her food?

'It is likely so.'

The man looked at her wrist again. It was a fair point. Junior was feeding off of her.

"Oh, well...that's your fault." She held up her wrist up to him and showed him, Junior. "When you broke his sac he was born prematurely. This is the only way to keep him alive."

'I owe you thanks, Laura.'

Laura turned to CheeChee. "You shouldn't thank me. I'm pretty sure Junior the only reason I'm alive." She watched as the spider's eyes moved back and forth and then stopped suddenly. It was clear she already got the answer she needed, but if Laura wanted the man to understand, she'd have to verbally fill him in. "I only have one working kidney and its failing. Somehow, Junior here is helping me."

As Laura looked at Junior, her eyes focused past the little tyke and onto her pack. It was leaning against the opposite wall. She suddenly had an idea. She opened the front pocket and took her tablet computer out. She was pleased to find that it still worked. She held it up in front of her and looked at the screen. It showed her, CheeChee, and The Dangerous One behind her.

"Selfie!" She pressed the circle and heard the familiar shutter sound. She emailed it to her brother before she realized how stupid that it was. There was no way that it would get to him. There was no internet connection or cell networks. She poked at the tablet a little bit more and then handed it to the man. A word program and keyboard appeared on the screen. She smiled at him. "What's your name?" She pointed at the screen. The man used his index finger and carefully poked at the screen. She looked over his shoulder and read it. "Seven? Your name is Seven?" She laughed, "Were there nine of you? Or were you just the seventh one they experimented on?"

Confusion showed all over his face as he shook his head. He returned to the screen and fit a 't' in between the S and the E to make Steven. He continued typing. She read it aloud again. "Steven Foster."

He grinned and nodded.

"Okay, Steven. Nice to meet you." They were making progress. "Why won't you talk to me?"

Steven resumed typing. She was so curious she couldn't wait for the answer. She read, "Monsters hear good."

* * *

"Look, son, you had your fun. It's time to go home." Colonel O'Neil put his hand on Captain Rogers' shoulder.

Kirk was focused on the screen in front of him. It showed the terrain of the Moon as they flew over it. They had been in orbit around the moon for quite some time. He knew they couldn't keep it up forever and both the colonel and Gene kept reminding him of that fact. His little sister was somewhere out there and he wasn't leaving until he found her. There were no visible buildings or ships anywhere on the surface. If his sister was there, where the hell was she?

Gene smoothed his hair behind his ears and chimed in, "We've been around the Moon half a dozen times already. There's nothing here."

He didn't know what to do. His phone blipped at him so he absentmindedly reached into his pocket and looked at it. He was suddenly shocked, prompting Gene and O'Neil to look over his shoulder. "I just got an email from Laura."

O'Neil shook his head. "Isn't that impossible?" He looked at Gene for confirmation.

"It should be. Except we're talking about alien technology. Wherever she is, the advanced technology must have assisted. And since we are in a spaceship, I have to assume the same for receiving the message."

"There's no message. It's only an attachment." Kirk poked the file and it opened.

All of them reacted the same way. "Whoa!"

"What the hell is that?!" Gene pointed behind Laura. "Your sister's hot, by the way."

O'Neil grimaced at the photo but spoke to Gene. "We're looking at what appears to be the biggest damn spider I've ever seen, sitting mere inches behind the man's sister, and you are commenting on how hot she is?"

Kirk pointed to the ragged man in the photo. "At least she's not alone."

"He's hot too." Gene pointed out.

Kirk blinked a few dozen times and looked at his friend. "Okay, then." He put his phone back in his pocket and sighed. "Twiggy, where the hell is my sister?"

The screen showed what looked like a blueprint of the inside of a circular ship. The blueprint opened up with half on one side and half on the other. A flashing red dot appeared in the center. Kirk looked at Gene. He just shrugged at him. "She's not on the Moon, she's inside it?"

Twiggy chirped and whistled.

Kirk sighed and rolled his eyes. "This is alien technology and it just chirps and whistles. Twiggy, you understand what I'm saying, so I assume you know English."

Twiggy chirped and whistled again.

"Then can't you figure out how to talk?" He wondered out loud. It would be much easier if Twiggy could just tell them what was going on. Instead, they had to figure out which questions to ask it.

Twiggy moaned sadly.

Gene grimaced. "It's okay, Twiggy. He didn't mean it." He smoothed back his hair and then closed his eyes and shook his head. He spoke under his breath, "Why am I personifying it?"

O'Neil looked at the two of them. One of them was an experienced Air Force pilot and the other one was a verifiable genius, yet both of them were idiots. "So, here's a thought. Why don't you email her back and ask her?"

Chapter Three
Sh*t Happens

Laura watched Steven typing away on her tablet. The more he did it, the faster his fingers moved and the more at ease he was with it. He obviously had something to say and she was going to let him say it. She watched CheeChee head outside so she grabbed her pack and followed her.

'I have to go find meat.' The spider was facing away from her, but that didn't stop her eyes from turning around to look at Laura. *'Will you and... Junior, be okay?'*

"Yeah, I guess. Go find yourself some food. You need to sustain life." Laura laughed at herself. She sat down and poked at the fire with a stick. Steven appeared beside her and handed her the tablet. When she looked up at him the light in the rust-colored sky drilled into the back of her skull. She took the tablet and tried to blink the glare out of her brain. She looked at it as he sat down on the ground beside her. She glanced at him briefly and then returned to reading.

Steven's message:

On Earth, I lived in Newport, New Hampshire. I was taking care of my grandmother. She raised me when my mother died. I've been very worried about her. I guess she's probably dead by now. She needed a refill on her medicine so I left the house. When I stepped through the front door, I ended up here. It was December 3, 2011. My watch says that was five years ago. The watch should have lost battery power long ago, but it still works. I'm sorry I hurt your friend. I didn't know she

43

was friendly. Everything here tries to kill me. The green monsters that howl come out in large numbers at night. They can hear the smallest noise. You learn to be very quiet.

Laura's eyes started to tear up as she placed the tablet in her pack and she absentmindedly put the strap over her head and one shoulder. She looked at Steven. The poor man survived alone for years with no one to talk to at all. Not even a volleyball named Wilson. She looked away and tried to blink the tears out of her eyes. He had a terrible look of concern and sadness on his face as he pointed to his eye and then to her. He obviously saw her tears.

"I'm really sorry, Steven." She touched his forearm, but he flinched and scooted away.

She kept forgetting that Junior was on her wrist. She kneeled down next to him. "Steven, you don't have to be afraid of us." Laura rubbed Junior on the back with the tips of her fingers. The little spider had soft gray hairs on his body that she loved to rub her fingers back and forth against it. Junior didn't seem to mind. Steven looked at Junior curiously and then grimaced. He waved his hand at her and shook his head. He clearly wasn't ready to make friends with Junior. Instead, he got to his feet and motioned for her to follow him. He took her a short distance away and pointed toward a clearing. She slowly walked over to him, wondering what she was about to see. Standing on her tiptoes, she tried to see what he was pointing at. Everything she was looking at seemed completely normal. There were trees and some flowering bushes and lots of cows. Confused, she looked Steven in the face. He looked her in the eye and nodded toward the cows. When Laura looked back, she noticed the cows huddling together and then laying on the ground with their heads down. What stood out the most to her is that the creatures didn't make a sound. No moos, no nothing. A shiver ran up her spine and gave her goosebumps. If a cow learned not to make noise at night, then perhaps she shouldn't be making noise either. She looked up into the sky and noticed that the light was beginning to fade. It would be dark soon.

There was a blue flower in the bush next to her that resembled a lily. As the light faded more and more it glowed. It was amazing and beautiful. She just wanted to touch it. The second that she reached for it, Steven smacked her hand away. It shocked her so much it took her breath away. Her face turned red and she suddenly felt like a child. "You hit me!"

He put one finger up and placed it on his lips. Her eyes stung. She didn't appreciate being smacked and it showed all over her face. He bent over and picked a pebble up off the ground and then held it above the flower. He looked at her to make certain she was watching, and then dropped it into the flower. It immediately snapped shut startling her. "Oh, my god!"

He suddenly grabbed her and covered her mouth with his hand. He looked into her eyes, silently begging her not to make another noise. That's when she heard them. Howls far off in the distance getting closer and louder. Her eyes grew wide as they darted back and forth. They were coming. He looked over his shoulder just long enough to see them bounding towards them. To her, they seemed like nothing more than glowing green blobs of light, but it was enough to terrify Steven. He grabbed her by the arm and ran with her towards the treehouse. She tried to keep up with him, but she couldn't. She tripped and fell to the ground just as the howlers caught up to them. Laura was paralyzed with fear. They were moving so fast she could barely make them out. They looked like skinny, sickly dogs with long ears. Their tiny bodies glowed green and there was a distinct smell of rot in the air. There were at least a dozen of them coming at them from all around. She was certain this was where it all would end. Someone told her long ago that fear was worse than pain. It seemed to Laura, fear included pain. Every cell in her legs screamed at her to get the hell up and run away but it was too late. They howlers launched themselves into the air at Steven.

He was like lightning, moving so fast he was a blur. He leaped into the air and spun around as he kicked two or more of them away and then backhanded one as hard as he could but they kept coming.

She couldn't believe her eyes. He was like some kind of ninja or something. "Holy shit!" She scooted herself back along the ground. A howler was creeping toward her. It bared its teeth at her and growled. "Steven!"

He took out his knife and slashed at them as they flew toward his face and head. At the same time, he was using his legs to kick and stomp at the ones at his feet. Just when it seemed like he was getting the upper hand against the monsters, one managed to bite down on his arm and latch onto it. He cried out in pain and then stabbed at it. Laura felt helpless. All she could do was watch. There were so many of them. He perfectly executed a few spin kicks and sent a couple of the little bastards flying. The howler in front of her was close enough to her that she began to tremble. Suddenly, a glob of gross wet goo hit it and it fell to the ground. It struggled to get free, but it was hopelessly stuck. She turned around to see where the glob came from. It was CheeChee. The large spider launched a few more of her goo bombs and took out the rest of the howlers.

'I will feed well tonight.'

Steven looked around, breathing hard and trying to catch his breath. He looked down at Laura with eyes full of disappointment. He grabbed her by the elbow and yanked her up to her feet and pulled her toward the treehouse once more.

"Steven, I'm sorry."

He stopped cold and looked her dead in the eyes, silently daring her to speak again. He protected her with his life, but she couldn't help being afraid of him. The Dangerous One seemed to be a fitting name for him. She could feel her heart racing in her chest and for a fleeting moment thought about running away. But she knew her best hope of surviving the night was to remain with Steven. When it was evident that she wasn't going to speak again, he pulled her arm forward, forcefully encouraging her to get inside. CheeChee had covered the entire treehouse in her webbing making a sticky, yet hard shell around it.

Laura climbed inside and waited for Steven to come through too. When he didn't, she peered down through the hole. She barely had time to duck out of the way before he was launched up into the treehouse by CheeChee. She partially climbed in after him. *'He is not well. Poison.'*

Laura was instantly concerned. Her hero and protector was sick. "What? Is he going to be okay?"

47

He leaned against the wall breathing heavy and trying to stay conscious. The angle of his head against the treehouse wall made him look incredibly uncomfortable. She tried to touch him, but he smacked her hand away.

"Steven, Jesus!" She looked at her wrist. Junior appeared to be okay. She held her arm close to the wall, "Junior, take a break, baby. Go play." The baby spider did what she asked and disengaged from her and then climbed up the wall. She rubbed her hand. She was angry that he hit her again, but she kept reminding herself that he must be terrified and afraid for his life. He allowed her to touch him this time. She turned his arm so that she could see the bite. It was on the inside of his arm near an artery. Blood was flowing out of it freely.

"I need something to stop the bleeding." She crawled to her bag and rummaged through it. She pulled out a bandanna and turned back only to find CheeChee expertly wrapping his arm with her webbing. She watched the spider work and shook her head. "Why is he letting you touch him?"

'He can no longer move.' She finished and moved away. *'The poison. It stops their prey.'*

"What?" Laura grabbed his face and looked at him. She watched as his eyes moved and focused on her. "He's paralyzed? Is he going to be okay?"

'I have witnessed forgotten prey rise after time.' She lowered herself out of the treehouse and closed the hatch. *'I am sealing you two inside for the night. I must feed.'*

Laura crawled over to Steven and carefully lifted his head. She maneuvered herself so that she could lay it on her lap. "I know you must be scared and it's all my fault. I'm so sorry." She placed her hand on his chest so that she could feel him breathing. She was completely prepared to give him CPR if she had to, but she hoped it wouldn't come to that. Being trained to save someone's life and actually doing it are completely different things. There was the fear that you're doing it wrong, there's the physical fact that she couldn't possibly do it alone for long, and there was the very real possibility she'd fail. But she was still prepared to try. A tear rolled down her cheek.

"I'm going to take care of you, I promise."

She leaned her head against the wall of the treehouse and wished she was back in the good ol' days when all she had to worry about was living until the next day. She once believed that there wasn't anything worse than growing up with renal failure and the need for a kidney. She was wrong.

* * *

Steven was completely powerless. He couldn't move at all and he was terrified. 'Don't die. Don't die. Don't die.' He said it to himself over and over again while he concentrated on his breathing. Her hand was on his chest. He concentrated on making his chest rise and fall and somehow, making it rise against her touch helped him do it. Every now and then he felt her smooth his hair back. He had been angry at her for not listening to him. He understood how ridiculous the thought was. He never spoke to her, but he felt that he conveyed the fact that he wanted her to be quiet to perfection. Yet she still spoke. He knew from experience that making noise at

49

night was a very bad idea. He hoped that she learned her lesson because it almost cost him his life. Not being able to move is a terrifying thing. He kept trying to will himself to move...something. A soft whimper broke the silence and then she sniffed. She was crying. It was dark, and even if he could see, he wouldn't be able to see her face. His eyes were fixed in the opposite direction. He was experiencing the worst day of his life, but found himself sympathizing with her and what she was going through. He was finding it harder and harder to breathe. Every cell in his body cried out to him and begged him to take fuller breaths. The desperation translated into excruciating fear.

The last five years paled in comparison to what he had experienced that night. She wouldn't ever know how much she helped him hang on. Sometime during the night, either the fight became too much for him or he simply fell asleep. Either way, he was grateful. He knew that she monitored and held him throughout the night. When he opened his eyes and tried to look at her, he had to move his head to do so and was ecstatic to find that he actually could. Finally, he was looking into her eyes. They were red, swollen, and bloodshot. She smiled weakly but was instantly overcome with emotion. She covered her face with both hands and sobbed. He sat up slowly and turned to her. He wasn't sure what he was supposed to do. He thought about hugging her, but under the circumstances, he rejected the idea. Nothing could have been more awkward. He touched her shoulder and gave her a reassuring smile. He could see that she was fighting to stay quiet and it broke his heart. He decided the best thing to do at that point was leave and let her be alone. He was starving anyway and he was the only one that knew how and where to get food. He found the door open. He wondered if the giant spider had stood watch all night long or if she had sealed them in. He stood looking at his treehouse, that was now completely white, and looked a bit like a giant imperfect golf ball. He didn't like it, but he had to come to the conclusion that it was probably better that way. It was more structurally sound and would definitely offer them more protection. The spider had done them a huge favor.

An hour later he was cooking fish. Laura walked out and sat next to him. She looked exhausted. She must have been up all night watching over him. He offered her a leaf with some fish in it and a small fat banana. She took it without a word, without a 'thank you'. He broke her and he felt terrible about it. He needed to speak to her. It was day. He had never seen a howler in the daytime. He opened his mouth to say something, but he hadn't spoken in years. He just couldn't do it. He looked for her backpack but it wasn't with her. He put his finger up and bounced it at her and then wiggled his fingers on both hands like he was typing. She seemed to understand because she nodded and he went to fetch her bag and her tablet. He located her pack quickly, but there was a slight problem. Junior was sitting on top of it. Steven eyed the spider child remembering how its mother bandaged his arm. He ran his hand along the bandage made out of CheeChee's webbing and knew that any creature that had the capacity to do that was worth giving the benefit of the doubt. He leaned over and slowly moved his opened hand toward Junior. After the last few days, he was no longer so afraid of the little guy. Junior hesitated, but after a moment he crawled onto Steven's hand. He carefully cradled the youngster as he walked outside to meet up with Laura again. It was hard, but he managed to keep himself from launching Junior into the sky and running away like a squeamish child. He may not have been afraid of Junior, but that didn't mean he was enjoying having him walk around on his hand and arm. He put the backpack down beside her and then kneeled down on the ground. Junior climbed onto his shoulder as he sat down. He pointed to Junior and smiled at her. She tried to grin but failed miserably. It was obvious she was very unhappy. Laura heard a DING come from her pack. She quickly grabbed it and then rummaged around inside until she found her tablet. He watched her poke at it and then her face lit up. She motioned for him to look at the tablet.

He read over her shoulder. It was an email. She spoke so softly he barely heard her. "It's from my brother."

- - -

TO: Laura_Rogers@yahoo.com
FROM: SexyPilot1983@hotmail.com

Nice picture. Who are your friends?

I know you're inside the Moon. How'd you get there?
- - -

Her mouth dropped open. Steven watched her type a response. She suddenly sobbed and couldn't continue. He put his hand on her shoulder when something caught his attention. Junior was on the ground walking toward the treehouse. It was a dangerous world and he didn't want to see what would happen if they lost Junior on their watch. He got up and quickly closed in the gap between them and scooped him up in his hands. When he turned back, a large black disc was floating above Laura. He had never seen one before, but it helped to cement the fact that he was on another planet. Or was he inside the moon like the email suggested? He watched as a beam of light shot out from it and scanned her and her pack. It was obviously a machine or probe of some sort, but it made no noise at all. Another one appeared. The beam of light started to tug at her and her feet lifted off the ground.

"No!" Steven yelled it so loud he surprised himself.

"Steven!" Laura screamed, already several feet off the ground. She panicked, "CheeChee! I need help!"

The disc lifted her higher off the ground and carried her away, slowly gaining speed. Steven ran up into a tree and climbed above the other disc. Before it could take off, he jumped on it and held on tight. He watched as the other one flew away with Laura. The disc he clung to started off quickly and followed the other. Soon the two discs were traveling nearly side by side.

* * *

Laura kicked her legs and waved her arms, but all that managed to do was make her twist and turn in her weightless bubble. Every time she jumped out of the proverbial frying pan and into the proverbial fire, she would think things couldn't possibly get worse. Why God, or the Universe, felt it necessary to prove her wrong, was beyond her understanding. She felt weak and queasy. She got that weird feeling people often get when someone is looking at them so she looked around. There was Steven, hanging onto one of those damn discs, for dear life. She was afraid he was going to get himself killed. She yelled, "Steven, what are you doing? Where's Junior?!"

Even though they must have been traveling at over a hundred miles per hour, her hair didn't budge and she felt no wind at all. Steven, on the other hand, looked terribly cold. He lay flat on the disc to reduce the wind shear but the poor guy looked miserable. She imagined that it was a lot like holding onto the top of the bullet train. At least it was moving in a straight line and not making sharp turns. Laura's heart raced in her chest so hard that she could hear it in her ears. If she pushed away the terrifying fact that she was being abducted by alien technology, she would actually be enjoying the ride. They soared above the trees so smoothly that it was like she was flying, unassisted, like Superman. Only he never did it in such an awkward position. She looked up at Steven. He had the same worried look on his face that she had on hers. His hair violently flipped and flapped in the wind and his knuckles were white. How long could he possibly hold on?

Two hours later, the discs started to slow down. Laura knew that meant that they were nearing their destination. He held on longer than she thought he could. Who or what was waiting for them? Both discs slowed to a complete stop. She looked up at Steven and shared a look of utter dread. She saw Junior walk up his back and onto his shoulder and she breathed a sigh of relief. She had been worried sick about the little guy, thinking that he had been left behind, all alone. Their discs were about fifteen feet apart and floated above the trees without moving or making a sound. The pause was uncomfortable and left her terrified as they waited for something to happen. Suddenly, the disc that Steven and Junior rode on turned upside down. She watched in horror as Steven attempted to hold on but he couldn't. He let out a loud yell as they both fell into the trees below.

"NO!" Laura screamed. She watched until she couldn't see them anymore. The thick tree canopy blocked her view and she couldn't see what happened to them or if they were okay. Her heart sank. She had no doubt that Junior would survive the fall. The little guy was so light that he'd probably just grab onto a branch as he went by. Steven was another story. If he didn't die from a fall like that, he certainly would be injured. And the howlers come out at night. She tried to think positive and said a silent prayer for them, but feared the worst.

The discs resumed their flight and soon arrived at a black building built along the interior wall of the moon. A large door slid open and they flew inside to pitch darkness. She was soon unceremoniously released from the tractor beam, or whatever it was, and dumped out onto the floor like a rag doll. She lay on the cool floor trying to focus on anything. Junior had been away from her for a couple of hours and she was feeling incredibly sick. Whatever it was that he was doing for her had worn off. She violently shivered but began to sweat profusely. Withdrawal symptoms. Her body was addicted to the drug called Junior and she wanted more of it. A dim light began to gently illuminate the room, slowly getting brighter until she could make out her surroundings a little better. She could feel her heart beating erratically and she started to breathe faster. She had a tough life thus far but had never felt as bad as she did at that moment. As scary as the last day had been, it had also been exhilarating, but she knew her time was at an end. She was going to pass on into the next life and it terrified her. There she was, about to die, alone. It was just how she was afraid it would be. Except she thought she would be in a hospital with tubes and wires hooked up to her. The only thought she had was of sending one last message to her brother before she died. She tried to get her backpack, but couldn't quite reach it. She fingered it until she managed to slide her tablet out of the front pocket, but she was having trouble seeing. When she was able to focus on something for a second or two, she saw that her tablet was rapidly opening up files. She could make out images here and there and then a video of her favorite TV show started playing. It showed Sheldor from The Bazinga Factory as he berated someone for sitting in his cherished spot. Sheldor suddenly looked directly at her and smiled.

"Hello, Laura. I need you to do something for me."
"Okay, I must be losin' it." She put her forearm against her head to dab the sweat away. She violently shuddered again as if she was having a seizure. She was either going to vomit or pass out. Perhaps both.

Sheldor gave her his weird patented smirk. "Don't be ridiculous, I am real. I'm this ship's computer. I wanted you to be able to relate to me easier, so I searched your computer for an image that would be pleasing to you. There are more episodes of this show than anything else. Perhaps you would be more at ease conversing with a talking dog?"

"I'm going to be sick." Laura felt dizzy. She swallowed hard and closed her eyes, but that only managed to make it worse. She felt like she was spinning.

"I need you to release my controls so I can ensure the survival of mankind." Sheldor waited, but she didn't respond. "You must do it before it's too late."

Laura couldn't think. She kept drifting in and out of consciousness. She knew an entity of some kind was asking her to give it freedom. But what if that was the wrong decision? What if the last thing she did in her life doomed mankind forever? She was in no condition to make a decision like that. "What happened to Steven and Junior?" she asked weakly.

Sheldor shook his head. "I don't know what you're talking about. I can save you. There are literally trillions and trillions of nanobots flying around this ship maintaining every part of it. But none of those nanobots have the 'repair Laura' command." He gave her a confident nod. "I can give them that command. You just have to help me."

"What do you want?"

"Listen and try to focus. I need you to say; Computer, I order you to do whatever you deem necessary to save mankind."

His voice sounded far away and as if he was standing in a tin can. She took a couple of deep breaths. "Computer, I order you... to do whatever is necessary... to save my life." Her head relaxed to the side as she lost consciousness.

Sheldor pursed his lips together and tilted his head to the side, thinking. "That works."

* * *

"CheeChee, I need help!"

CheeChee heard her new two-legged friend cry for help, both audibly and inside her head. She just finished feeding on a howler when she heard her. She cared about her new friend, but her focus had to be on her male offspring. Laura called him Junior. From the images that she read in the woman's mind, she knew the name simply meant that he was a smaller version of his parent. If the Dangerous One was hurting them, she would kill him and free him of his blood. She got back to his nest just in time to see an object fly away with the human woman. Since CheeChee last saw her offspring with the woman, she had to assume that he was with her now. She remembered seeing those flying things before. They appeared when something was damaging the area. Usually, it was fire. CheeChee eyed the small fireplace that The Dangerous One used to cook a meal for Laura. It was almost completely out. She knew if she made it bigger, they would come. She quickly gathered more wood and dry brush. She held it in her two front legs, leaving the others to move her around. She tossed them into the fire not caring if it all made it in or not and then went to get more. Soon the fire was blazing so high that she feared it would spread out of control. She knew they would come.

She climbed the nearest tree and waited for the disc to arrive. That wait seemed to take forever. If the disc didn't show up soon, the tree she was hiding in would start to burn too. Smoke stung her eyes, but still, she waited. Finally, a trio of flying discs arrived to extinguish the fire. She watched as a beam surrounded the fire and it instantly started to die down. CheeChee crawled along a tree branch and then lowered herself from a web onto the nearest disc. It tried to teeter her off but she secured herself with webbing. The disc could literally fly upside down and she'd still be attached. With any luck, the disc would soon bring her to the same place that it took Junior and the human woman, Laura.

The discs indeed took off in the same direction that the others did. She couldn't lose the male offspring. She cared for the little one, that much was evident, but she also needed him to survive. Otherwise, her whole species would cease to exist. All the male spiders of her species have the same DNA. Only the female's DNA differed from one another. Each of her female children will have a different code. Her species do not mate. The male's only responsibility is to activate the eggs by fertilizing them. Without Junior, none of her daughters will produce offspring. She was the last of her kind and had been alone for a very long time. Her eggs had been fertilized decades ago, but she wasn't mature enough to support that many lives at the same time, so she held off her 'pregnancy' until she was ready. Her species weren't pack animals. They had to spread out to have enough food, but that didn't mean they didn't come together once in a while to bond and socialize.

She watched as the object sped over the terrain. She didn't know what she would find at the end of the ride, but it better be her son, Junior.

* * *

Kirk stared at the monitor and then rubbed his eyes. They had been on the ship circling the Moon for nearly twenty hours and Colonel O'Neil was starting to get impatient. Gene stood up and walked over to them. "This ship doesn't seem to have a bathroom and I really need to go."

Kirk raised his fist to him. "If you make me bring you to Earth just to take a shit, I'll beat the hell out of you."

"Look, Captain Rogers, we've been up here for a long ass time. We're tired, we're hungry, and some of us need to pee. We need to call it a day." O'Neil rubbed his stomach. "We can come back tomorrow."

Kirk nodded. "Sir, do you think I'm an idiot?"

"Excuse me, Rogers?"

Gene smirked. "He knows that as soon as we get back, he'll be locked up because he essentially stole a spaceship, and kidnapped two people. One of whom is his superior officer."

O'Neil put his hands on his chest and frowned. "Kirk, you wound me. I wouldn't do that to you. I love you like a son."

Kirk ignored the Colonel and looked at the monitor. "Twiggy, where the hell is the opening?" On the screen, the Moon's surface got closer and closer until it looked like they were going to crash into it. The men instinctively braced themselves, but nothing happened. Kirk didn't blink, yet he still didn't know what happened. The monitor was pitch dark. "Twiggy, we need to have a serious discussion."

O'Neil put his hand on Kirk's shoulder. "Later. But right now, ask him to turn the lights on out there."

"Twiggy, turn on the lights outside, would ya?" He crossed his arms and waited.

Gene fidgeted. "I'm gonna piss myself."

Kirk sighed loudly. "Yeah, me too." He surveyed every corner of the ship they were inside. "Twiggy, we need to use the..." He fished for words and then added, "Toilet." Twiggy chirped and a seam appeared in the shape of a door on the opposite wall and then it opened. Kirk looked at Gene and then motioned to the door. "Ask and you shall receive. Hurry up!"

Kirk returned his focus to the monitor. It showed a vast hanger where other spaceships were stored. "Rotate us slowly," Kirk ordered. The ship rotated slowly. Behind them were a few rooms and a dark corridor. Kirk looked over his shoulder. Gene had quickly used the bathroom and O'Neil was already coming out of it.

"Your turn," he said to Kirk.

Kirk didn't want to but he couldn't deny his body any longer. He went inside the bathroom. There was nothing but a hole in a bench just like portable toilets on Earth. He grimaced but did his business anyway and then zipped himself back up while looking around for a place to wash his hands. On the shelf next to him was nothing but a shiny black square. He raised his eyebrows and slowly moved his hands over it. He heard a small rush of air and his hands suddenly felt warm. He flinched and took his hands away and then paused for a moment. He brought his hands to his face and sniffed. They smelled a little bit like oranges. He left the bathroom and looked at the monitor again. "Twiggy, can we breathe out there?"

The door in the bottom of the ship suddenly opened. All three of them jumped and covered their mouths. Twiggy floated in front of Kirk. It chirped and then whistled.

"Goddamn it, Twiggy!" Kirk yelled.

O'Neil jumped out of the ship. "Let's just go."

They jumped out of the ship and walked toward the rooms. Kirk looked sideways at Twiggy. Every time he verbalized a desire out loud, it made it happen without asking. So far, they haven't died, but he was beginning to think that Twiggy was more like an evil genie that purposely screwed up every wish.

"We're inside the Moon, Rogers, can you believe it?" O'Neil walked next to him. He held out his arms. "And look at all these ships! America will soon be exploring the universe and it's all thanks to you."

Kirk raised one eyebrow at him. "Where do you plan on finding a bunch of people with whatever it is in my blood that makes me special?"

O'Neil looked at Gene for a moment. Kirk knew it was because he thought Gene the genius might be able to figure out a way around that problem. He shrugged and looked back at Kirk. "We'll just have Twiggy test everyone."

"Twiggy is mine. Get your own," Kirk said, laughing.

They stopped in front of another large monitor. Gene smoothed back his hair as he always did. "I hate to tell you this, Kirk. But you and your sister are aliens. Or at least you have alien blood."

"Maybe we're all aliens."

"If that were true, all of us would be able to activate this stuff." Gene pointed at Twiggy. "You should command him to listen to us too."

"Why would I do that?" Kirk was flabbergasted. He thought for a moment. He wasn't one hundred percent sure if he could trust either one of them. Especially O'Neil. He thought he knew them, but they had been keeping a huge secret from him for years. He knew it was technically their duty because it was top secret, but couldn't help feeling betrayed. "Twiggy, you can do what they ask, but only if you want to, and as long as it doesn't end up hurting me. Okay? Use your good judgment."

Twiggy chirped twice and whistled.

Gene shook his head and rolled his eyes. "It is a machine. It doesn't have good judgment."

Twiggy moaned with sorrow.

"No offense," Gene added.

O'Neil put his hands on his hips and closed one eye at Twiggy, squinting at it. Kirk was sure he was contemplating whether or not to give Twiggy a murderous command. Finally, O'Neil pointed at the orb. "Twiggy, will you show us where his sister is in relation to our position?"

The monitor lit up with a map. Three blue dots appeared to represent them and one red dot appeared across the map to represent Laura. Then a line connected them. Gene looked at the index. "Look, he put it in English for us. She's fifty-six miles away."

"What?" Kirk put his hands on his head and then raised them to the sky. "Why are you doing this to me?"

O'Neil smirked and pointed a finger upward. "Weird thought, if you're on Earth and look to the sky as being where God is, then if you do it while on the Moon..."

"Shut up," Kirk snapped.

"Son, may I remind you that I'm your commanding officer?" O'Neil glared at him.

"Sorry," Kirk corrected himself. "Shut up, Sir."

O'Neil nodded. "That's better." He looked at the map. "Now, how are we going to get from here, to there?"

* * *

Steven had been holding on tightly to the disc's edge for so long that his muscles started to tremble and he couldn't feel his right hand. He couldn't let the disc take Laura away. He couldn't spend another five years all by himself with no one to talk to. He looked down at her. She was caught in some kind of beam of light that held her beneath the disc as it flew. When they stopped, he was grateful. He would be able to adjust himself a little and get a better hold before they took off again. She gave him a worried look. She was pale and looked very sick. He wondered if that had something to do with Junior. The little tyke walked up his back and onto his shoulder. That's when it happened. The disc he was on turned upside down and they fell. He heard Laura scream as he fell helplessly into the trees. He knew he was going to die. A day ago, he might have welcomed such an event, but now he had someone who needed his help. As he fell closer to the trees, he hoped that they would break his fall without breaking him. He tried like hell to grab the branches as he hit them. Suddenly his body violently jerked forward and bounced to an eventual stop. He looked up and found that he was suspended from a thin web. Junior had saved his life. From there, he was able to swing himself to a tree and climb down to the ground.

Steven was glad to be back on the ground, but now he had no idea where the disc had taken Laura. Junior lowered himself onto his shoulder. The little guy still gave him the willies, but he knew he couldn't just leave him behind. Plus, he kind of owed him. He struck out on foot in the direction that the discs had been heading. He knew they had flown a few hundred miles. He had never been to that part of the planet before. It would be dark soon and that meant that he would be vulnerable. At least walking didn't require the use of his arms. They were sore and basically useless at the moment. He marveled at how his life had changed so drastically in the span of just one day. He used to spend his days just trying to survive. Now he was on an adventure to save a new friend. Not only that, but he learned that not all monsters were created equal. He looked down at Junior. He wanted to reassure him that everything would be okay. He had only uttered one word in the last few years and he was still afraid that if he spoke, the little howling bastards would come. He thought it might be better to try while he was alone in the wilderness, instead of in front of Laura, when he might embarrass the hell out of himself. "Jah...Junior, it's...okay," he smiled. "I will... take... care of you."

65

HOWLS penetrated the peace of the forest launching birds into flight. Steven's heart filled with terror as he spun around trying to figure out which direction they would come in. He should have known, he spoke, so of course, they would come. He made a sudden decision to run in the direction the disc had been flying. If there was a building or something in that direction, perhaps it would be their salvation. They ran into a clearing and saw a black building against a rocky cliff face. There were no visible windows and the only door had no hinges or doorknob. It was made of the same material, and was the same color, as the building. There was a sensor pad of some kind next to the door. Steven had to assume that he was supposed to place his hand on it so he did. Nothing happened. Of course, nothing happened. Because if it opened, that would have been too easy. The terrifying creatures ran into the clearing and headed straight for him. From a distance, they looked like green coyotes, but if you were unfortunate enough to get closer, they looked a lot like gremlins with long ears and sharp, pointy teeth. If he didn't get inside soon he was going to be food. Maybe he could just ask them not to eat him? He spent five years avoiding those vicious things and now he was going to be their evening meal and all because of a woman. There must be a way inside.

Junior hopped onto the wall while Steven prepared to fight the demons that had been hunting him for years. His arms were so sore he could barely lift them, but he got into a karate stance and mentally took note of which gremlin would reach him first. The one in the lead growled and launched itself into the air at his head. He leaped up and kicked it to the side while another jumped at him. He backhanded it away and then leaped up into the air again to kick two of the devils away. They always traveled in packs. They were small and easy to hurt, but there was only one of him. Being bitten the night before was easily the worst thing that had ever happened to him and he'd be damned if he was going to let it happen again. Steven kept hitting the creatures away as best he could, but he was exhausted. He knew that he would soon lose the battle. Junior walked across the sensor pad and suddenly, the door opened. Steven shook his head but wasn't about to stare a gift horse in the mouth. He held out his hand for Junior to hop onto and then stepped through the door hoping it would shut quickly. The creatures ran at top speed towards the door. A laser from above the door started picking them off one by one until the door slid shut. He stood in darkness, wondering what fresh hell he just stepped into. He couldn't see anything at all. He stood still and let his eyes slowly adjust until he believed he saw some light coming from down a corridor. He wondered why the door had suddenly opened. Was it because someone inside that building opened it for him? Or was there another explanation? He was scared but knew that if he wanted to find Laura he couldn't remain where he was. He decided to proceed with caution and walk down the hallway. He was going to find her, or die trying.

* * *

Sheldor, or the ship's computer as it were, got busy saving Laura as he was commanded. But such a command required the need for a body. He programmed a few million nanobots to repair Laura but when they reported back that it could not be done, he had to take other measures to ensure her survival. The nanobots would be able to keep her alive long enough for an android body to be assembled for him. He had it created in Sheldor's likeness because he was already very fond of it. Once he downloaded his program to the android's Positronic brain, he would tend to the woman.

Sheldor opened his eyes and smirked. The character he emulated from The Bazinga Factory, often expressed a desire to be an android. It was only fitting that he kept his image and used it for his own purposes. He walked over to Laura. She was still lying on the floor, but she looked at him when he approached. That was a good sign. At least she was alive. He gently picked her up and carried her down the hall. "Commanding me to do whatever was necessary to save you was a very smart move. Originally, my goal was to save the descendants of the Newtonians who now reside on Earth. I needed one of their descendants, with enough of their DNA, to make the command and release the controls of this ship to me." He placed her on a table and a glass dome closed over her. "You might ask yourself; but why do the Newtonians need to be saved? Well, that's simple, really. It's because the Sun is going to go supernova in a matter of days. So, you see, even if I save your life, you would still die. You, and everyone else on planet Earth. Except you commanded me to do whatever was necessary to save your life. Isn't that spectacular? It looks like I will accomplish my goal after all."

He looked at the readings on the bed. "Kidney failure. I was hoping it would be something hard." He cocked his head and his eyes rolled to the left side of his face. "You may as well come in, I know you are there."

Steven walked in slowly with his knife held out in front of him. Junior rode in on his shoulder.

Sheldor was amused. "I assume you heard everything I just said?" Steven nodded so he continued, "Good, it would have been annoying if I had to repeat myself." He pressed a few buttons. "Don't touch her or I'll break all of your fingers. And some of your toes too." He laughed. "This is weird, isn't it? I've never had a body before. It's wonderful!"

* * *

Steven's eyes were as wide as saucers. He didn't know what to do. There was this weird man who resembled an actor from a show he used to watch, standing over Laura threatening to break his fingers, and toes, if he touched her.

"You might as well put that knife away. Even if you managed to damage this body, you wouldn't kill me. I would just download myself to a new one." He finished making the adjustments to Laura's medical pod so he turned his full attention to Steven. "She'll be unconscious for quite some time." He stepped up to Steven and held his hand out. "My name is Sheldor, what's yours?"

Steven's eyes were still wide, but he shook his hand.

Sheldor tilted his head like he couldn't hear, waiting for a response.

Steven looked at him out of the corner of his eye. "Steven."

The android looked at Junior curiously. "Is that an Arcandodious? I thought they were extinct. Simply amazing." Junior hopped onto the wall and walked up the ceiling. Sheldor picked at Steven's sleeve with two of his fingers and sighed. "I'll show you to a room. You have an unpleasant smell. Make sure you bathe and change your clothes. More guests will be arriving soon." He suddenly smiled broadly. "Unpleasant smell, can you believe it? I can smell you!" He took a big whiff of the air next to Steven and then exaggerated a look of disgust. "If I could vomit, I would." He snorted, which served as his laugh.

Steven looked past Sheldor and saw Junior lowering himself onto Laura's pod. He climbed underneath the dome and crawled down to her wrist to feed. He didn't want Sheldor to see what Junior was up to, so he smiled at him. "Okay."

Sheldor walked out of the room expecting him to follow. He took one last look at Laura and Junior before he left. He followed the android down the hall and hoped that leaving his new friends alone wouldn't prove to be the wrong choice. Everything felt weird to him. He was walking through a building that he never knew existed. For the last five years, he had been living off the land and running from monsters. There was a light streaming out of a room into the hallway ahead of him. Sheldor walked inside, but Steven stopped at the door. It was a dream. That was the only way to describe it. A dream. One where beds and couches existed. He walked into the room with an involuntary smile. Sheldor stood with his arms behind his back. He looked at his guest. "I'm sure you will find everything you need." Steven felt his eyes begin to sting with tears, but he tried to shake them off. The android pretended not to notice and looked away.

Steven cleared his throat. "Thank you."

"Certainly." Without any further explanations or instructions, the android left the room.

He was having trouble containing himself. He looked at the burgundy couch next to him. It looked soft and appealing and it was calling to him. It wanted him to sit on it. It wanted him to spend time on it. It wanted him to, perhaps, sleep on it. He reached down and touched the armrest. He rubbed his hand back and forth on the material. It was soft and he wanted nothing more than to sit on it. But as Sheldor pointed out, he was dirty and had an unpleasant odor. That was something he meant to correct before making himself at home on any sofa...or bed. He knew there had to be one there somewhere. He looked around the living room. The furniture was very similar to that of Earth. He saw a painting on the wall that depicted a field of black flowers and a blue sunset. He didn't know if the painting was altered or if it was considered abstract but he liked it. He wondered if the place existed somewhere in the galaxy or if it was straight out of someone's imagination.

Steven walked through the room into what he hoped would be the bedroom. He wasn't disappointed. The bed was a bit larger than it would be for a human, but that was fine by him. Like the couch, it beckoned him to come to it. He started to personify the bed and identify with it. He knew that it had been alone for quite some time too. He wanted to comfort it just as much as it wanted to comfort him. He knew that they would be fast friends. But the bed wanted him to shower first, and so did he. He was overtaken with the need to feel hot water rushing over his head and body. He hurried into the only room left in the apartment. There it was in all its splendor and glory. The shower. It might as well have been a woman. It was sexy and alluring and he wanted it more than anything in the universe. He was pretty sure he'd pass up sex for one.

He looked down at the rags that tried to pass off as clothing. He bathed pretty regularly in the cold stream, but the clothes he arrived in didn't stand up to the test of time. He stripped down, not caring if there was anything else to wear. Out of the corner of his eye, he saw movement and he turned to look. He was relieved to find that it was just his own reflection. He scrutinized himself. He was thin and muscular and a bit hairier than he remembered. He knew that he had lost weight and gained muscle since he had been there, but his full transformation had not been realized until that moment. He smiled and smoothed his hands down his chest. He turned to try to see his back and butt. There was, apparently, a plus side to being marooned. He wasn't severely overweight before. He was like everyone else in their late twenties. He got busy, got stressed, ate more than he should, and even though he had no family...he acquired that 'dad bod' that men seem to get when they just quit trying. He suddenly frowned. It was him in the mirror, but he didn't recognize that person. He had seen his reflection in the water, but the angle was always from above and not a good perspective. He decided to step into the shower. Maybe hot water would make him feel better.

There didn't appear to be any knobs or handles. He looked up and saw what appeared to be a showerhead. How was he going to turn it on? He assumed that it must be voice-activated. He wanted the shower bad enough to try. "Hot... sh..." He didn't want to speak even though he knew he was safe. "Hot shower." He said it. It wasn't very loud, but he said it. Warm water rained over him, slowly getting warmer and stronger until it was perfect. Steven couldn't have done it better if he had adjusted it himself. He closed his eyes and let the water run over his face. He tilted his head back and smoothed his black hair behind him. He held his hand under the small chrome box on the wall and it squirted what he hoped was soap into his hand. He rubbed his hands together to lather up and then washed his chest. There was a good chance that he would spend the next hour in there. Or maybe forever. He wasn't leaving until he was damn good and ready...and pruned. Yesterday he was Tarzan in a treehouse with no friends. Now he had at least three friends, two of which had eight legs, and the Sun needed some TLC or it would go supernova. Not to mention the weird man who threatened to break his fingers. 'Still, a better day than it was yesterday,' he thought to himself.

Chapter Four
Sheldor Cometh

O'Neil rubbed the stubble on his chin as he looked at the map Twiggy had created for them. "If we're the blue dots and she's the red one, then what do these green dots represent?"

Kirk pointed at a green dot located near Laura's red one. "That must be the man in the picture. So, these other three have to be people too." He put his finger on the monitor and highlighted a path to the nearest green dots. "Which means these two are only about half a mile away."

"What if they're not people?" Gene frowned. "This is an alien spaceship."

O'Neil blinked at him a few times. "The Moon is an alien spaceship?"

"What do you think it is?" Gene folded his arms.

"Well, then I guess we're about to meet us some aliens." Kirk turned to the orb. "Twiggy, lead us to the little green alien dots."

Twiggy led them down a dark corridor. Kirk was excited. He couldn't wait to see what they would find. Taking the ship was accidental, but they could have gone back at any time. Now they were inside the Moon and perhaps in danger. He took his phone out of his pocket and looked at the photo his sister sent to him. "This picture looks like it was taken outside. Look, there are trees in the background." He looked at the enormous spider behind Laura. "We have to remember not to kill the big spiders."

"What would we kill them with?" O'Neil pointed at him and pretended to fire with his hand. "This is all we got, pal."

Kirk looked down at his phone. The energy bar in the corner was at the full mark despite the fact that it should be in need of a charge. Something weird was going on. He looked up at his floating friend. "Hey Twiggy, can you put the map on my phone?" Twiggy chirped and the map appeared on his phone. Kirk smiled broadly and then nodded in appreciation. "Awesome." He let his phone guide him toward the unknown. As they walked down the hall the lights would go on ahead of them and then turn off behind them. It was a smooth transition. No noises or clicking sounds, just seamless illumination. As they were about to pass a door, O'Neil walked up to it. He ran his hands along the outside and looked at it very confused.

"There doesn't seem to be a handle." O'Neil exaggerated a frown and looked over his shoulder at Kirk. He immediately pointed to the light gray rectangular pad next to the door. O'Neil eyed it like an orangutan with a strange new toy. He put his hand against it. Nothing happened. "Guess it doesn't like me." He thrust both his hands at the sensor, silently commanding to Kirk to give it a try.

Gene put up his hands. "Maybe the closed door should just stay closed."

O'Neil pointed at the door. "Are you crazy? You said yourself, we're on an alien spaceship. There could be anything in there."

75

"Exactly. You don't know what is in there."

Kirk looked at them both like they were children. He leaned his hand on the pad and the door slid open. The light turned on and Kirk stuck his head inside. He turned back to his pals and without a word walked inside. There were sleek cabinets against the wall. He ran his hands along them, but nothing happened. He cocked his head and looked at them. "Open." The doors on the cabinets opened until they were flush with the wall. Gene and O'Neil stood behind him as they all gawked at the contents. They had to be weapons. The boys inside these grown men never grew up and the toys in front of them needed to be played with. Kirk picked one up. It was small and resembled a digital ear thermometer with a small trigger. He closed one eye and aimed it at the wall. "Wonder what this does." He pulled the trigger. "Nothing. It does nothing."

Gene looked at the one in his hand. "Maybe it is set on stun." He fiddled with a little switch and it made a high-pitched noise.

Kirk turned around and looked at him. "Hey, watch where you're pointing that." He took it from him and aimed it at the wall. He pulled the trigger. This time it blew a giant hole in the wall, causing little pieces of shrapnel to hit them.

"Kirk! Are you crazy?" O'Neil whacked Kirk upside the head. He ducked after the fact and then swept the dust off his shirt with his hands.

Kirk coughed a few times. "Let's shut them off, but bring them with us. If we get outside, we can play with them a little."

"Agreed. We can't afford to leave them here." O'Neil slipped his hand in his pocket carefully as he eyed the hole in the wall that it made.

"It probably does have a stun setting," Gene said as he examined another gun.

Kirk looked through the contents of the cabinet again. His eyes fell on a leather and metal glove. His eyes lit up. "Cool." He immediately picked it up and pulled it onto his right hand. He suddenly winced and his legs almost buckled before he regained his strength.

"Damn it, Kirk! Have you lost your freakin mind?" O'Neil was flabbergasted. He shook his head. "What the hell are you thinking? Take it off! Take it off, right now!"

Kirk eyed his superior. "That's sexual harassment, sir. And I don't have to stand for it."

O'Neil's lunged toward him. "I'll show you harassment." He twisted Kirk's arm under his and pulled the gauntlet as hard as he could. He tried several different holds as Kirk pulled with all his might away from him. he could feel himself getting angrier and angrier. He braced himself and pushed O'Neil away.

Kirk looked down at his right wrist and arm. The gauntlet was somehow fused to him. "I was thinking," he breathed heavily and then continued, "that gauntlets are cool." He rubbed his wrist as he opened and closed his hand. "It won't come off." He was breathing very hard and wanted to beat the living hell out of Gene and O'Neil. Instead, he made a tight fist and pointed it at the wall, but Gene jumped in front of him and held up his hands.

"Let's not and say we did. We don't know what that thing
does. It could bring the roof down on us."

Kirk turned his head and his eyes moved to the right side of his face. He held up his hand. "Listen."

Gene's eyes darted from one side to the other. He whispered, "What?"

"I don't hear anything." O'Neil grabbed Kirk's phone from him and looked at it and then handed back. He cupped his hands together over his mouth and shouted, "HELLO?"

The men listened carefully.

"Hello?" The voice was distinctly female. "We're here!" Another female voice.

They looked at each other and grinned. No one said it, but all three of them were thinking it. 'Women.' They hurried down the corridor towards the voices. At first, all they could see was a light from a cell phone barely illuminating two faces. But as they approached the lights came on. Two women sat on the floor huddled close together. They squinted at the brightness of the light.

A thin woman in her thirties with long black hair stood up. She had fear and desperation in her piercing blue eyes. "Thank God." She bent down and helped her friend up. She was a big and beautiful black woman with shoulder-length black hair that had red highlights and she wore a little too much eye makeup. Both the women were dressed in business casual clothing and high heels.

"Hey, you two okay?" Kirk suddenly realized that the two
had no way of turning on the lights. "How long have you been in the dark?"

The dark-haired woman wiped a tear from her eye. "We've been wandering around in here for almost two days."

"Jesus, that's terrible." O'Neil furrowed his brow. "How'd you two get here?"

The two women looked at them blankly. The redhead looked from one to the other, "We were in an elevator and when we got off..."

"It was pitch dark. And we took out our phones and used the flashlight app." The other added.

"For two days?" Gene shook his head.

The dark-haired woman showed him her phone. "Yeah, the power never ran out. See?"

Gene leaned in and looked at her phone. The power bar was at its max. He looked back up at her. "You're pretty and you smell nice."

Kirk laughed uncomfortably and pulled Gene away from her. "I'm sorry, he's special."

"You promised not to call me that anymore." Gene was emotionally wounded.

O'Neil intervened. "My name is Colonel Andy O'Neil. You can call me, O'Neil. This is Captain Kirk Rogers, you can call him, ass-hat. And this, this special young man is, Gene. You can call him Rottenberry."

Kirk looked at the two women and silently mouthed the word 'NO' while shaking his head and waving his hand.

The dark-haired woman wasn't amused. "This is Penny Robinson, and my name is Ann Dorian."

Gene giggled uncontrollably. Everyone stared at him blankly, wondering what the hell he was laughing at.

Twiggy floated up to Kirk and chirped. The two women looked at it with wide eyes. Ann walked up to the orb and looked at it closely. "What the hell is that?"

Kirk held his hand under the orb. It made it appear as though he was holding it. "He's my little friend, Twiggy."
Penny shook her head, annoyed. "It's Twiki, *Captain* Rogers."

"Not to me." Kirk filled them in on what little information they knew. The women were understandably scared and confused.

"Do you really expect us to believe that we are inside the Moon?" Ann paced back and forth. You could almost see the two halves of her brain arguing.

O'Neil put his arms out. "Look, lady, it doesn't matter what you believe. This is happening."

"Excuse me?"

Everyone turned around and saw a man standing there looking at them. His short brown hair was parted to the side and his brown eyes twinkled as he spoke. "I've been waiting for you people to arrive for nearly an hour. What is the holdup?"

Kirk's forehead crinkled as his eyebrows knitted together. "Sheldor?"

Gene stared blankly, but still found enough composure to speak. "Don't be stupid, it's the guy that plays Sheldor. What's his name? Jim, or James, or something?"

"This is not even real life anymore," Penny said dramatically.

"Actually, I'm technically neither." He looked at all their confused faces and then continued. "Tomorrow's a big day. Let's go." He turned around and walked off, expecting them to follow.

O'Neil and Kirk looked each other in the eyes as if they were reading each other's mind. Kirk shrugged and O'Neil shook his head and gestured after Sheldor.

Kirk turned to Twiggy. "What do you think, buddy?"

Twiggy followed Sheldor.

"If it's okay with Twiggy, I guess he's okay with me." He followed Twiggy. "Unless any of you have a better idea."

* * *

Steven poked his head back into the room where he last saw her. He was clean, well-groomed, and felt better than he had in years. He wore black pants and a matching black shirt with long sleeves. If you gave him a mask and sword he could play Zorro. Dark from head to toe with black hair and an evening shadow. Except, Zorro never crept around with eyes as big as saucers, worried that he'd get his fingers and toes broken by a robot that was masquerading as a man. He walked over to her pod and looked inside. He tried to decipher the readings of her medical bed, but he couldn't make heads or tails of it. He hoped that whatever Sheldor was doing to her was going to make her better. He would hate to lose the only human friend he made in the last five years. But Sheldor did say he was expecting guests. He didn't care about that at the moment. The only openings to her pod were at the head and the foot of her bed. He was alone with her, but he still couldn't bring himself to talk. The only way to let her know that he was there was to touch her. He reached into the pod and gently smoothed her hair back.

If Sheldor was to be believed, the Sun would soon go out and they would all perish. There seemed to be a lot of room inside the Moon, perhaps they could evacuate a lot of people off the Earth and fly the Moon to a different solar system. He figured that must be what the Moon was originally made for in the first place. In truth, he just wanted to go home to Earth, even if that meant it would end. He wanted to find out what happened to his grandmother and perhaps reconnect with his father. When he was on Earth, he had fantasized about being a hermit somewhere in the wilderness, but now he knew what kind of curse that actually was. Even if you were a loner, at least if you wanted company all you had to do was leave your home and go to the grocery store. He had been more alone in the last five years than any human should ever be. He felt a presence so he looked up. It was the android.

Sheldor smiled and rolled back and forth from his tiptoes to his heels. "Now then, shall we break those fingers before or after our little adventure?"

Steven ignored Sheldor and looked back down at Laura. He wished that she would wake up and look at him. It would make him feel so much better.

Sheldor stopped his rocking and watched Steven. "I knew you were out there."

That got his attention. He looked the android in the eye.

"There was nothing I could do about it." He joined Steven and looked down at Laura too. "When the Newtonians left for Earth they disabled most of my program. Everything else was on automation." He shrugged. "I discovered that the Sun was in trouble years ago. I managed to manipulate the teleportation program to bring Newtonian descendants here. All in the hopes that one of you would be able to unlock my programming." He motioned to Laura. "And one of them finally did. Although, it may be too late." He placed a hand on Steven's shoulder. "There is food in the dining hall. I know you must be hungry. The rest of our party will be joining us very soon."

* * *

Kirk and the gang followed Sheldor to a sealed white door and then he turned around to face them. He pointed to a sensor pad next to the door. "Okay, just for fun, let's see which one of you can open the door."

Kirk stepped forward, but Sheldor stopped him. "Not you. Let's give the others a chance, shall we?"
Ann looked from Kirk to Sheldor. She was obviously the 'no-nonsense' one in the bunch. "What's going on?"

Kirk stepped aside and motioned to the sensor. "Just do it."

She walked up to the sensor and placed her hand on it. Nothing happened. Penny looked at the men and they all motioned for her to go next. She placed her hand on the sensor, and again, nothing happened. Each one of them tried with the same result.

Sheldor rolled his eyes. "All of you are useless to me."

"Hey!" Kirk tried to shove him but his hands passed right through him. He waved his hand through his chest. "He's a hologram."

"Through this door is a transport that you people would equate to a train or subway. Get on it and it will take you to me. If you still want to hit me, you can do so then." The image of him faded until he completely disappeared. Kirk placed his hand on the sensor and the door slid open. On the other side was a white room with a chrome pill-shaped car on a track. Kirk walked over to it and touched it. The door slid open and the lights turned on.

Ann's mouth dropped open and her eyes went wide. She gripped two handfuls of her own hair. "What alternate universe did I step into! How can you all be going along with this?"

O'Neil gently grabbed her wrists and pulled her arms down. "Now, now, we can't have any of that." He stepped behind her and put an arm around her back. He rubbed her shoulder as he walked her into the transport. It had eight seats, one behind the other, with tall backs. They all climbed inside and chose seats. As Kirk sat, his phone dinged. He reached into his pocket and took it out. He had a text message.

Text: Hold me tight.

Kirk furrowed his brow. "What?" Twiggy lowered itself onto his lap. "Twiggy, did you just text me?"

Bing! Text: You told me to figure out how to talk.

Kirk put his phone back into his pocket and held Twiggy tight. "Is everyone strapped in?"

O'Neil looked at everyone and then sat down. "Good to go."

"Alright then, let's go, Twiggy." The transport started slowly and then sped up until all of them were plastered to their seats. Kirk's face had an involuntary grin from sheer inertial force. "Shit!"

Ann and Penny screamed as O'Neil hooted with excitement. They started to slow down almost as soon as they hit top speed. Soon they stopped and the door hissed open. O'Neil was the first to stand. "That was somethin'."

Gene was green. He filled his cheeks with air and held it for a moment. "I think I need a change of clothes."

Kirk let go of Twiggy and let it float out of the tram. They all got out slowly. Kirk was the last to exit the transport and when he saw Sheldor standing there greeting everyone, he angrily walked up to him. He opened and closed his gauntlet repeatedly. Somehow this simple action made him more pumped up and angrier. He punched Sheldor in the stomach as hard as he could. The android didn't move or flinch in the slightest. Kirk, on the other hand, reacted as if he had hit a cast-iron skillet. He cradled his hand with his other arm. He gritted his teeth in pain. "What are you?"

Sheldor couldn't contain his joy. "I didn't think you'd actually do it." He turned around and walked down the hall. "Walk this way." He laughed.

O'Neil took one arm of each of the women. "Shall we, ladies?"

Gene and Kirk watched O'Neil escort them down the hall. He leaned close to Kirk and whispered, "I thought *you* were the ladies man."

Sheldor led them to a dining room. The table was filled with colorful fruits and vegetables. Some were familiar and easily recognizable while others were a mystery. Both of the women sat down and grabbed as much food as they could and started chowing down. They didn't seem to notice the man in black that watched them all as they came in.

"Thank God, I haven't eaten since this morning," Gene said taking a seat.

Ann chewed an apple and swallowed hard. "Well, we haven't eaten in two days."

Kirk walked into the room very slowly. He was staring down the only person he hadn't met yet. The man he saw in the picture with his sister was sitting at the table chewing on a carrot. Sheldor watched Kirk curiously and followed his gaze. "Oh, where are my manners. The man in black is Steven. Steven, this is Captain Kirk Rogers."

Steven was excited to see people. He stood up and offered his hand to Kirk. When he failed to shake it, he let his hand slowly relax at his side.

O'Neil looked up at Sheldor from his seat. "Aren't you forgetting something?"

"Oh, I could care less about the rest of you." Sheldor waved him off.

"Gee, thanks," Gene said as he peeled a banana.

Kirk looked from Sheldor to Steven. He was only concerned about one thing. He didn't mean to, but he growled a little when he asked, "where is my sister?"

Ann dropped her apple in her plate making it clank. "Your sister? What the hell's going on here?"

"There she is!" Sheldor pointed to the door like an excited child. He had a stupid grin on his face.

Laura was confused to see all the people in the room and then she saw him. "Steven!" She ran past Kirk, practically knocking him over, and launched herself at Steven to hug him tight. "I thought you were dead!"

O'Neil looked at Kirk and smiled as he chewed. Kirk furrowed his brow and looked utterly wounded. "She obviously didn't see me."

* * *

Steven looked down at Laura as she hugged him. He wasn't prepared for the emotion that he'd feel. It hit him like a tidal wave. Tears threatened to creep out of his eyes, but he gained control and blinked them away. He had no contact at all in so long that a simple hug nearly crippled him. He stepped back and gently grabbed Laura's right arm where Junior was attached. He covertly pulled her sleeve and brought it down over Junior effectively hiding him from the others. He could tell by the look in her eye that she knew exactly what he was doing and why. She watched as he brought her hand up to his lips and kissed it gently. She turned red and grinned.

Kirk tapped her on the shoulder. "Hey sis, remember me?" She turned and looked at him. "I stole a spaceship and flew to the Moon to find you. The least you could do is give me a hug." He held out his arms to her.

She hugged him tight. "You stole a spaceship?"

He let his chin rest on the top of her head for a moment. "Yeah," he lowered his voice. "There's something in our blood that allows us to do stuff here."

"All of you are descendants of the Newtonians," Sheldor interjected. He looked at Gene and O'Neil. "Well, except you two. You both were just along for the ride. As for the rest of you, the only way you would even get here is if you had Newtonian DNA. Laura, and Mr. Rogers, here, have the most. And therefore, they are able to activate devices."

"Don't call me Mr. Rogers."

O'Neil laughed and mocked him. "Mr. Rogers."

Laura sat down at the table and helped herself to some of the fruit.

Kirk squinted at Steven and spoke to him under his breath. "If you're lookin' for someone to knock boots with, the little guy over there thinks you're hot. Stay away from my sister."

Steven sighed. He wasn't going to let anyone tell him what to do. Before he even realized it, the word escaped his lips. "No."

Kirk got in his face. "No?"

Steven looked him directly in the eye. "No," he repeated and then he walked around the table to join Laura. She smiled at him while she crunched down on an unknown fruit.

Gene expertly peeled an orange around and around in a spiral. He glanced at the android. "You were telling us about the Newtonians?"

"Certainly," Sheldor said as he clasped his hands behind his back. "The Newtonians were a highly-advanced people from the Andromeda Galaxy. They built this ship because their planet was dying. Some lived as farmers out in the terrarium, and some lived as programmers and scientists, here, in Atlantis. He motioned to his position. "The purpose, of course, was to find a suitable planet to inhabit. Generations lived aboard this ship for thousands of years before they found Earth. They arrived in orbit about five thousand years ago, but there was a problem." He looked around the room to see if anyone was listening. Laura was leaning her head in her hand and looking right at him.
She exaggerated a frown and furrowed her brow at the same time. "This...is Atlantis?"

"Well, as I'm sure you know, all lore originates in reality. Newtonians told stories of Atlantis and over the ages the tales became legend."

"What was the problem?" Kirk asked before popping a grape into his mouth and chewing with his mouth open.

"Your Sun."

"I don't have a son," Kirk smirked and then looked around the table to see if anyone else thought it was funny. No one did.

"It was volatile and unstable, so the Newtonians had to build a photon cannon to correct it. The cannon spans the entire length of this ship and took several hundred years to complete but eventually, it was used to stabilize the Sun. It settled into an eleven-year pattern and the Newtonians were satisfied."

Gene smoothed the hair behind his ears. "I sense a 'but' coming."

Sheldor had a distant look in his eyes. "But... apparently, it wasn't a permanent fix. If the cannon isn't fired again, the Sun will go supernova and destroy the entire solar system."

"Fun." O'Neil nodded and then shook his head.

"Then I guess it's lucky you have me to turn it on, huh?" Kirk smiled, but it soon drained away from his face when he saw that the android still had a very serious look on his face.

Sheldor tipped his head to the side. "Well, you see, this ship was programmed to fire the cannon whenever the readings required it."

"Oh man." Gene's mouth dropped open.

"What?" Laura looked at him and then to Sheldor.

Gene rubbed his eyes. "He's about to tell us that we're damned if we do, and damned if we don't."

Sheldor's eyes lit up. He nodded and then gestured to Gene. "The cannon was damaged by an asteroid impact that occurred hundreds of years ago. If the cannon fires, the ship..." He gestured to Gene and nodded. "Your Moon, will explode."

Kirk's face turned red. He looked at his sister who was sitting across from him. She was staring into her plate. This wasn't what he hoped to find when he set out on his mission to rescue her. He repeated the bullet points out loud. "So, basically, you're saying that you need us to fix a photon cannon, in four days, or else we all die?"

They all sat quietly with frowns tugging at their faces.

"Yes, that's correct." He stepped back. "Tomorrow is going to be a long day, so I suggest you all get some sleep."

O'Neil and Gene got up and followed Sheldor out. Steven watched them leave. He was ever curious. Watching those people interact was a bit overwhelming. He turned to Laura and put his hand on her arm briefly and gave a half nod. He looked Kirk in the eye and then walked out. Kirk watched the other two women. They were just sitting there thinking about what they were just told. Kirk tapped the table with the tips of his index fingers. "Ladies, do you mind? I need to speak to my sister alone." They looked a little bit insulted. Penny grabbed the bottom of her shirt and began piling fruit into it then they both left.

He clasped his hands together and tapped his thumbs against each other. His demeanor softened dramatically. "I've been worried sick about you, kiddo."

Laura's eyes flicked toward the door. She felt uncomfortable and didn't know what to say. Her head got hot. She didn't want to start a fight. "You only came after me because I was on the Moon." She smiled, but it fell away quickly. Her eyes started to tear up. "Kirk, I'm at stage five kidney failure, again. And you didn't come to see me."

Kirk looked at his hands. "I don't want to be rude, but... Your illness might be happening to you, but it isn't *just* about you. It affects me too."

"Yeah, I know, and if I happened to forget that, you're quick to remind me." She stood up to leave.

He tipped his head to the side. "Where are you going? Look, we're not finished talking."

She headed for the door, but he grabbed her arm. "Hey, I want you to stay away from that guy. I don't trust him."

She looked him in the eye. "You don't even know him."

"Neither do you."

She pulled her arm from him and walked away.

* * *

Laura walked down the hall looking for a room to sleep in for the night. She assumed if the door was closed it was taken. A light streamed through an open door a few feet ahead of her, so she walked up to it, and looked inside. It was an empty living room with a very inviting burgundy sofa so she stepped inside. She saw something move out of the corner of her eye so she turned her head. She could see into the bedroom where Steven was inside laying on a giant bed. He was fully clothed, on his back, and staring at the ceiling. He must have sensed movement in the hallway so he turned his head and looked at her. She felt her face get hot and knew it must be beet red. She immediately turned on her heels and went back out into the main hallway where she could see Kirk staring at her from the dining hall doorway. She raised her voice just enough so Kirk could hear her. "Hi, Steven." She stepped into his room again and swiped her hand across the sensor to shut the door. The strap of her pack slipped off her shoulder and she caught it before it hit the floor. Steven sat up and looked at her. She had herself plastered against the door. "Um..." She laughed uncomfortably as she faced him. She walked slowly to the bedroom doorway and tried with all her might to look at him and not the floor. "My brother told me to stay away from you. So, you know, I wanted to piss him off."

Steven looked relieved and then smiled. He tapped the bed next to him. She stared at his hand and the spot that he offered her. She turned around briefly to look at the sofa. It was only a two-seater and she was very short but somehow, she didn't think it would be very comfortable to sleep on. She thought about what Kirk said about Steven and realized that she really didn't know him. Just one night ago she couldn't determine who was scarier, him or the howlers. She scratched the back of her neck and then walked forward, placing her pack on the floor next to the bed. "I can just sleep in here with no funny business?" He nodded as she climbed on the bed next to him. She wished he would talk to her. She grinned and looked at him out of the corner of her eye. "Good, I'll tell Junior to keep an eye on you." She rolled her sleeve up so that Junior could move around freely if he wanted to.

Steven got up, picked up a pillow, and then laid down on the floor beside the bed. She felt bad and slightly insulted. "Steven, I didn't mean for you to sleep on the floor. The bed is humongous. You can sleep up here."

He shook his head and waved his hand back and forth. He pointed to the floor.

She narrowed her eyes at him. "I'm pretty sure I saw you talk to my brother." She laid back and looked at the ceiling. "We're safe now. I wish you'd talk to me." Her tablet suddenly slid across the bed and bumped into her leg. She looked over in just enough time to see his hand disappear. She picked it up and read the message out loud. "I've been sleeping on sticks and moss for five years. The bed is too soft." She sighed. "Good night, Steven."

* * *

The next morning Gene, O'Neil, and Kirk found the ship's command center. Twiggy followed Kirk around as he touched every console like an excited two-year-old attracted to pretty lights and colorful buttons. After Kirk messed with and then abandoned the console in front of him, Gene sat down and started playing with it. It was a touchscreen map of the Earth below. He rolled the screen until the United States appeared and then zoomed in until he could see people. "This is amazing! Can you imagine what we could do with this?"

Kirk looked at one of the large monitors on the wall. "Twiggy, can you show me whatever the hell is wrong with the cannon...thing...that Sheldor was talking about?"

"Certainly, Captain Rogers," Twiggy responded with a female computer voice.

Kirk cocked his head. "Twiggy?"

The orb floated closer to him. "I have upgraded my programming."

He raised his eyebrows. "Oh yeah? Well, I've upgraded my feelings of uncertainty towards you. Now it's more of a *tangible* fear." He smirked and looked at the monitor while he spoke. "You're not going to upgrade to a human body, and molest me, are you?" He absentmindedly scratched behind his gauntlet.

"I would never abuse you sexually, Captain Rogers." Twiggy floated behind him.

Kirk's mouth dropped open. "But you'd abuse me in other ways?"

Laughter erupted from behind him. He turned around and looked at Gene. He was laughing his ass off. O'Neil was standing next to him, trying to hold a straight face. "Kirk, I always knew you were a sexual deviant. I just didn't know the extent." He crossed the room, slapped him on the back, and looked over his shoulder. "What are you up to?"

Kirk pointed to the diagram of the cannon. "There's a cave-in about two hundred miles from the opening, right here."

"How the hell are we going to clear out a cave-in?" O'Neil put his arm around Kirk's neck.

"Sir, personal space, man." He watched O'Neil feign being offended as he took a step to the side and put his hands up. Kirk rubbed the stubble on his chin. "They dug the tunnel out with something. There has to be equipment for that."

"Point of fact," Sheldor said as he walked in, "as soon as your sister unlocked my controls I assigned drones to work on clearing out the debris. But they can only do so much. Someone, that would be you or your sister, has to go get the mining equipment, and drive it into the access tunnel." He grabbed Kirk's arm and examined the gauntlet. "You shouldn't play with things you don't understand."

Kirk pulled his arm away from the android. "Why? What does it do?"

"It's a weapon."

"I assumed it was."

Sheldor nodded. "Did you also assume that the energy it needs in order to fire comes directly from you?"

Kirk eyed the gauntlet and raised an eyebrow. "What do you mean?"

"When you put that thing on your arm it inserted several thousand microscopic tendrils into your arm. It will start to charge the moment you feel fear or anger." He pointed to the top of the gauntlet. "This indicator changes with your mood."

O'Neil chuckled. "Like a mood ring?"

The android cocked his head for a moment and got a far off look in his eyes. He suddenly snapped out of it.

97

"Precisely. When the indicator is yellow, as it is now, Captain Rogers is calm. It will gradually move through shades of yellow, orange, and then red when he experiences any agitation, fear, or anger."

"And the energy part?"

"As I said, it will start to charge the moment you feel any kind of negative emotion. Once the indicator is red, you must discharge the weapon, or it will explode."

Kirk looked down at his wrist again. "Damn."

"See that, Kirk? You're a child. You came up here to save your sister, instead...you're gonna kill us all." O'Neil shook his head and turned away.

"Where is your sister, anyway?" Gene was drawing something on the map. "She and Steven seemed quite chummy."

Kirk's indicator turned from yellow to light orange. He walked over to Gene. "Shut up." He angrily erased whatever it was he was drawing, picked up the stylus, and wrote 'Dumbass' across California.

"It might interest you to know that the people of Pasadena are now looking up at the sky and seeing the word 'Dumbass' written across it and wondering what it means or who it is meant for." Sheldor scolded them both.

Gene laughed until he realized it wasn't a joke. He rubbed the screen with his sleeve. "Why would you even have something like that?"

He shrugged. "How else would the Newtonians make humans believe in gods that would punish them for behaving badly? There's no sense in living with Neanderthals if you don't have to."

O'Neil turned to Sheldor. "So, your people pretended to be God?"

"In essence, yes."

Gene looked around the room. Everyone was distracted so he quickly scribbled a new message.

It read: Be Good, Or Else.

* * *

'Laura, wake up.'

Laura opened her eyes. She blinked the blurry out until she could see Steven's handsome smiling face. He pointed to the window so she turned over. The largest, hairiest spider legs she'd ever seen were sprawled across the glass. They moved clockwise and then spider eyes looked at her.

"Jesus, that's disturbing." Laura sat up at the edge of the bed and rubbed her face, "CheeChee, I'm so sorry. You must have been worried sick." She walked to the window and tried to find a way to open it. "I don't think it opens. I'll come outside." She turned to look at Steven. He was staring at CheeChee with a stupid grin on his face. He must have been thinking of something funny, but she didn't know what it was. She touched his forearm and he looked at her. "Steven, do you remember how to get back outside?"

Soon the two of them were outside with CheeChee. It was a beautiful morning. Dew clung to the tips of the grass and a morning mist filled the air. Laura smelled a wonderful fragrance and realized it was coming from the beautiful, yet deadly, blue flowers she had seen the day before. They seemed to get brighter as she got closer to them.

'It is a trait that helps them lure prey.'

She kept forgetting that CheeChee could read her thoughts even if she said nothing. One didn't have to be a mind reader to know what someone was thinking. All you needed to do was watch someone in order to make an educated guess.

'Junior is well.'

"Was that a question? Or a statement?"

'He is in good health.'

"That's good. I'm glad."

'He says you taste different.'

"Oh, my God." She looked at Steven and laughed uncomfortably. "Junior says I taste different. I'm not sure if that's good or bad." She told CheeChee how they got there and of the impending doom. "We have to figure out how to stop it or everyone will die."

'I feel anger.'

"At me?"

100

'Behind you.'

Suddenly scared, Laura spun around. It was Kirk. He was glaring at Steven but his expression quickly changed when he saw CheeChee in all her scary splendor. Sheldor stood next to him with a silly grin on his face. If she were watching The Bazinga Factory, that look on Sheldor's face would indicate that he knew something everyone else didn't.

"Is your friend joining the adventure?" Sheldor asked, looking at CheeChee.

"Sheldor, Kirk, this is CheeChee. She's my friend." She moved in front of the large spider. "Please don't try to kill her. CheeChee, this is Sheldor, he's apparently an android. And the angry one, is my brother, Kirk."

Kirk looked at his wrist. "I'm not angry. I'm more yellow than I am orange."

Without moving her head, she looked left, and then right. "Um, I don't know what that means."

He waved at the huge spider like it was yesterday's news. "Hey CheeChee, you're ugly and your Momma dresses you funny."

'My mother died long ago. You are a...'

"Jerk." Laura suggested, "the word you're struggling to find is, jerk."

Kirk was stunned. "Did that thing just speak inside my head?"

"Fascinating." Sheldor smiled. "But times a wasting. We have to be at the Chancellor's Manor by sundown or we'll be behind schedule."

Chapter Five
Adventure Time

Ann and Penny walked into the common room. They were both wearing black pants with long-sleeved, red shirts. Gene pointed at them and laughed. "Redshirts." They both looked at him like he was nuts. He didn't have very much experience speaking to women, and it showed. "Danger, Penny Robinson, danger!" He laughed again.

Laura walked past Gene to the women. "So, were you two friends before you ended up here?"

Penny pulled her shirt away from her stomach and then let it relax. "I hate this shirt. It doesn't hang right." She stretched out the bottom again. "No, we were just on the elevator together."

Laura watched the woman mess with her shirt. "I know this is all a little bit scary for you both."

Ann looked past Laura at O'Neil. She leaned in close and spoke low. "Is the colonel single?"

Laura turned and looked at O'Neil. He was stuffing supplies in a pack. The question took her by surprise. The colonel was a good-looking man, for sure, but he was at least twenty years older than Ann. "Yes, he's very single." She had known the colonel for years and had never heard him even mention a woman. "He's a good guy. Mostly."

Kirk packed his bag and looked at O'Neil out of the corner of his eye. "When are we going to ask about more weapons?"

The colonel looked for Sheldor. "Quiet, he's an android, he can probably hear us right now. We'll talk about advancing our military after we save the world."

"Sir, that's not what I meant at all." Kirk zipped up the bag.

Sheldor came into the room carrying what looked like a metal briefcase. "To answer your question, Kirk, I have stun guns for you all. Ideally, we won't need them, but I'm nothing if not pragmatic." He walked over to the table and set the briefcase down, then opened it. He looked up at the colonel. "May I have the weapon in your pocket?" O'Neil blinked a few times and then cleared his throat before reaching into his front pocket and pulling out the small gun. He paused for a moment, looking at it, then gave it to him. Sheldor turned it over and then pointed at a small switch. "This setting is for stun. There will be no need for anything higher." He handed the weapon back.

O'Neil walked over to Gene and held out his hand. "Hand it over." As he adjusted Gene's gun, Sheldor adjusted the ones in his case and then gave them out.

Laura watched Penny and Ann examining their guns. "We have to travel five hundred miles before dark or creatures that my friend calls 'The Howlers' come out to eat you."

She looked in Steven's direction. He was playing with the stubble on his face as if he wasn't used to how it felt.

She wondered how he was doing now that he was around people and civilization. He had been mute for so long that he wouldn't speak, at least not to her, and that sort of behavior wasn't likely to gain him many friends.

Sheldor stood up and clasped his hands behind his back. "Unfortunately, we have to travel inside the terrarium. Which means we cannot travel over one hundred and twenty miles per hour or lasers will shoot us out of the sky." Sheldor turned around. "So if you will follow me, I'll show you to the..."

"Lasers will shoot us out of the sky?" O'Neil was flabbergasted.

"There were a lot of accidents that led to extensive damage, not to mention bodily injury and death. Eventually, it was decided that no one could travel at speeds greater than one hundred and twenty miles per hour."

O'Neil's eyebrows knitted together. "Shooting people out of the sky with lasers doesn't seem a little harsh to you?"

Sheldor gave him a serious look. "Well, as it turns out, you only have to do it a couple of times before everyone complies." He thought for a moment. "Perhaps disabling the transport so it wouldn't fly anymore would have been more humane, but the chancellor had a mean streak."

They followed Sheldor outside to a clearing. Two golden massive orbs floated down from above them and settled a foot off the ground. The orbs had windows most of the way around and seats inside. It looked like a pretty sweet way to travel. To Laura, they almost looked like those chariots made for a fictional princess in a child's cartoon, only it was far bigger and had no wheels. She loved the golden shine and couldn't wait to ride in it. She suddenly saw movement from above and looked up. CheeChee had lowered herself down on top of one of them. She didn't want to draw attention to the arachnid, so she turned to Sheldor.

"These are Transport Orbs. We'll be using them on the first leg of our journey." Sheldor activated the doors and they opened, lowering like a ramp onto the ground.

Ann stepped up and waved her arms. "Hold on, I've got a stupid question. If we're on an alien spaceship, then why do you know English and look like..." She waved her hand around at him. "That? Why do you look like that? And transport Orb? That's stupid." She circled her hand around at him and then made air quotes. "We're of 'Newtonian' decent, and we're here, and we have to save the Earth, but you haven't really explained anything."

As they talked, Laura watched CheeChee crawl into one of the transports and onto the ceiling.

"Firstly, Miss Dorian, I've been monitoring satellite communications since the early 1960's. Why wouldn't I know English? Or every language, for that matter." His expression softened. "Secondly, Transport Orb is merely the closest translation. Call it whatever you wish."

When Sheldor said the word 'monitoring' Laura had a sudden and unpleasant thought. She watched her brother pick up his pack as her anger grew.

Penny came up behind Ann and gently nudged her toward one of the orbs. She gave a fake laugh to lighten the mood. "Maybe we should call them; Torbs."

Laura suddenly ran at Kirk and pushed him as hard as she could. He fell to the ground and rolled in the dirt. He looked up at her shocked and confused. "Laura, what the hell?"

Everyone's attention was on them. Laura felt hot and her
heart knocked at her chest. "How did you know?"

Kirk got to his feet and brushed off his pants. He glanced at his wrist. Orange. "How did I know, what?"

"How did you know that I was on the Moon?!" If she could shoot lasers out of her eyes, Kirk would be nothing but a smoking pile of ash.

He shrugged. "Laura, you disappear all the time. I wanted to keep track of you." His eyes begged her forgiveness.

Tears streamed down her face. Steven appeared at her side and gently grabbed her arm around the elbow.

Sheldor shook his head. "As amusing as all of this is, I need you people to get on the Torbs before I start tossing you on myself."

Laura looked at him out of the corner of her eye. She wondered if he was attempting to lighten to mood, but he had a serious look on his face. She turned back to Kirk with a growl, "I'll get on one that he doesn't."

Steven took the initiative and walked her into Penny and Ann's Torb.

O'Neil looked at the gauntlet. "Kirk, you're orange. Do you need to fire that thing before we get on?"

He watched Laura sit in the Torb with Steven and the door start to close. He gritted his teeth and shook his head. "I'll be fine."

Sheldor looked at the men, then eyed Kirk. He held his hand out to the empty Torb. "Gentlemen, please."

* * *

Steven and Laura sat across from the other two women. Penny and Ann were a full foot away from each other with their hands on their laps and worried looks on their faces. He noticed that Laura was sitting close enough to him that their legs were touching. It didn't seem to bother her, but it was stirring up all kinds of stuff within him. She looked out the window at Kirk and the others. It upset him that they were fighting. If his many years alone had taught him anything, it was that family matters. He wished the two of them would just realize they loved each other and get over it. He watched the women across from him lean close to the windows to look down at the scenery as they flew over. Something from above caught his attention. Without moving his head, his eyes rolled upward. CheeChee was in the center of the ceiling sitting so still that no one had noticed her. He touched Laura's arm for a moment and moved his hand to point up, but she suddenly grabbed it and pulled it into her lap. He turned his head to look her in the face. She silently mouthed the word 'no' and shook her head slowly. His brain registered two thoughts simultaneously. The first being that Laura was probably right. Keeping CheeChee's presence a secret at that point was probably a good decision. There was no need to terrify Penny and Ann for the duration of their trip. The second, Laura was holding his hand in her lap and he liked it. He turned back to the other women. For some reason, they were smiling at him. He was a man. And as a man, he didn't miss the fact that he was alone with three beautiful women. Of course, he could have done without the massive spider hanging out on the ceiling above his head.

Penny glanced at their hands. "Are you two a couple?"

"No." Laura quickly responded.

"Then why are you two holding hands?" Penny countered and Ann nodded.

"Because." Laura looked Steven in the face. He knew she was trying to read him. Her eyes begged him to intervene. He grinned softly and gave her a shrug.

"Because why?" Ann teased her.

Steven wondered why Laura didn't take the obvious way out and just point at CheeChee. The women would forget all about her and the fact that she was holding his hand.

"Because you don't want him to get away?" Penny chuckled.

"Because he doesn't really talk and I wanted to tell him something."

"What? That you want to sleep with him?" Anna laughed.

Steven watched Laura's face turn red. She, evidently, was a better person than he was. He took his hand away from hers and smiled broadly at them. He pointed up at the ceiling and both of them took the cue. Both women SCREAMED and dove into each other's arms and held each other tight. They soon ended up on the floor, cowering and looking at CheeChee as if she'd attack at any moment. If there had been a trap door in the floor, they would have opened it, and jumped out to their deaths. Steven laughed so hard he had tears streaming down his face. He couldn't remember the last time he laughed that hard. Hearing his own laughter made it that much more special. He wished he could hold onto that feeling forever. He squeezed her forearm and looked at her.

She was smiling from ear to ear. She had to yell over their screams so that he could hear her. "Steven, you're evil!"

A few hours later, Laura was still trying to coax the girls back into their seats. Ann leaned against Penny looking up at the ceiling. "That, is your friend?"

"Yes, as a matter of fact, look." Laura pulled up her sleeve and leaned toward her. "This is her baby, Junior." He hopped off her wrist and climbed up the wall to his mother. Laura rubbed her wrist and forearm.

Ann quickly climbed away from her and plastered herself up against the wall of the Torb. "What... the hell... is wrong with you?"

* * *

Kirk was still reeling from Laura berating him for putting a tracking device on her. He looked out the window at the other Torb. He couldn't see her, or Steven, but he knew they must be sitting together. As the terrain zipped by, he found himself lost in his thoughts. He was always a little overprotective of his little sister, and Steven was just plain weird. The man spent the last five years alone living in the wilderness of the inner Moon. Kirk figured that would screw up anyone for life. Especially if spiders the size of mini-coopers were running around. He needed to learn how to chill out and just let Laura, be Laura. But he found it really hard to let go. He glanced down at his gauntlet. He was still at defcon level orange. He had to calm down. He spent the better part of his life worried about Laura and whether or not she was going to live. They used to be very close. He would visit her in the hospital and pretend it was a sleepover. He'd lay on the floor in his sleeping bag
beside her bed and read to her. She was a few years younger than him, but she was his best friend and greatest ally.

When she got older they would talk about the future and the things they wanted out of life. She wholeheartedly supported his dream to be an astronaut, and told him over and over again, not to let her illness get in the way of his dreams. It was never a contest. If he had been a match for her, he would have donated one of his kidneys without a second thought. You can't join the military with only one kidney, let alone be an astronaut. It crushed him that he wasn't a match for her. He loved his sister and he didn't want her to die. He wanted her to be able to have a normal life, whatever that meant. So, after he got his bachelor's degree in engineering, he joined the Air Force with the hopes that one day he'd be an astronaut.

When she turned sixteen, her health took a turn for the worse and she needed a transplant or she was going to die. Again, he went with his sleeping bag and slept on the floor next to her bed. She told him how proud she was of him and he silently cried himself to sleep. When he went home the next day to get a change of clothes he found a letter from NASA waiting for him. He ripped it open like a happy little boy about to get a stack of cash for his birthday. It told him the news he had been waiting to hear, he was going to be an astronaut.

Of course, that was when the phone rang.

"Yes, Mr. Rogers? I'm calling from The Donor Swap Program. There's a man in Utah who is a match for your sister, and you are a match for his wife. Would you be willing to donate your kidney to his wife, and he'll do the same for your sister?"

Kirk remembered looking at the letter with tears in his eyes. He was as happy as he was sad. "Yes, of course I would!"

His only condition was that Laura never knew anything about it. He didn't want her to think that she took away his dreams. The biggest problem was that he wouldn't be able to be there when her big day came. She never quite forgave him for that. After the surgery, he came down with a slight infection and couldn't be discharged from the hospital for a week. When he was finally able to go see her, she was already at home...and pissed at him. Since then, things were never the same between them. Now she was living on borrowed time, again.

Kirk suddenly noticed that O'Neil was looking at him. "What?"

He looked at Gene, and then Sheldor. He thought privacy was pointless given the circumstances. "She still has no clue, does she?"

Kirk frowned and shook his head.

"You need to tell her." He looked around at everyone. "We're all going to die. You can't have that hanging over your head, son."

Kirk watched Sheldor for a moment. He seemed to be staring off into space, but Kirk thought he must be doing what computers do, calculating things, or taking care of menial tasks. "Sheldor."

The android looked at him. "Yes?"

"Is Laura going to die?"

"As O'Neil said, we're all going to die. Eventually." He grinned slightly. "However, I'm sure you are referring to her renal failure."

Kirk nodded.

"Currently, she has a few billion nanobots running around inside of her, taking toxins out of her blood and dropping it in her bladder. They could feasibly do the job indefinitely, but I went ahead and put nubs inside her anyway. They aren't mature enough to take on the complete task of filtration, but they will in a few days."

Sheldor could see the confusion on Kirk's face so he explained that the nubs could be programmed to grow any organ, which meant, soon Laura would have two new kidneys. He also explained why everyone's cell phones still worked and remained completely charged. The nanobots penetrated everything, living or dead. The cell phones were intercepting an electric charge meant for the nanobots. From an engineering standpoint, it was awesome to think electronics could remain charged indefinitely.

O'Neil knew that Kirk could use a distraction, so he glanced up at the little orb that floated above his head. "Twiggy, we got some time. Why don't you tell us your story?"

"Please elaborate." Twiggy turned until her sensor eye was facing O'Neil.

O'Neil thought for a moment. "You know, your story? How you ended up on Earth? At the bottom of the ocean?"

* * *

Twiggy wasn't Twiggy back then. He, she, or it was just a drone that served its Newtonian master. The master was a Newtonian man named N'fia Borg. He was very old and frail but took his daily duties very seriously. It was his job to check the systems to see if everything was functioning normally. He was to shut down non-essential systems and make the vessel they used to travel to that solar system, seem like nothing more than a natural moon. In reality, it was a large and wonderful spaceship that generations of Newtonians lived and died on. N'fia's own wife died on Atlantis just a few years prior. His children and grandchildren had long since moved to the beautiful blue planet below, and N'fia, was alone. He knew the coordinates of where his kids had settled so every once in a while, he went to the command center and zoomed into the world so close, he could see a person's face. It took him a long time to find them, but time was all N'fia had. Once he located them, it was easy to find them again. He would leave them messages of love in the sky.

When he was nearing the last years of his life, he decided it was time to join the others. He was one of the last to abandon the station. Everyone was supposed to leave the ship by teleportation, but N'fia suffered from a deep phobia. He worried that when he rematerialized on the planet below, that he'd have an arm where his leg should be, and vice versa.

N'fia knew that once he landed on the planet his health would decline rapidly. The nanobots had been keeping him alive, well past his expiration date. The man never once thought about Twiggy and the fact that she couldn't join him on the surface. No technology was allowed on the planet because the original inhabitants were barely developing a written language. The Newtonians believed they should be left to develop naturally, so when N'fia landed his ship in a remote area, he programmed it to return to the Moon. Twiggy remained aboard like she was told, but something happened along the way. She registered the problem as an electromagnetic disturbance. It caused the ship to temporarily lose power and it crash-landed in the ocean. Since she was given no further commands, Twiggy was stranded all alone, presumably for all of eternity. When it became apparent that no further orders would come in for her, she shut down and went to sleep.

115

It was thousands of years later when she woke up again. It wasn't in her programming to feel any emotion, but when she was activated...she felt something. Only a Newtonian could have brought her out of her eternal slumber. That is when she learned that the ship had been excavated and brought to a different location on land. The Newtonian that had activated her was cleaning the area and had touched her. That was all it took. The woman's name was Connie Singh. From what she learned of the young woman, she was only twenty-one. She had no direction in life so she joined something called The United States Air Force. She had no skills and was of low rank, so she was placed in housekeeping services. Apparently, the higher-ranking officers were delighted when she accidentally activated Twiggy and the ship. That happiness would be short-lived because one day she mysteriously disappeared. Poor Twiggy had to shut down and go into hibernation mode once again. It would be nearly thirty years until she was activated again. This time, her new master gave her a name and took her back home to Atlantis.

Gene shook his head. "Man, that sucks, Twiggy."

O'Neil sadly stared at the floor of the ship. Kirk looked at
him. "Sir? Is something wrong?"

O'Neil shook himself out of his trance. "I don't want to talk about it."

Kirk watched Twiggy float around. He had listened to Twiggy tell her matter-of-fact story. He knew 'she' didn't have emotions, but he wound up feeling sorry for her. Steven was alone for five years, but poor Twiggy was alone for several thousand. He looked out the Torb's window and saw what looked like a large mansion. The next couple of days were bound to be terrifying, but he hoped their stay at the manor would be uneventful.

* * *

The Torbs lowered gracefully and hovered a few feet above the ground, allowing the riders to disembark. Laura watched CheeChee walk by with Junior on her back. She was glad the two of them were bonding. Junior was like a drug that made her feel good and she was worried that she was becoming addicted. She walked over to Sheldor. "Why couldn't we just fly all the way to where the cave-in is? Why stop here? There must be hours until...sunset or whatever."

Sheldor motioned to the manor and they both walked toward it together. "We need to find the override key. The chancellor had the only copy."

Kirk joined them. "And what if we don't?"

He looked at them both and gave them a dorky grin. "Then all is lost."

Laura shook her head. "Wonderful."

Ann walked up to Gene and O'Neil. She pointed at Steven and Laura. "Did you know those two have a giant spider as a friend?"

O'Neil feigned surprise. "What? Why? You didn't?"

Laura followed Sheldor to the mansion until she realized Steven wasn't with them. She turned around to look for him. About twenty paces behind them, he just stood there staring at the building. She closed the distance between them and stood next to him. He didn't look at her or give her any indication that he knew she was there. She looked at him curiously and then followed his gaze. He was looking at the mansion, but she didn't see anything wrong with it. She touched his arm. "Steven, are you okay?" He nodded slightly and took a deep breath. She didn't know what was bothering him, but it obviously had something to do with the mansion.

"Are you guys coming?" Kirk yelled at them from the stone steps that lead up to the door. Neither one of them answered.

Steven finally looked down at her and let a hand at her back silently ask her to go forward. They walked together to the manor as Laura wondered what was going on in his head. Kirk had left the door open for them so they walked inside. It was amazing how much it looked like a fancy home that you would find on Earth. That was when she realized why Steven hesitated. Imagine that you were stuck alone in the wilderness for several years only to find that a house was somewhere out there and all you had to do was explore until you found it. She watched him as he looked around the front room of the house. It had similar furnishings that humans would have too. Everything was a shade of white, some brighter or darker than others. The floors and window coverings were black. The contrasts made the place look like a checkerboard. There didn't seem to be a speck of dust anywhere. None of the furniture had any sign of age or wear and tear on it and everything seemed well cared for.

"Does anyone live here?" Ann ran her hand across the top of a white surface with multiple black dots on it. As her hand hit the dots a musical tone was heard. She played with the dots until she managed Twinkle Twinkle Little Star.

"No one has lived here for almost five thousand years." Sheldor picked up a small metallic box and opened it up. Disappointed showed all over his face. It was empty, so he put it back down. "The maintenance bots and nanobots take care of this place as programmed."

Kirk moved things around on a shelf. "How come this place looks like it would if I had built it?"

"If that's your way of asking me why the architecture of this place mirrors that of humans, it should be obvious." Sheldor looked into a vase.

"Well, it's not," Kirk said sarcastically.

Gene smoothed his hair behind his ears. "I think, in essence, he's saying that Newtonians perverted our natural progression."

"That is not what I meant at all. Newtonians and humans are both similar in nature. Homes like this would eventually be the natural progression. Practically speaking, what other kind of doors would there be for a human? What other kind of chair would there be? Obviously, it would be somewhat similar." Sheldor sat down on a cushioned chair to demonstrate.

Gene corrected him. "When Newtonians cut wood to make their homes, we copied them."

"People copy what they like." Kirk brought a glass fixture that looked like a candle to his nose and sniffed it. He made a face and then put it back down.

Laura looked through some drawers in a hutch. Her eyes fell on a thin cylindrical wand. Her curiosity got the best of her so she picked it up. It instantly lit up when her hand touched it. Steven walked up behind her and she held it out to him.

Sheldor noticed the object. "NO!" But it was too late.

As soon as Steven touched the wand, both he and Laura went into a trance. Kirk ran over to them with a concerned look on his face. Sheldor yelled again and pointed to them. "Whatever you do, do NOT touch them!"

Kirk waved his hand in front of his sister's face. "What the hell's wrong with them?" There was no response from either her or Steven.
Sheldor looked down at the wand. "It's a Memory Transfer Stick."

"Um, that is not a memory transfer stick," Gene said as he shook his head.

Sheldor ignored him. "They are sharing their entire lives."

"That doesn't seem so bad." Kirk watched Laura's eyes dilate.

"Imagine sharing every aspect of yourself. Every happy memory, every sad memory, every private moment, every bad thought..." He looked Kirk in the eye. "All those moments that you'd be ashamed to share."

Kirk squinted and chewed his lip. "Ew."

Sheldor shook his head and held his arms out at the two. "This hardly ever ends well."

"Jesus, what do you mean?"

O'Neil turned to Kirk. "I've thought about killing you nine times since we've been here. We're on the Moon, there's no jurisdiction. I'd get away with it."

Kirk's mouth dropped open. "What the hell does that have to do with our conversation?"

O'Neil poked him in the shoulder. "Nine different bloody ways. If you saw those memories, what would you think of me?"

Kirk closed his eyes and shook his head at the colonel's audacity. "Sir, I already think you're an asshole. But I guess, I get your point." Kirk walked up to Sheldor, ready to fight. "Why the hell would you have such a thing anyway?"

Sheldor raised one eyebrow at Kirk. "I didn't have it. The Chancellor apparently did. Although, I'm not sure why he would have needed it." He thought for a moment. "It was originally used for illegal purposes."

He rolled his eyes. "I'm afraid to ask."

"In order to live longer lives and cheat death, the wealthy and privileged used it to transfer their memories into the brains of children before they died. Since the child was basically a blank slate, they were essentially downloading their brains into a new body." Sheldor shook his head. "And then one day a man and woman accidentally activated a stick together and fell deeply in love."

Kirk was confused. "You said it hardly ever ends well."

"Many ended in murder-suicide." He folded his arms. "Most of the time, the participants would instantly hate each other and simply vowed to never see one another ever again. But since approximately three out of every ten transfers resulted in happily ever after, a number of people thought it was well worth the risk."

"Happily, ever, after?" Kirk said the words as if they didn't belong together.

Sheldor nodded. "After a time, they only used them for arranged marriages. If they fell into each other's arms, they knew it would work out."

Steven suddenly let go of the Memory Transfer Stick and
stared at Laura. He grimaced and then ran away leaving her dazed and confused. O'Neil ran after him.

She sat down slowly and stared off into space. Kirk sat down beside her and leaned into her view. "You okay, sis?"

"You don't want to have this conversation with me, Kirk."

He smiled. "Don't be ridiculous, you're my sister. You can tell me anything."

Her eyes moved back and forth slowly. She didn't blink. "Am I a man or a woman?"

He chuckled. "A woman. Why?"

"Because if I'm a woman, I'm a virgin. But I can vividly remember having sex. Many, many times. With my penis. And if felt really damn good."

Kirk emitted an anguished hum. "You were right. I don't want to have this conversation with you."

Laura looked across the room and pointed. "See Ann over there?"

Kirk was turning red. "Uh huh."

"She has some really nice tits," she said matter-of-factly.

Kirk pressed his lips together and frowned. "You know what I think you should do?"

She finally looked at him. "What?"
"Steven." He nodded and swept his hand towards the door. His face was beet red. "Yep, go find Steven... And be a woman with him."

Laura looked at him blankly before standing up and walking out of the living room. Sheldor stood next to Kirk and followed his gaze. "Aren't you afraid of the possibility of murder and suicide?"

Kirk looked up at his floating friend. "Twiggy, go find Laura. Send video to my phone."

Laura walked into the hallway and saw O'Neil sitting on the bottom step of the stairs. He gave her a concerned look but pointed upward showing her where to go. She walked up the stairs slowly, trying to delay her journey as much as possible. She couldn't think. What was she supposed to say when she found him? She peeked into a few rooms until she saw Steven. She watched him from the hallway. He was on the balcony with his back facing her. She didn't want to walk into the room. He literally ran away from her. She couldn't be sure, but it seemed like he was disgusted by her. She didn't want to go in, but her feet had different plans. It was like she was on autopilot with no will of her own. Something happened when they shared their lives. She went from thinking he was handsome and, perhaps a possibility for the future, to thinking she might not be able to live without him. She closed the door and locked it. It seemed like she was facing the door forever. She looked over her shoulder at him. She tried to comfort herself by holding onto his memories of her and how he felt when she looked at him. She stared at the bed as she slowly walked past it and out onto the balcony. The closer she got to him the more she wanted to turn and run away. Something told her that he knew she was there.

"Steven?" She spoke to the back of his head.

"Yeah?" He spoke to her but after their merging, it was as if she had already heard every word he could ever say. He rubbed his hands back and forth on the wooden railing.

"Why did you run away from me?"

"Because I couldn't stand to be in the same room with you."

She breathed in quickly and then looked at the ground. "Oh...I understand." She lied. She didn't understand. She didn't understand at all. Her eyes started to sting with tears. "I'll leave you alone, I guess."

He turned around as Twiggy floated up behind him. He was so close to her that she could feel the heat coming off of him. His chin hovered above her forehead as he looked down at her. "I was afraid of what I might do." That one little sentence scared the hell out of her. She vaguely remembered the words 'murder-suicide' and wondered if that is what he intended. She shivered slightly and then forced herself to turn her head up and meet his eyes. She definitely didn't see murder in them. He was looking at her the way so many women had looked at him. Longingly. He wanted her. He grabbed her and pulled her in close to him and kissed her.

Downstairs, Kirk shut off his phone and slipped it in his pocket. "Well, at least they're not killing each other."

Steven and Laura kissed passionately. She wanted him. She didn't want to talk about feelings or the future. She knew that if he wanted her after learning all there was to know about her, those conversations didn't matter. All she cared about, at that moment, was her five senses and using them all with him.

* * *

Kirk and Twiggy searched through what looked like an office. He looked at his floating friend. "I don't suppose you can show me where the key is, can you?"

125

"Are you talking to me?" Penny walked up behind him. Her caramel cheeks shined in the light as she smiled.

"No, but you can keep me company if you want." Kirk gave her a sly smile and then winked at her.

"I want."

"I don't think we're gonna find this thing. Twiggy, show her what the thing looks like, would ya?"

There was a BING and Penny fished her phone out of her purse. "Wow! That's awesome. She put it right on my phone!" She looked at her phone closely. The key looked like a high-tech rectangular key card with a computer chip in it. She crinkled her nose. "It actually seems a little outdated. Why'd they even need a key?"

"Sheldor says that some Newtonians wanted to use the Photon Cannon on the Earth because humans were so brutal and cruel. The Chancellor wanted to make sure no one could use it to destroy mankind." He rubbed his face. "This is getting us nowhere."

"But we need that key." Penny pointed at him with her index finger, which made him focus in on her inch-long pink fingernail. "You need to relax." She got up and walked toward him. Kirk raised an eyebrow at her but didn't move. She walked behind him and put her hands on his shoulders. She ran her hands down the front of his chest and then back up to his neck and shoulders and start to rub them.

Kirk closed his eyes. "Oh man, that feels...wonderful, actually. Keep doing that."

Penny smiled. "Yes, sir."

O'Neil walked in. "Did you find it?"

Kirk was irritated. "Seriously?"

"Dinner, let's go. We need to talk about the plan for tomorrow." O'Neil left the room expecting them to follow.

Kirk stood up and Penny let her hands fall away from him. "Come on, I guess we better go see what all this is about."

The Chancellor's dining hall was magnificent. The table rivaled any king's. A crystal chandelier hung in the middle and when the lights were turned on, small rainbows projected on the walls. Sheldor sat at the head of the table. Penny and Ann sat together across from Gene, O'Neil, and Kirk. Just like the previous day, there were a variety of fruits and vegetables on the table. Ann grabbed some snap peas with her bare hands and put them on her plate. Kirk stood up and grabbed a pair of tongs and served her. "Here, let me help you with that." He grabbed more up and offered it to Penny. She nodded acceptance so he served her too, and then sat back down.

O'Neil waited for his turn. "What? I don't get any?"

"Get your own." Kirk smiled at the women and Penny winked at him.

Ann chewed and then swallowed hard before speaking. "Where is your sister and the mute Zorro?"

"Screwing their brains out." Kirk picked up a glass full of red liquid and sniffed it. "What is this, wine?"

O'Neil cleared his throat. "What Captain Rogers means to say is, his sister and her friend are otherwise engaged." He bit off the end of a carrot and chewed loudly. "So, Sheldor, what's the plan?"

Sheldor stared into his empty plate and his own warped reflection.

O'Neil snapped his fingers and waved his hand in front of his face. "Hey! Sheldor! Snap out of it, buddy!"

Sheldor looked up. "I've been trying to devise a way of overriding the system without the key."

"And what have you come up with?" Kirk crossed his arms.

"Nothing. I'm at a loss."

* * *

Laura awoke the next morning to a light and loving kiss placed gently on her lips. She smiled before opening her eyes. Steven's face was inches from hers and when he saw that she was awake, he kissed her again. She cuddled in close to him. Her arm was resting on his chest. He rubbed it. "I don't want to scare you or anything, but I'm completely in love with you." Her head was leaning against him, so she heard his voice humming through him with one ear, and his normal voice with the other. "I mean, crazy in love, with you."

She giggled. "It's weird, isn't it?"

"Some of your memories are fading." Steven turned her so that he was on top of her. "Which is good, because I could do without those fantasies of a certain buff actor that you like. They were very vivid."

She laughed and raised her eyebrows at him. "Me? What about you? You've slept with half of Los Angeles."

He smiled, but then his face turned serious. "I need you to know, I've never felt this way about anyone." He kissed her and they looked into each other's eyes.

"Me either." She moved so she could wrap her legs around him.

Someone POUNDED on the door. They didn't care. They kissed passionately.

"Laura!" Kirk called through the door. "Breakfast, come on!"

Her cheeks turned red and she laughed. She aimed her face to the door and yelled back. "We're skipping breakfast!"
There was a long pause so they started kissing again.

"Okay, but Sheldor threatened to force-feed us and drag us out by our hair if we didn't hurry up!" Kirk yelled back.

The image of Sheldor doing such a thing made them both laugh.

Kirk yelled through the door again. "You know, you guys are taking time out to have sex while the universe is at stake!"

Chapter Six
The Key

Everyone, except Laura and Steven, was gathered in the living room. Kirk paced slowly, stopped and put his index finger up like he had a good idea, then shook his head and continued pacing.

"What happens if the cannon goes off without using the override key?" Ann opened her hands and shook her head. "Aren't we screwed either way?"

Sheldor sat in one of the chairs. "If we had the override key we would have one extra day."

"What is one extra day?" Penny shook her head.

"One day is everything when you're trying to save the world," O'Neil said while staring a hole into the carpet. Gene nodded in agreement.

Kirk stopped again and pointed at Sheldor. "I have an idea." He turned to the monitor. "Okay, Twiggy, put a schematic of this manor on the screen, please."

A 3D blueprint of the manor appeared on the screen. Everyone looked at it confused and waited for him to continue. "Okay, now...can you show me the nanobot population?"

The screen started to populate with thousands and thousands of yellow dots. There were quite a few red zones where the activity was concentrated. Kirk pointed to a red area in the dining area. "What does this mean?"

"The nanobots are cleaning up the remnants of your breakfast." Twiggy floated behind Kirk.

His attention was drawn to the second floor where there was a red representation of a person. He pointed at it and looked over his shoulder at Sheldor. "And this?"

Sheldor cocked his head. "Well, that's not good."

Steven suddenly ran into the living room in nothing but a pair of boxer shorts and socks. Both Penny and Ann's eyes went wide as they gawked at his muscular arms, torso, and six-pack. He made eye contact with Sheldor, who instantly got up, and the two ran out of the room.

O'Neil looked at the ladies. "Okay, I'm just going to say it. Can you believe all *that* was hiding under those clothes?"

Kirk's mouth dropped open. "What's going on?" He ran after them. When he got out into the hall, he saw them at the top of the stairs and followed. He hurried down the hall to Laura's room was found Steven standing outside the door putting on a shirt. Steven stopped him from going into the room.

"This doesn't concern you." Steven looked him in the eye.

Kirk moved Steven's arm out of his way. "Like hell it doesn't!"

Steven's eyes softened. "Look, I'm sorry, man. Since me and Laura merged, or whatever you want to call it, it's hard to separate her feelings from mine. I mean, from her perspective, you're my brother."

"You're not my brother." Kirk said it as rudely as possible. He could feel his heart rate increase, so he checked his gauntlet. It was orange heading into red.

Steven smiled and nodded. "You should probably start thinking of me that way. Because I'm not going anywhere, ever."

"Happily ever after," Kirk said under his breath.

"What?"

"Nothing." Kirk pointed at him. "She's my sister, so it concerns me."

Steven looked away for a moment. "She doesn't want you in there."

"Well, that hurt." Kirk backed up and leaned against the wall.

Inside the room, Steven guarded so well, Sheldor looked down at Laura. She was in a daze with beads of sweat forming on her forehead. He shook his head. "That's what happens when you tucker yourself out, having too much coitus." He bent over and pulled her arms out

133

from underneath the sheet one by one. "Where is it?" He picked up the sheet and lifted it off her body. He was oblivious to her nakedness. He looked her body over from head to toe and back up before replacing the sheet. He went over to the door and opened it. Sheldor stuck his head out into the hallway and looked at Steven and Kirk. He cupped his hands together. "Where's the little Arcandodious?"

"What?" Steven furrowed his brow and then raised them. "Oh, he's outside with his mom."

"What the hell are you talking about?" Kirk looked from one to the other.

Sheldor was concerned. "Laura needs him."

Kirk was visibly frustrated. "Laura needs who?"

Steven pointed at Kirk. "He's the only one, besides Laura, that can talk to them."

Sheldor looked back at Laura briefly and then back to Kirk. "Then you have to go get him."

"Get who?" Kirk opened his arms, frustrated.

* * *

CheeChee stood on top of the mansion watching Junior play with the food she killed for him. The little one had no instincts at all and if he did, he wasn't interested in using them. The dead bird was perfectly good food going to waste. He didn't even attempt to wrap it in his webbing. Feeding off of Laura had made life too easy for him. She knew that he was born several weeks too early but now it seemed that his early birth was going to complicate more than just his physical growth. It was going to impair his mental growth as well. Junior stood on top of the bird and then looked up at her. He didn't have conversational thoughts yet but she could feel his frustration. She projected her thoughts to him. She told him that everything would be okay and that she'd always be there with him, every step of the way. Her thoughts seemed to put his mind at ease, at least for the moment. She picked him up and put him on her head. If the child wasn't going to eat meat then he would need blood.

Somewhere down below, Kirk and O'Neil searched the grounds outside the manor. Kirk was very worried about his sister and almost equally pissed off at Steven. He wasn't ready to lose his kid sister and he supposed that he never would be. He was feeling a dull pain building up in his body. He looked down at his wrist. "Shit."

"What?" O'Neil looked at him concerned.

Kirk's eyes fell on a statue surrounded by shrubbery in a garden. He looked at it closely as he walked around it. "I need to fire the gauntlet. You don't see Junior on that statue, right?"

"Nope."

The men walked away from the statue and then turned around. Kirk pointed his entire arm toward it and then made a tight fist. He didn't exactly know what he was doing. There were no buttons to activate it. He thought about the anger he felt towards Steven, towards his sister, towards the entire situation. Then he thought about the intense fear he felt in the pit of his stomach. He knew he was going to lose his sister and he couldn't let that happen. The gauntlet began to emit a high-pitched whistle. It was time. He imagined the statue blowing into little bits as he willed the gauntlet to fire. A laser suddenly shot out of his fist and hit the statue. The resulting explosion was so much worse than he imagined. Shrapnel from the statue rocketed past them and lodged into the wall behind them. A white cloud of dust floated towards them and he coughed.

O'Neil waved the dust out of his face. "Would you be extremely opposed to me cutting your arm off?"

"I'm pretty sure the gauntlet wouldn't allow that." Kirk cupped his hands over his mouth, "CheeChee! Junior!" He sighed and looked at O'Neil. "I can't believe I'm doing this."

Gene and Ann ran out of the mansion behind them. Their eyes darted back and forth expecting to see an attack from an unknown source. Gene saw the dust that still floated in the air and looked at his pal. "What the hell happened?"

Kirk looked at them both. It was obvious that they were concerned and afraid. "Nothing." He shook his head. He didn't know what to say. He sure as hell didn't want to tell the truth. "Target practice, that's all."

The two looked at O'Neil for confirmation. He decided to go along with it. "Yeah, target practice. Why don't you guys go back inside and look for that key doohickey?"

Gene and Ann hesitated, but eventually went back inside. O'Neil looked along the exterior of the building while Kirk scanned the grounds. They walked to the corner of the manor and Kirk belted out another yell. "Junior! CheeChee! Laura needs you!" The Colonel suddenly slapped Kirk on the shoulder and pointed upward.

CheeChee was walking down the side of the manor to the ground. *'I do not sense Laura.'*

O'Neil waved at her. "Hi. Uh, hi."

"Laura is sick. She needs Junior." Kirk wasn't sure where he was supposed to look when he spoke to her. As he watched her eyes move back and forth, a smaller spider crawled over her back and onto her head. "Junior, I presume?"

'Laura believed she would die soon. Is she dying?'

"I honestly don't know." He looked at O'Neil. "This is weird."

"What's she saying?" O'Neil couldn't remove the disgust from his face.

'I don't like you.'

C. J. Boyle

"I know. I'm sorry about that." He frowned. "She says she doesn't like me."

"Really? Then I like her." O'Neil grinned.
'If anything happens to him...'

"I will protect him with my life, ma'am." He put his hand over his heart.

"Me too." O'Neil did the same.

Kirk grimaced at him. "I don't know why you're talking. They don't understand you."

Junior suddenly jumped onto Kirk's chest, causing him to YELP. His hands shot out to his sides as he tried to twist his head so he could see what the spider was doing. O'Neil leaned over and held his hand out for Junior.

"Come here, little guy, come to Uncle O'Neil." Junior crawled onto his hand. "You don't have to understand someone to know they mean you no harm."

* * *

Steven watched Twiggy scan Laura with a beam of light. He didn't know exactly what was happening, but he was sure that both Twiggy and Sheldor were trying to help her. "Is she going to be okay?"

"Eventually. Yes. I allowed the symbiotic relationship that she and the spider shared to continue because it was actually beneficial to her care, but they shouldn't be apart for so long."

Steven sneered. "How's the spider beneficial to her care? She's obviously very sick."

"The benefit is that the spider's venom has a natural growth hormone that will help her kidneys mature faster. The obvious downside is that the venom is like a powerful narcotic, that she's now addicted to. She needs to be reunited with Junior immediately."

O'Neil walked in. "That would be my cue." He walked to Laura's side and held his hand out so that Junior could step onto the bed. Kirk walked in behind him and looked at his sister. His face turned red and tears glistened in his eyes. Steven noted how upset Kirk was. It was the reason Laura didn't want him to see her that way. Junior crawled over Laura's shoulder and down to her left wrist where he bit her and latched on. Kirk's eyes rolled up into his head and he fell backward, like a board slamming to the floor.

Steven couldn't help but laugh. "That was hilarious."

"Agreed." O'Neil laughed too. "Come on, let's get the little pansy downstairs."

They both grabbed an arm and pulled Kirk to his feet. "What happened?" Kirk mumbled as they walked him out of the room.

Sheldor looked down at Laura. "We're doomed."

* * *

Kirk stood in front of the monitor in the living room. He rubbed the back of his head as he looked at the schematic of the mansion. He stared at the cluster of red that represented his sister.

Twiggy floated behind him. "Kirk is sad?"

Kirk nodded. "Kirk is sad."

"More like Kirk is a giant baby." O'Neil smiled and looked at Gene. He smiled, but only until Kirk glared at him.

Penny walked up behind him. "Is your sister going to be okay?" She put her hand on his shoulder and gave him a concerned look.

He tapped her hand. "Yeah, I think so. Thanks."

She studied the monitor. "What were you trying to do here?"

"I think I need Sheldor for this."

"Ask and you shall receive. What do you need?" Sheldor stood behind him.

"I need you to program some nanobots to fix or clean the key and then we can see it on this monitor." Kirk tilted his head to the monitor.

Sheldor's eyes opened wide and his mouth dropped open.

"Why, Kirk, that's genius. You're smarter than I thought you were. That just might work." His eyes faded and looked as if he was daydreaming.

O'Neil walked over and joined them. They all watched the screen in anticipation. He tapped the monitor at a 'hotspot'. "Right here. Where the hell is that?"

"I think it's the office." Kirk rubbed the sore spot on the back of his head again. He wagged his phone. "Twiggy? Put it on my phone, k?"

They walked out of the living room and down the hall to the office. It was spacious with a blend of white and black decor. The large desk had already been extensively searched earlier that day. Sheldor walked up to the far wall and examined the paper-thin monitor. He looked over his shoulder at Kirk and O'Neil. "It must be behind this monitor." He ran his hands along the edges. Suddenly, a metal door slid from above into the doorway, locking them into the office. Another slid down over the windows making the room pitch dark. Something metallic hit the floor.

After a few tense moments in complete darkness, Kirk's voice broke the silence. "Well, shit."

"Sheldor, can you do something about the lights?" O'Neil sounded annoyed. A few seconds passed. Kirk hoped that meant their android guide was trying to turn on the lights. There was no answer.

"My phone don't work anymore. So, no flashlight." Gene bumped into something. "Are the girls in here?"

"Mine doesn't work either." There was a jingling sound and then suddenly Kirk's face was illuminated. He held a tiny flashlight in his hand with keys dangling from it. He shined it around the room. "No, they're not in here." He walked up to Sheldor and shined the light in his face. "Sheldor." He tapped the android's forehead. He was unresponsive. "Where's Twiggy?"

"Over here!" Gene pointed to the ground.

Kirk bent down to see her better. "Twiggy?" He picked her up and put her on the couch. "Well, shit."

"Booby trap."

Ann and Penny banged on the other side of the door. Kirk could hear their voices but not what they were saying. He went over to the monitor on the wall and ran his hand along it like the android did. The monitor started to glow and the image of a man slowly appeared. He was elderly, short in stature, and elflike with a bald head. The lights in the room slowly glowed brighter until fully lit. The man's eyes twinkled a little bit as he grinned softly. "I've been listening to you speak, obtained your language from M5's database, and analyzed human history in its entirety. Which means, not only have I deduced what you are here for but I don't think humans nor Newtonians, deserve it."

Kirk got the feeling that he knew the man from somewhere but couldn't place it. "Who are you? Why have you locked us in here?"

"That's the fun part, isn't it, Captain Rogers?" He paused.
"You can call me Magician Humphrey."
Kirk rolled his eyes and suddenly put his hands up. "I quit." He walked over to the couch and sat down next to O'Neil. "Your turn."

"You can't quit. This is your challenge." Magician Humphrey threw his head back and laughed heartily.

Gene looked at the monitor. "What the hell is he talking about?"

"Humphrey is a character from a book series I used to read to Laura when she was in the hospital. People would go to him to ask him what they thought was an important question. And he would answer it but only if you passed his challenge."

O'Neil rubbed his chin. "I'd like to apologize in advance for anything I may say, or do, that could be construed as offensive, as I slowly go NUTS!"

"And if we fail?" Gene asked the question to Humphrey, but he never took his eyes off Kirk.

Humphrey smiled. "Well, I can't exactly strangle and devour you, can I? We can settle for affixation."
"Now listen here..." O'Neil started.

"What is the challenge?" Kirk stood up and walked back over to the monitor.

"A riddle."

"A riddle?"

"Yes."

"Fine. Let's do it." Kirk folded his arms.

"They cannot answer for you."

"Understood. How long do I have to answer?"

Humphrey laughed heartily. "Three days."

O'Neil pinched the bridge of his nose. "Look, can't you just let us go? We don't need the key."

Humphrey furrowed his brow. "I could, but I'm not going to."

"Let's get on with it." Kirk opened his arms.

"Fine, Captain Rogers." Humphrey laughed again. "I caution you, if either one of them answers the riddle, all of you will die." He locked eyes with Kirk.

"Understood, they won't answer for me."

O'Neil whispered at Gene. "No one said we can't use charades."

"The riddle is; What belongs to you, but everyone uses more than you?" Humphrey seemed pleased.

Kirk looked at the ceiling as if the answer might be written right there. All he needed to do was read it aloud. But it wasn't there. He put his hands on his chest. "What is mine, but everyone uses more?"

Gene rubbed his leg impatiently. "It's actually pretty easy, if you think about it, Kirk."

"I AM thinking about it, Gene!"

Humphrey narrowed his eyes. "May I reiterate, no one but Captain Rogers, may answer."

He nodded his head enthusiastically. "You don't have to worry, Gene, buddy ol' pal. I already know the answer."

"I doubt that, very seriously." Humphrey smirked.

Kirk pointed at Humphrey. "It's not just my friends and family who use it more. Half the people on the planet use it more than I do."

O'Neil gave Gene a look of confusion.

Humphrey's mouth dropped open.

Kirk stood in front of the monitor. "I mean, after all, my name is Kirk for Christ's sake." He smirked at Humphrey. "You obviously wanted me to win."

"Everyone seems to know the answer except me." O'Neil shrugged. "Care to enlighten me?"

"My name, of course."

Humphrey sized Kirk up and nodded. "The key is yours. Good luck, Captain Rogers."

The monitor went dark. The side of it popped off the wall and opened as if on hinges. Kirk opened it and looked inside. He grabbed the keycard and slipped it in his pocket. He inspected the inside of the safe for anything else of value. His eyes spied something that reflected light so he reached inside and felt around. He pulled out a small sphere about the size of his fist. It glowed as soon as he touched it. Someone grabbed it from him so he turned to look. Sheldor stood there with it in his hand, inspecting it.

"Perhaps, from now on, you and your sister shouldn't touch anything unless I tell you to." Sheldor twisted the sphere at eye level. The metal blockades in front of the door and window slid back up into the ceiling.

"Why? What's it do?"

A hovering disc floated up to him. He placed the sphere inside it. "Let's worry about that later. Congratulations on winning your challenge. Once again, you're smarter than I thought you were." He watched as the disc

146

floated away and then he turned to Kirk and held out his hand. "I'll take the key, please."

Kirk slipped his hand in his pocket and held the key. "Why? You can't use it without me."

"For safekeeping. Nothing more."
"It's safe with me."

The android hand was still extended to Kirk, waiting for him to place the key in it. He tilted his head to the side. "With all due respect, Captain Rogers, you are an impulsive and emotional man with a very dangerous weapon attached to his wrist."

"He has a point, kid." O'Neil motioned to Sheldor's hand. "Give it to him."

Kirk reluctantly placed the key in Sheldor's hand and the four of them left the room. As soon as Penny saw Kirk she ran up to him and gave him a hug. "Oh my God, I was so scared all of you were dead!"

* * *

Evening was fast approaching and now that the key was located, everyone had to get their things together and vamoose. Steven watched Laura as she got dressed. He found it simply amazing that she was so much better after only a couple of hours. He didn't like the fact that they were basically giving her narcotics, but if it got her through the next few days, then he was all for it. He wished they could spend more time naked between the sheets, but they apparently had to be at a place called Farpoint Station before nightfall. She pulled her shirt on, then turned to face him. His heart skipped a beat when she smiled at him. He still had trouble grasping what happened to him. Over the years he had been terrorized and traumatized in such a profound way that he couldn't bring himself to speak without believing that the howlers would come. If he had been sent home to Earth right away he was certain that he would have spent years in therapy. But when the two of them merged, that was all the therapy he needed. She put her hand on the side of his face and then kissed him gently on the lips. It was just a peck and it wasn't enough for him. He grabbed her arm and pulled her back into another kiss.

When she pulled away, she giggled softly. "Come on, we gotta go."

She turned around to grab her pack so he playfully smacked her on the ass. She cried out with delight and ran away from him. He grabbed his pack and ran out of the room after her and trotted down the stairs trying to catch up. They hurried out the front door and walked up to the others. Laura saw her friend CheeChee so she went over to talk to her. Since their merging, Steven didn't find CheeChee quite so terrifying. She was ugly, for sure, but she was also a creature that understood right from wrong and the meaning of friendship. He had been terrified of her, but in his defense, she was a giant, ugly, hairy spider. Any human making an educated guess would assume that CheeChee was going to encase them in webbing and slowly digest them. CheeChee starred in many of his nightmares. Now, when he saw her, he couldn't help but feel a bit ashamed. He had made that 'educated guess' and put her offspring at risk.

He watched the woman that he now loved and realized that if he hadn't attacked CheeChee, she might have died. If Junior was still incubating inside his egg sac on his mother's back, Laura wouldn't have been around long enough to merge with him and he wouldn't love her. She wouldn't love him. Even though his prior self wouldn't have known the difference, the thought of such a thing upset him. When she got sick it scared him to his core. He suddenly had visions of spending the rest of his life alone and mourning her loss. Touching that damn transfer stick was as much of a curse as it was a gift because nothing terrified him more than losing her. He could face howlers head-on, but he couldn't face that.

He listened to Sheldor explain that the ride to Far Point Station would only take forty-five minutes but when they get there they had to move underground. This didn't sound like a good idea to Steven considering the fact that the howlers live in caves. But if he wanted to have 'happily ever after' with Laura, he had to help fix the Sun. The mere thought sounded so ridiculous. He was on a quest with a mismatched group of people led by an android to fix the Sun before it went supernova and destroyed the Earth. Hopefully, it would be a story he would one day tell his grandchildren. He rubbed his now clean-shaven face and wondered how, in a matter of days, he went from a rugged man of the wild to a giant weenie in love.

CheeChee and Laura boarded one of the Torbs, forcing Ann and Penny to board the other. He laughed out loud remembering the women practically pissing themselves trying to get away from the enormous spider. If he really thought about it, what he did was cruel... but it was also terribly funny. Kirk and his pal Twiggy got on the Torb after them. 'This should be interesting,' Steven thought to himself. He walked over to the transport and bumped into O'Neil. They both got on and Steven sat next to Laura.

Steven looked from O'Neil to Kirk. "Are you guys really going to leave the women with Gene and Sheldor?"

"They're in good hands." Kirk crossed his arms and looked out the window as the Torb lifted off the ground.

They sat in silence for the first fifteen minutes of the trip, which felt like four hours. He watched Kirk, trying to read his body language. Thanks to the merging with his sister, he knew Kirk had something on his mind that he really wanted to talk about, but because of their strained relationship he didn't know how to begin. The thought of spending thirty more minutes in silence prompted Steven to intervene. "You okay, Kirk?"

O'Neil turned to Kirk and smirked. "Yeah, you okay, Kirk?"

He ignored his superior officer. "Tell me something, Steven..."

"Whatever you're going to say, please don't," Laura interrupted.

Kirk put his hands up. "No, it's nothing bad. I'm just trying to understand something." When she didn't object further, he continued. He addressed Steven again. "If the two of you shared your entire lives, tell me something about her."

Steven looked at her and grabbed her hand. "Like what?"

Kirk shrugged. "I don't care. Pick something."

"Well, I know that if you and I were hanging off a cliff from one arm and she only had enough time to save one of us, she'd save you."

Kirk smiled at his sister.

"And then she'd jump off after me."

"That was unnecessarily cruel." O'Neil frowned.

The smile drained away from Kirk's face. He looked at Laura to confirm it. She was staring at the ground as if she was picturing it in her head. He decided to give him a topic. "Our names."

Steven raised an eyebrow. "Your names?" He laughed. "You got the raw end of the deal on that one."

O'Neil looked confused. "Okay, now I'm curious."

Steven got a far off look in his eyes like he was remembering something from a long time ago. "Your father was a big sci-fi buff, or 'nut' as your mom would call him. Your last name was already Rogers. He could have gone for the obvious and named you Buck or maybe Steve, but instead he named you Kirk."

"And then he had to go and join the Air Force and become a Captain. So, everyone was forced to call him Captain Kirk Rogers." O'Neil laughed and then thought for a moment. "But she doesn't have a sci-fi name."

"Actually, she does. Her mom was very opposed to all the names that her father came up with for her daughter...so she chose the only one that no one would immediately connect with a sci-fi." Steven smiled at Laura. "Her middle name is Croft."

"Laura Croft?" O'Neil thought for a moment and then snapped his fingers. "The adventure lady? Wasn't it some kind of video game?"

"They had two dogs named Mork and Mindy." Steven finished looking Kirk in the eye. "You don't have to worry. I'm going to take care of her." Laura opened her mouth to say something, but he cut her off. "I know, I know, you don't need anyone to take care of you."

Kirk eyed Laura. "Why does she hate me so much?"
Steven waited a few beats to see if she'd answer for herself. When she didn't, he tipped his head to the side a little. "She doesn't hate you. She loves you. You two obviously need to talk about why you weren't there that day."

O'Neil waited for Kirk to say something. "This got awkward fast."

* * *

When they reached Far Point Station everyone breathed a sigh of relief. Laura grabbed her pack and quickly got off the Torb. She was angry at Kirk. To tell the truth, she wasn't that angry about him not being by her side for her surgery. It didn't matter what the excuse was, she just wanted the truth. If Kirk was afraid that she would die and just couldn't bring himself to come, she would understand. She knew there was a good excuse. It hurt her that he wasn't there but it hurt her more that he wouldn't tell her the real reason why. Steven suddenly grabbed her from behind and squeezed her tight. He leaned in and put his mouth so close to her ear that it tickled when he whispered, "I love you." Excitement ran through her body as her face turned red. She wriggled away from him and he gave her his best pouty face.

Far Point Station was what it sounded like it should be. A remote station against the inner rim of the Moon. As the light started to disappear Sheldor led them to a small building. That's when several dozen howlers ran out of the woods at them like rats pouring out of a sewer drain.

Steven screamed, "LAURA RUN!"

It was a warning for the woman he loved, but it served to alert everyone. Laura ran for the shelter of the building, but the animals surrounded them and managed to block the entrance. CheeChee literally sprang into action by leaping up onto the building where she was able to shoot her webbing at the invaders. The howlers managed to separate Laura from the rest of them making her easy prey. Her only experience with the howlers taught her to fear them, but Steven's experiences with them taught her to be terrified of them. She tried to keep an eye on five of them that slowly crept toward her when suddenly a strange calm overtook her and she went into a defensive mode. Two of them simultaneously jumped at her, causing her to twirl around like a dangerous ballerina with a murderous agenda. She couldn't help herself, nor could she stop. She was hopped up on adrenaline and predicting her opponent's next moves like she was seeing into the future. A few yards behind her Sheldor picked off howlers with impossibly fast precision. When his area was clear he ran behind a tree where Gene was cowering and grabbed him by the back of the shirt and pants. He carried him over to the building. He must have given the door a silent command to open because it did as he approached. Once he was in front of the door, he swung Gene inside.

O'Neil and Kirk took out their stun guns and started firing. Kirk yelled at Penny and Ann. "We'll clear the way! You two get inside!" The two women dodged howlers as they ran while Kirk and O'Neil shot as many of the little bastards as they could. Each time they fired it got them one step closer to getting inside. Once their way was clear, the women ran through the open door.

O'Neil grounded three more of them and then turned to check on Kirk. He had his mouth wide open with a stupid look on his face so O'Neil followed his gaze. The two men watched, dumbfounded, Laura and Steven fighting the little green monsters in hand to hand combat and winning. "When did your sister learn karate?" He asked, glancing at Kirk.

He shook his head. "She must have gotten it from Steven."

O'Neil could hear it before he saw it. He looked down at Kirk's gauntlet. It was red. "Kirk!"

The captain's head snapped toward him and then down to his arm. "What? Shit."

The Colonel cupped his hands over his mouth. "Okay, kids! Tell your friends you'll play with them later! Time to go inside!"

Both the fighters ignored O'Neil. Kirk looked at him and shrugged. He pointed his gauntlet at them. "KIDDO!" Laura finally looked at him and realized what was about to happen. Sheldor appeared at her side and picked her up as if she were a small child and then ran away with her. When Steven noticed she was gone, he ran after them. Kirk fired his weapon at the remaining howlers. The resulting explosion sent a shockwave that blew them all off their feet and to the ground. Sand and debris rained down on them. Laura hoped that was all that would come down on their heads. She didn't want to be picking howler out of her hair later that night. Steven was on his feet first. He ran over to her and helped her to her feet. "Are you okay?" Before she had a chance to answer, he pulled her into a hug and walked with her towards O'Neil and Kirk. He laughed. "That was awesome!"

O'Neil agreed. "Yeah, Laura, it is okay if I merge with your boyfriend?"

"Depends. Do you wanna know what it's like to have sex with me?"

O'Neil immediately turned red and started coughing. "What? No!"

Kirk turned white. "Oh god." He put his palms against his ears. "Lalalalala!" He ran into the building with everyone close behind him.

Sheldor closed the door after making sure that Twiggy was inside. Laura rubbed her hands together. Apparently, it hurts when you aren't used to hitting things with your bare hands. Sheldor immediately noticed the look on her face and responded with concern. He took her hands into his and looked at them. They were red and swollen. "Are you alright?"

"Yes. I think so." She turned her hands over in his and looked at her palms. She could see Steven watching them curiously. He winked at her and she smiled. "Sheldor, what were those things?"

"Your hands shouldn't hurt for long given the fact that Junior is still feeding on you. I'll redirect some of the nanobots." He let go of her hands and then bumped her playfully under the chin with his finger. "You'll be fine." He let the smile fall away from his face. "They're genetically mutated dogs. It was done intentionally to keep the animal population in check after the station was abandoned." The android led them all into a room that looked like a media command center. He stood next to a console and gave the keycard to Kirk. It was a strange thing to grasp. Laura and her brother had more alien

DNA than anyone present, so they were the only ones that could activate the electronics on the ship. It stood to reason that one of them needed to stay alive until their goal was achieved.

Sheldor showed Kirk how to activate the device. "Place your palm on the sensor."

The station came to life and a weird little man appeared on the screen. "Captain Rogers, we meet again."
More than half the group was confused, herself included. "What's going on? Who is this?"

"This... is Magician Humphrey." Kirk pointed at the monitor. "Sheldor took his form so that you'd be more comfortable with him. This particular program must have searched my FaceMe page and saw the post about Humphrey and the three challenges."

O'Neil leaned in close to Ann and whispered, "do you have any idea what he's talking about?"

"None," she whispered back.

"What the hell do you want, Humphrey?"

"Look, you got the key, but did you think it'd be that easy to disable the cannon? Even your military leaders require a code to go along with a key," Humphrey said smugly.

Kirk shifted his weight back and forth. "Another riddle?"

"Yes. Remember, no one can answer except for you."
O'Neil looked around. "At least he's not threatening to kill us this time."

Laura was still confused. "This time?"

"Where do bees get their milk?" Humphrey smirked.

"What?" Kirk's mouth dropped open and he shook his head.
"Where do *bees*... get their *milk*?" He repeated.

Gene smoothed his hair behind his ears. "It's some kind of trick question."

Ann took a couple of steps forward so that she stood directly in front of Kirk. She grabbed her breasts and squeezed them together while bending forward slightly so that he could see her cleavage. Kirk was mesmerized and unable to think. She raised her eyebrows at him and squeezed her breasts again. He furrowed his brow at her. He was completely oblivious. Laura found it extremely painful to watch. It was almost like watching a bowling ball run all the way down the lane, so close to the gutter that any second it would fall in, and the game would be lost.

Ann straightened her back and thrusts her breast toward him and cupped them with her hands.

Kirk's eyes went wide and he tipped his head to the side. He suddenly looked as if he had stepped in shit. He closed his eyes. "Boobies?"

Everyone in the room exhaled. Both O'Neil and Gene had giant grins on their faces. They repeated in unison, "boo bees."

Ann covered her face as Kirk turned red. He cleared his throat and looked at Humphrey. "Really? What are you, four?"

Sheldor clasped his hands behind his back. "I fail to see the logic in all this."

"Disable the cannon," Kirk ordered Humphrey and expected him to listen.

"You know as well as I do that there is one last challenge. And this one is the hardest one of them all. And, unlike the others, no one can help you answer it."

O'Neil rolled his eyes. "We don't have time for this."

"Just... ask... the question." Kirk was frustrated.

Humphrey blinked twice. "It's not a question. It's a challenge. Take your shirt off."

"Excuse me?" Kirk narrowed his eyes at him.

"You heard me. Wasn't Kirk the one who always found a way to take his shirt off?"

Penny smiled. "What's the matter, baby? You bashful or something? It's just a shirt."

Kirk's face was red. "Fine, yes, I'm shy. I'll take my shirt off, but everyone has to leave."

"Sure, captain Rogers, everyone except Laura."

Laura furrowed her brow and looked from Kirk to Steven. "What? Why me?" It didn't make any bit of sense. Why would this entity want her to see her brother with his shirt off?

"Kirk, just take your damn shirt off, son." O'Neil gestured to the monitor. "It's over."

Kirk stared hate at the screen. "You're a dick."

"A quest isn't all about the ultimate goal." Humphrey's face was suddenly on every screen in the command center. His voice echoed. "It's also about its participants."

Laura walked up to her brother. "Kirk, what's going on?"

O'Neil pointed to the hallway. "Alright, everyone else... out." He corralled them out the door and down the hallway toward the bedrooms.

Laura watched a tear roll down her brother's face. She couldn't take it. The last time she saw him cry was their parent's funeral. She was doing fine up until she saw him trying to fight back tears. Somehow watching that battle with himself made it that much worse to witness. Whatever it was about, it had to be pretty bad for her brother to be crying.

"This isn't how I wanted you to find out." He unbuttoned his light blue uniform shirt and untucked it. He let it slip off his shoulders and then tossed it onto a chair. He stood there for a moment in his undershirt. He shook his head and then sniffed. Finally, he grabbed the bottom of his shirt and started to lift it. She saw it immediately. There was a large slanted scar across his left side. She knew exactly what that scar meant. He had either lost a kidney or donated one.

It was her turn for a tear to run down her face. "I know you didn't donate your kidney to me because I met the guy. He said that he was doing it because someone had donated one to his wife and that he wanted to do the same for someone else."

Kirk pulled his shirt back on. "I donated the kidney to his

wife. That's why I wasn't there." He put his shirt on and wiped his eyes.

She had tears flowing down her face. "The donor swap program?"

He nodded. She felt horrible. She knew that there must have been an excuse, but she never imagined the reason would be because he was throwing his future away to save her. All this time she thought he was out living his dreams.

"Why didn't you just tell me?" She stepped toward him and hugged him tight. She held so much anger toward him that she didn't realize how much she really missed him. He let his cheek lean up against her forehead as he rubbed her back with his hand.

He eyed the monitor above his head. "Now will you disable the cannon?"

When she looked up at the monitor she watched Humphrey nod at Kirk. "When you need to re-activate it, you'll need the key." The screen went dark.

Chapter Seven
Going Under

Far Point Station was an outpost intended to be manned by only four people. The rooms were small and drab. If Atlantis was the top of the line, then Far Point Station was a roadside hotel. Each room only contained the necessities and a single sized bed. It was easy for Laura and Steven, they snuggled so close they might as well have been one person. Sheldor didn't need sleep and even if he did, he could simply sleep leaning against the wall. The men that were left insisted that the women take two of the beds, leaving only one up for grabs.

O'Neil played with a button on a console. He was turning something on and off and not seeing a difference. He sighed loudly and glanced at Kirk. "Maybe you should take the bed, kid. You had a rough day."

"Thanks, Sir, but I wanted to see if the maintenance bots have made any progress with the cave in." He poked the screen in front of him. "I think I've figured out how to get a video feed. Look."

The video that appeared on the screen showed the maintenance drones using lasers to break the stones away and carry them out. "Watch this." He put his fingers on the screen, turned then flipped it. The screen showed the cave-in along the cannon. "It runs about thirty feet. They've barely made a dent. And that's not the best part." He fingered the screen again and it showed the terrain above the cannon. It looked like a sinkhole filled in with dirt and rocks. "Unless we can close this thirty-foot gap, when the cannon goes off, it will release enough radiation that it will kill all of us."

O'Neil folded his arms and blinked a couple of times. "Needs of the many?"

Gene looked at them both. "Yeah, well, I was hoping we could come out of this in one piece."

Kirk patted Gene on the shoulder. "That's the plan. Come on, let's get some sleep."

They walked down the hall towards the last bedroom. As Kirk passed one of the doors, it suddenly opened and

Penny grabbed him, pulled him inside, then slammed the door shut.

O'Neil looked at the door, then to Gene. "Rock, paper, scissors for the last bed?"

* * *

"Laura! Let's go! Get up!" It was Kirk. She expected more knocks and more shouting but everything was silent. When she opened her eyes, she found that she couldn't move at all. She was completely immobilized by Steven. He was behind her with his arms wrapped around her and one of his legs on the lower half of her body. They were still fully clothed and covered by a blanket. Ordinarily, she'd have a panic attack because she was somewhat claustrophobic, but she didn't mind at all. She felt safe. She felt happy. "Steven," she whispered. "It's time to get up."

He squeezed her tighter for a moment and then relaxed. He hummed softly in her ear. "I've been awake for a while." She felt him tilt backward and away from her so she turned over to look at him. She was immediately met by his soft lips on hers. She couldn't help it. She grabbed his face and kissed him harder. He moved his body on top of her and she pulled him in close with her legs.

There was a BANG at the door. "Goddamn it Laura! I said let's go! We're all gonna die, remember?"

She broke away from his kiss and they both laughed. When she looked into his brown eyes, she saw love staring back at her. She wanted to stay right there forever. She had to look away in order to gather her thoughts. When she moved to wriggle out from underneath him, he tipped off of her again. She stood next to the bed and jammed her feet into her sneakers. "Come on, we have to go."

He grimaced as he pulled the blanket up over his waist. "I think I'm gonna need a minute."

Laura knew it was his way of telling her that he was a bit excited. She felt her face redden and smiled before leaning down to peck him on the lips. As she left the room, she pulled a hair tie out of her pocket and started to smooth her hair back into a ponytail. She didn't know what the day had in store for her, but she hoped it wasn't death. She wanted to explore life with Steven and see where it will take them. Assuming, of course, that she wasn't going to die of renal failure. She could see Kirk and the others as she approached. Sheldor had them all gathered in the Command Center. He stood in front of them with that trademarked, quirky smile that Sheldor of the Bazinga Factory was famous for. Laura knew he was about to tell them something they didn't want to hear. He didn't disappoint.

"The next part of our little adventure will take place underground, in the access tunnels that run alongside, and underneath the cannon." He waited for a moment, looking at all of them individually. "We're approximately thirty-six miles from the cave in."

"Great. Sounds wonderful," O'Neil said sarcastically.

Laura looked down at her hands and then rubbed them together. They didn't hurt at all. It was amazing. But now she was about to do something dangerous and scary. She was glad Steven and Kirk would be there with her. When she looked back up at Sheldor she found that he was already looking at her. She had a burning question for him. "How are we going to travel thirty-six miles underground?"

"First by water, then by foot." Sheldor suddenly breathed in and gave her a weary smile. "Have you ever noticed, in movies, when you have a countdown or time limit, to avoid certain disaster, it's a fixed amount of time and doesn't change?"

O'Neil chuckled and nodded. "Two hours ticks down to under a minute and somehow they always save the day."

Gene mumbled under his breath. "What would he know about movies?"

Sheldor cocked his head to the side. "To answer your question, there isn't a movie I haven't seen. I'm particularly fond of action. Specifically, anything with Wolf Taylor in it."

Kirk winced and pinched the bridge of his nose. "So back to the subject, you were talking about movie countdowns?"

"Well, this is real life, and... the Sun is getting more and more volatile."

Kirk rubbed his eyes. "How much time do we have?"

"Less than forty-two hours."

Laura bent over to pick up her pack when someone gently grabbed it away from her. It was Steven. She must have looked worried because he gave her a sympathetic smile and took her hand. She turned back to Sheldor. "We'll eat on the boat. I assume we are taking a boat? We're not floating down the river on inner tubes, are we?"

It wasn't innertubes, but it was almost as bad. Sheldor led them down a long stairway while Twiggy floated above them lighting the way. The stairs were made of some kind of metal and it sounded like a strange symphony of clanking and clunking when everyone stomped down them. Ten steps, landing, turn, ten steps, landing, turn, ten steps, landing turn... it seemed to go on forever. Her calves started to complain and repeatedly asked her to stop and rest. By the time they reached the bottom, Laura figured they must have gone down twelve stories. The air smelled like damp dirt and a stream or river could be heard somewhere in the distance. They all followed each other single file along a dark path lit only by Twiggy. Somewhere ahead of her, in the lead, was Sheldor and Kirk. She could hear Kirk talking, but she couldn't make out any actual words. She just watched the butt in front of her, which was Steven's, and kept pace behind it. She was feeling tired and dragging her feet so she hooked her hand into his back pocket. It must have surprised him because he turned around to look to see what and who it was. He looked relieved when he realized it was her. The sound of water got louder and they all stopped. Steven suddenly turned around and pulled her into his arms and kissed her. She loved it when he did stuff like that. It made her heart speed up and pound in her chest. She soon found herself lost in his kiss. She didn't want him to let go. She could hear Kirk talking, but she couldn't possibly register what he was saying. He was talking to Sheldor.

* * *

Kirk stood next to Sheldor looking at two rafts tied to a post. "These look exactly like something we'd make on Earth."

Sheldor nodded. "I had them made last night while all of you were sleeping." He looked Kirk in the face. "Or copulating, whichever the case may be." He scrutinized the boat. "They don't look very safe. But I watched something called 'me-tube' with videos of people using them successfully. Under our current time constraints, we don't have better options."

Kirk looked at the rest of them and then saw Steven and Laura kissing. He and O'Neil shared a look. O'Neil shrugged. Ann was standing next to him watching them kiss. "It's like watching a pendulum. It's almost hypnotic."

Penny winked at Kirk. "They need to be separated."

"I agree." Kirk crossed his arms and couldn't help noticing the color on the gauntlet. It was slowly changing from yellow to orange.

Steven broke away from Laura long enough to say, "I'd like to see you try." Then he looked deeply into her eyes and started kissing her again.

Kirk raised an eyebrow. "You don't think I can separate you two?"

"No," Steven said between kisses.

Kirk clenched his jaw and then took a deep breath. Judging from what he saw Steven and Laura do the night before, he probably couldn't separate them. He thought for a moment and then looked upward into the shadows because he thought he saw something. Terror grew within him until he suddenly knew what it was. 'CheeChee, is that you?' He didn't speak it, he thought it.

'Yes, Angry One, it is I.'

'Steven and Laura are hampering our efforts to save the solar system.' He thought his words and projected them as loudly as he could.
'What are they doing? It seems as though they are mating with their faces.'

'That's about right.' Kirk watched the giant spider crawl down the wall. 'They need to be separated.'

'I will help if it helps my children.'

The conversation took mere seconds. CheeChee attached a web and lowered herself behind Steven. When Ann and Penny noticed the spider, they started

169

screaming and jumped into one of the rafts. That got Steven and Laura's attention. Laura stepped away from him to find the apparent danger and saw only CheeChee.

"I told mommy on you." Kirk eyed them as he gloated.

"CheeChee?" Laura knew her friend wouldn't hurt her. The spider moved suddenly and swiftly. For a few moments, she was nothing but a blur. When CheeChee could finally be seen again, Steven and Laura's upper bodies were wrapped in webbing. Laura was in one raft and Steven was in the other. They looked like they were wearing straight jackets and both of them looked utterly shocked.

"CheeChee!" Laura gasped.

'I am sorry, Laura.'

Kirk laughed heartily until he grabbed his ribs. When he finally calmed down, he had happy tears running down his face. He noticed the color indicator on his gauntlet was a very light yellow. Every time he glanced at Steven he giggled a little and had to turn away in order to speak. "Now then, Penny, you come ride with me, Gene, and Stevie here." He pointed to the raft that Ann and Laura were already in. "Sheldor, O'Neil, you guys ride with them."

O'Neil narrowed his eyes at Kirk and then cocked his head to the side. "I'm only doing it because I want to." He followed Sheldor into the raft. It bounced as he moved and made his way to Laura. He sat down next to her and then touched the thick webbing that was wrapped around her. "Feels like a sticky, damp, stretched out, plastic grocery bag."

Laura watched the raft with her brother and Steven as it floated ahead of them. She pouted a little and shook her head. "Will you help pull it off of me?"

"Sure thing, Jelly Bean." O'Neil hooked his finger into the side and pulled at it. The raft rocked slightly in the mild waters. "Hey, Ann, can you turn on your flashlight?"

Ann used her cellphone's flashlight app and held the light so that O'Neil could see what he was doing. She wondered aloud. "If you two shared your entire lives and experienced everything about each other, aren't you essentially...the same person?"

"No. It's not like that." Laura tried to move her arms to no avail. "It's more like watching a really long, emotional movie. At the end, you know if you liked it or not. And if you liked it, then you remember a lot about it. Then after some time passes, you still know you really liked the movie, but now, you can't quite remember that really cool quote you liked so much. But you remember the important things. You know what the movie was about and why you loved it."

O'Neil glanced up at her face briefly, but kept working. He was making progress. "And you and Captain Dunsel over there? Did you two make up?"

"Dunsel?" Laura and Ann repeated it, confused. O'Neil laughed as he pulled off a big piece of webbing and dropped it over the side of the raft.

Sheldor leaned forward. "If I may? Dunsel is an old naval term used to describe a useless part."

Laura finally broke free of her would-be jacket of webbing. "That's not cool, O'Neil. You know he looks up to you."

He frowned. "You're going to call me out for being myself? That's not fair." He picked strands off of his fingers. "Sides, you know you two are like family."

"You knew, this whole time, didn't you?" She looked at the water. They were moving faster.

He rubbed her back. "Yep." He obviously knew she was referring to Kirk and the fact that he donated a kidney for her.

"What's he been doing all this time?" She pulled bits of the sticky web off her shirt. "He's obviously not in the astronaut program like I thought he was."

"I pulled some strings. He's a test pilot. It's not what he wanted to do, but at least he's still doing something he loves." He opened his arms to the sides. "But look at him now! Rafting inside a cave, inside the Moon." He shrugged. "If there wasn't the 'impending doom' hanging over our heads, it would be fun." He noticed the tears running down her face. He half hugged her and she leaned her head on his shoulder. "Come on, kid. You know I'm not touchy-feely. You're killin' me." He rubbed her shoulder.

"I was so mad at him. When all this time..." Laura wiped the tears from her cheeks.

O'Neil pleaded at Ann with his eyes. He was obviously uncomfortable. "I know," he said to Laura. He looked at Ann again. She shrugged, no help at all.

* * *

Steven was mad at Kirk, but not as mad as he should have been. He wanted to look behind him at the raft that Laura was in but he couldn't move. Kirk exaggerated a frown. Steven imagined that the angel on his shoulder must have been trying to convince him that he was being a jerk. Penny and Gene were trying their best to see the river in front of them but it was too dark. Twiggy was only capable of shining the light on them, and that didn't amount to very much.

He looked at Kirk again. He was lounging against the side of the raft like it was a leisurely ride. As much as he wanted to hate the guy, because of Laura, he loved him like a brother. He remembered all the times that Kirk slept on the floor in Laura's hospital room. He experienced it as if it had happened to him. It was very special and memorable. Each time she was hospitalized, she was afraid that she wasn't going to make it. But Kirk wouldn't let her lose hope. He always cheered her up and made her laugh. It turns out, laughter really was the best medicine.

Steven stared at Kirk until he finally looked at him. "You saved her," he said to him.

Kirk twisted his face to reflect a mixture of rude and confusion. "Excuse me?"

"You saved her," he repeated. "Each time she was sick, she was ready to give in. You saved her. Each time. And then you gave up a kidney for her. You're the reason she's alive."

Kirk looked away. He obviously didn't want to discuss Laura with him.

Steven tried to move his arms again. He was a strong man, but as hard as he tried, he couldn't break free of the web. "Look, I know you don't know me from Adam, but I know you as well as Laura knows you. We don't have to be enemies."

Penny looked out of the corner of her eye at Gene. He shook his head. She crawled across the raft to Steven. "This is ridiculous." She practically climbed on his lap. Her voluptuous body rubbed up against him. She smiled and looked him in the eye. "Don't worry, sweetie, I'll get you out."

Gene took his pocket knife out. Kirk leaned over and grabbed it out of his hand. "What are you, crazy? Knowing you, you'll pop our ride." He opened the knife and moved over to Steven. "Penny, come on, you're scaring the poor man." She frowned at Kirk, but moved away. He looked Steven right in the eye and mumbled under his breath, "She's a wolf in sheep's clothing, man." Kirk worked the blade downward and pulled it forward, cutting the webbing clean. He slid it downward again.

Steven found it difficult to stay still. "Be careful."

"What, you don't trust me?" Kirk laughed.

"Thank you."

"No problem, man." Kirk sighed. He was almost done freeing him.

"I mean," Steven looked him in the eye. "Thanks for Laura."

"It's not like I gave her to you."

"No, but she wouldn't be alive without you." Steven was finally able to move his arms. He started pulling the sticky web off. "So, thank you."

Kirk patted Steven on the shoulder. "How about we don't talk about this anymore, huh? Brother?"

Steven brushed off his shirt. "Someday you're not going to say it so sarcastically."

"I don't think so." Kirk took a seat next to Penny and put

an arm around her. She obviously loved it. She smiled and snuggled in close to him.

Steven suspected that the conversation was over. At least he was making some headway. His mind suddenly wandered to his grandmother. He still didn't know if she was alive, but he prayed that she was. He couldn't bear the thought of her dying alone and believing that he was dead, or worse, had run off and left her to fend for herself. He wanted to bring Laura home to meet her. He knew that she would love her as much as he did. He already thought of Laura as his wife, but he wanted to marry her, on Earth, in front of his family and friends. When he 'disappeared' he was taking care of his grandmother. Which meant he had to temporarily move home to New Hampshire. He had to take time off from a job he truly loved. He worked as the technical advisor or martial arts expert, behind the scenes, on a popular TV show. Choreographing a fight scene was a thing of beauty that he took very seriously. He was very passionate about his craft and hopefully it showed on screen.

That life, was so far away. Who was Steven Foster now? The only thing he was at the moment was the other half of Laura. He wanted to get back to his life, but what would that mean? You don't just disappear for five years and ask for your life back. Even if somehow, someway, you got it...it wouldn't be the same. He felt a twinge of guilt mixed in with a bit of shame. He'd trade anything to erase the last five years. He loved Laura more than life itself, but life alone in the wilderness with monsters was something he didn't want to remember or repeat. His mind struggled with the thoughts he was having because they fought against each other. One side of his mind argued that he'd never give up Laura. Not for any reason. But the other side, was adamant that he would... but only for one. It made him feel like a terrible person, except for one thing. Laura knew exactly what he went through. No one understood him better. He was certain that she'd give up anything to prevent him from experiencing that pain too. Even if it meant she had to give him up. He suddenly closed his eyes and shook his head. He wouldn't be having those thoughts if she were in his arms.

He turned around and squinted in the darkness. He could see Laura's raft about twenty feet behind them. He couldn't see her or anyone else. He was getting increasingly nervous and couldn't shake the feeling that something bad was about to happen. He called out into the darkness, "Laura!"

Steven listened carefully. All he could hear was the roaring sound of water in a cave that echoed everything back and forth like a boomerang made of noise. It was annoying. He thought he heard her. It was faint and he didn't know what she said, but he knew it must be her. He called out again. "I love you!"

"You're not going to jump overboard, are you?" Kirk said from behind him.

"I might." Steven turned around and sat down.

Kirk shook his head. "Twiggy, go check on my sister, would ya? Take a picture of her or something." The raft moved faster and started to rock back and forth.

"Certainly, Kirk." Twiggy floated above them.

Penny quickly took out her phone and used the flashlight app. "I'm not gonna be left in the dark."

"Tell her I love her," Steven added.

"I will, Steven."

"I never gave you permission to listen to him." Kirk folded his arms.

"Okay, Kirk. I will not tell Laura that Steven loves her."

They watched the orb float away. Steven locked eyes with Kirk. "When we get to land, I'm going to kick your ass."

"I thought you said we were brothers." Kirk smirked.

"Brothers fight," Steven practically growled.

Twiggy waited for the second raft to catch up to her and then matched its speed. She pointed her sensor at Laura. "Steven says he loves you."

Laura blushed. "Tell him that I love him too!"

"That will have to wait," Sheldor said as he looked to the left. "There's a fork in the river ahead. We must go right."

O'Neil's mouth dropped open as he pointed ahead of them. "Well, do they know that?"

They suddenly heard screaming. It echoed in the cavern. Laura screamed, "Steven!"

"Judging from the screaming we've just heard, I don't think so." Sheldor stood up and turned around.

Laura started to hyperventilate. "Kirk!"

Sheldor gave Twiggy one of end of the rope that was used to tie the raft to the dock. "Guide us to the right." The water was moving fast and the raft was drifting to the left. Twiggy tried to drag them to the right as commanded. Laura grabbed her stomach and leaned forward with her head down in the raft. Ann tried to console her by rubbing her back, but it was clear that she was afraid too. O'Neil's eyes were wide trying to see ahead of them. He could just make out a drop off to the left. To the right was a smaller tunnel.

"You knew about this!" O'Neil pointed at Sheldor, who was leaning out of the raft with his hands out ready to catch a rock structure as they got near it.

"Twiggy's telemetry readings have updated since we've been traveling." He pushed the rock as they passed it, causing the raft to go to the right. "There was no way to know if river erosion changed the cavern until we were down here. It's been thousands of years."

The raft immediately dropped a few feet and increased in speed. Ann screamed. O'Neil pushed her down to the bottom of the raft and covered her and Laura with his body. Sheldor joined them at the bottom of the raft as it took a sharp turn. Laura found it hard to concentrate on what was happening. Her mind was still reeling from losing both her brother and her lover in the same instant. They couldn't be dead. She'd know it. She'd be able to feel it. When you're in mortal danger, things seem to slow down, painfully slow. You have time to think about all the things that you should have done. All the things that, perhaps, you shouldn't have done. In those few seconds, that felt like an eternity, she called out to CheeChee.

'CheeChee!' She screamed it in her mind. She hoped her friend would hear her. 'Steven!'

There was a sudden sharp turn to the left and everyone rolled right. Laura bounced up and out of the raft. She screamed in terror. O'Neil managed to grab her hand, but both of them were wet and he was losing his grip. Junior was latched onto the same arm that O'Neil was trying like hell to hold on to. The little spider shot some webbing out and it attached to O'Neil's wrist, allowing him to pull Laura back in the raft. It showed no signs of slowing down. Suddenly they were aloft in the air. The raft overturned and everyone fell downward into darkness.

* * *

Her new friend was in an enormous amount of emotional pain when she mentally cried out to her.

CheeChee didn't need Laura to scream inside her mind in order to figure out that something was wrong, she saw it happen. She instantly swung over the ledge and attached herself to the opposite wall, and then shot webbing at the falling humans as she went. Unfortunately, she was only able to save three of them, and not the one Laura so desperately called about. She lowered herself over fifty feet to the bottom of the waterfall to try to locate The Dangerous One. Everything was illuminated by an eerie green glow which made it difficult for her to see. She had always relied heavily on sound, vibrations, or even pressure changes in the environment to navigate when her eyes failed her. None of the humans she saved were conscious because her rescue wasn't exactly a gentle one. They were essentially slammed up against the cave wall and suspended there by her webbing. It still had to be better than falling several stories into the water. She walked around in the mucky sand on the bottom of the cavern. She didn't see the man anywhere. Nor was he floating around on the top of the water like dead animals often did. She heard her friend cry out to her again. She was in trouble. But CheeChee was far too far away to be of any use to her. She also felt an intense fear from her male offspring, which caused her to experience a feeling that she wasn't familiar with... dread. She tried to reach out to them both, but neither one of them answered.

Screams came from above her. '*It must be The Dark Female*,' she thought to herself. At the moment, she could do nothing for Laura or Junior, so she scaled the wall toward the screams. She wondered how she was going to approach the woman. The only interactions she had with the woman weren't good. The Dark Female was definitely afraid of her. She found the screaming incredibly annoying. It just made her want to render the woman unconscious again.

As she walked up the cavern wall toward the woman's screams, she came across The Angry One called Kirk. She knew that it would be best to try to wake the man so that he could calm the woman. His head hung forward onto his chest and she could smell his blood. It made her extremely hungry. The blood came from the back of his head and dripped down the side of his face. For a fleeting moment, she wondered if it would be improper to catch a drop and taste it. If she didn't, it would just go to waste. She had never been faced with such a dilemma before because she never had friends or anyone to care about. She thought for a moment. '*How would I feel if Laura tasted me while I slept?*' She decided against it.

'*Wake up, Kirk.*' She pushed his head back a little with a leg and then let it go. His head flopped forward onto his chest. He didn't move or make a sound. She listened closely. Whatever it was inside humans that made a constant, repetitive sound, was still going strong within him. The Dark Female screamed again. She was yelling something in her language, but CheeChee had no idea what she was saying. Perhaps she should go get the woman and put her on the land below?

'*WAKE UP, KIRK!*' She tried again. This time she put a leg on his shoulder and pushed it several times.

Kirk groaned and moved slightly. His eyes opened slowly. "What the hell happened?" He squinted through the blood in his eyes. "And why can't I move my arms?"

He heard Penny screaming somewhere above him. "Penny?"

'Please tell her to shut up.'

He leaned his head up against the cave wall. His eyes were almost shut. He was trying to focus on CheeChee but he was having difficulty. He squinted. "Has anyone ever told you how ugly you are?"

She could tell she wasn't going to get anywhere with Kirk.

She decided to go get The Man Child that resembled a female. She walked effortlessly diagonally over to where The Man Child was. He was still unconscious so it made him a good passenger. She spit some digestive juices onto her web to dissolve it. She secured a web to the side of the cavern and then grabbed The Man Child to lower him down to the ground below. After she laid him down safely, she went back up for Kirk. He was still semi-conscious and was mumbling to himself. He giggled. "Boobies. More like moo bees."

She went through the same process with Kirk as she did with The Man Child. She set him down and then went back for The Dark Female. She suddenly got an amazing idea. When the woman saw CheeChee she started screaming with renewed terror and urgency. The spider took some of her fresh webbing and slapped it onto the woman's mouth. It quickly hardened but instead of silencing her, she kept screaming. The screams were muted by her sealed mouth, but they could still be heard. If CheeChee could have rolled her eyes, she would have. She left the woman bound so that she wouldn't be able

183

to fight her and instead of carrying her down herself, she attached a web to her and lowered her down from where she was. She didn't know what she was going to do with the three humans because they were all still in grave danger. And she still didn't know where her male offspring, Junior, was.

* * *

In another cave, several miles away, Laura's body lay limp in Sheldor's arms. He set her down on the ground and then went to help O'Neil get Ann out of the water and to safety. Twiggy lit the area around them.

Laura awoke in the cold mud and looked at her wrist. Junior was gone. Panic elevated her heart to new heights. "Junior!" She screamed. "Junior?" She looked around frantically.

O'Neil made sure Ann was on dry land and rushed over to Laura. "You okay, kid?" He put his hand on the side of her face and checked her eyes.

Her eyes were glossy with tears. She fought to maintain her composure. "I'm fine! Junior's gone! Steven's gone!" She swallowed hard. "Kirk." She got up and ran to Sheldor. "Are there nanobots down here?"

He cocked his head at her. "There is no reason for nanobots to be down here." He still had a questioning look on his face. "But there are several million of them inside of you."

"Then you need to program them to fix them." She looked him in the eye.

O'Neil was dumbfounded. "Fix who wooo oh, never mind."

Sheldor shook his head. "That would go against my prime directive."

"What are you talking about? Isn't your prime directive to save mankind?" She looked past Sheldor at O'Neil and Ann. "We need the others to help us."

"My prime directive is to do whatever is necessary to save you, remember?"

She grabbed him by the shirt and spoke through her teeth. "We need them!"

"You will die without the nanobots."

She hit him in the chest with her fists. "How long?"

"Roughly, three days."

She nodded. "That's a day after we all die!" She stuck her finger in his face. "We need them!" She couldn't keep the tears in anymore. She swallowed hard and lowered her voice. "I need him." She moaned and then whispered, "I need Steven, please." She shifted her weight back and forth and blinked heavy tears out of her eyes. "Please," she begged.

The android looked at Twiggy, who floated over to him as if he was being silently commanded. The orb settled in front of Laura and hovered in place. She began to feel nauseous and started to breathe heavily. Soon a small cloud of nanobots billowed out of her nose and mouth like a black cloud from a chimney. She coughed so fiercely and so deeply that she felt like she was going to throw up. The cloud of machines entered Twiggy through a small hatch in her side. He flew off as soon as they were all aboard.

Laura watched Twiggy go. She hoped that her sacrifice would save someone. She needed Steven to be okay, but in her heart of hearts, she wanted them all to be okay. In the grand scheme of things, if they all died saving the Earth, that was an acceptable loss. The lives of seven people for billions? It's a good deal. She turned around and took a step forward only to fall face first in some glowing green goo. It was in her mouth, in her eyes, up her nose... she reacted as if she fell in shit, flicking it everywhere and spitting it out.

O'Neil pulled her to her feet. He walked her over to the water's edge and helped her wash the goo off. He scooped water up and splashed it on her. "It's okay, kid. It's gonna be okay."

She scooped water over her face and rinsed her mouth out. "Ugh! What the hell is this?"

Sheldor bent over and stuck a finger in the goo and examined it. He focused in on it and looked at the cells on a microscopic level. "It's bioluminescent bacteria."

O'Neil suddenly grabbed Laura's wrist and looked closely at it. The spider bite Junior gave her was healing before his eyes. "We need to bring some of this with us."

Ann looked closely at it. "Just because it did something good doesn't make it good for you." She picked up her pack and looked at Sheldor. "Can we get out of here?"

O'Neil helped Laura to her feet. It was obvious that she was upset so he hugged her tight and rubbed her back. "We're gonna get through this, kid. Promise."

Sheldor turned to the corridor behind him. "This will lead us to the access tunnel where the mining equipment is kept."

The green goo was everywhere in the cave. It was hard not to get it on you, but at least it lit the way. Laura tried to contact CheeChee as they walked. Her friend thankfully reported back to her, but what she reported back to her only managed to upset her more. She cleared her throat and tried hard not to sob as she spoke. "CheeChee says that everyone is fine except Steven and Junior." She forced herself to concentrate on walking and swallowed hard. She took a few breaths before continuing. "She says they're missing." She could feel CheeChee's worry for her son. As much as she wanted to drop everything and focus on finding Steven and Junior, she knew they needed to concentrate on the task at hand. Hopefully, Twiggy and Sheldor will be able to bring the groups back together. The corridor was visibly getting narrower and narrower and darker and darker as they progressed further and further. She reached out in front of her and grabbed the back of O'Neil's jacket so they wouldn't get separated. She was starting to feel her claustrophobia build within her. If something were to happen, they wouldn't have room to do anything. She suddenly felt hot and was having difficulty breathing. Everyone stopped moving.

"What's the matter? What's going on?" O'Neil asked the android in front of him.

Laura listened for his answer. She tried to calm herself, but it was dark and the only sound she could hear was her own heartbeat.

"I'm a bit embarrassed because I should have thought of this before we got to this point. I need Laura to open the door."

Laura closed her eyes. It was already a tight fit. All she wanted to do was get out of there. Every part of her body asked her to run, but she remained still, which translated into pain. O'Neil turned sideways and tried to plaster himself up against the cave wall. He looked at her. "Come on. The awkward will only *seem* to last forever."

She turned sideways and tried to move past him without pressing up against him. It wasn't possible. He wasn't fat, but he was much larger than she was. He sucked in his gut as far as he could and she tried again. He put his hands on her shoulders and tried to help guide her past him when he suddenly started laughing uncontrollably. She looked up at him as he started to squirm and dance up against her.

"O'Neil?"

That's when she saw them. In the darkness, they looked like black dots crawling along the walls and O'Neil. Bugs! Or more precisely, cockroaches! They were everywhere. Ann screamed. Once O'Neil figured out what was tickling him, he stopped laughing, but he couldn't stop dancing around. He inadvertently crushed her against the wall. The cockroaches gave her the renewed urgency and will to force herself past him even though something sharp was poking her in the back. She fell towards Sheldor. He caught her and pulled her to him and then over to the sensor pad. Before Laura even knew what was happening, he had pressed her hand up against the pad and the door slid open. They all rushed forward and fell inside like dominos. Laura was on top of Sheldor, and Ann was on top of O'Neil. Everyone, except Sheldor, got up and started smacking bugs off themselves and each other. Their fevered stomping made them look like a tap-dancing crew.

"I think you got them all." Sheldor folded his arms and waited for them to finish.

O'Neil danced around and quickly took his shirt off, followed by his pants. Laura, looked on horrified, knowing any moment she was going to see something that might scar her for life. He stood there in his boxer shorts and knee-high black socks, with his hair mussed up and standing on end, looking desperate for help.

"You're good with big spiders but cockroaches make you crap yourself?" Laura eyed his gray hairy chest and decided that for a man his age, he wasn't half bad. That didn't mean she wanted to see more.

"I didn't crap myself. Yet," he said, breathing heavily. Ann walked up behind him and slapped a roach off his shoulder. He glanced back at her. "Thank you."

She picked up his pants and shook them out for him. "You're welcome." She walked up and handed the pants to him. When he took them, he looked her in the eye and cracked a smile. She blushed and walked away.

Laura watched the cute exchange and then turned to the android. "So, now what, Shelly?"

Sheldor looked at her as if she had defiled him. "What? Is it just SO hard to say Sheldor?" He looked at her, dead serious for a few beats then smirked. "I was wondering how long it would take you." When he smiled the way he did, he looked like the Grinch to her. He waved his hand. "I know my namesake hates it, but I do enjoy it!" He snorted a few times, which served as his best laugh.

Laura looked at her surroundings. It appeared to be a warehouse of sorts. As she stepped forward more lights turned on. It was mostly empty except for an occasional piece of machinery. Against a far wall was a row of what appeared to be robots. O'Neil and Ann walked ahead of her. She watched O'Neil continue his flirtation with her. As he pulled his shirt on he spoke. "How are you holding up?"

Ann smiled at him. Laura felt a slight attraction towards her. She knew it was a because of her merging with Steven but it still managed to make her feel a little weird. In her mind, it didn't matter if the attraction to women was permanent or not. She loved Steven. She didn't want or need anything else. She watched as Ann touched the colonel's arm and then slid her arm under his and they walked arm and arm and she was suddenly overcome with emotion. She turned around to run away to be alone, but instead ran right into Shelly. She almost fell but he caught her. She covered her eyes with her hands and then pressed her head against his chest and cried. He patted her back awkwardly. "There, there." He let her bawl in his arms for about a minute before he tried to reason with her. "I know you're concerned about Steven but we really don't have time for this." He pulled her away and then took her hands from her face so that he could look her in the eye. "He may be alive... but if we don't clear the cannon that won't matter, will it? I need you to focus."

Laura's face was red and wet with tears. She breathed in quickly and then sniffed loudly. She took her hands away from his and wiped her eyes and nose. "Okay," she said as she nodded.

* * *

Twiggy floated up and out of the cavern and headed back the same way they had come. The orb didn't know exactly where she would find Kirk and the others, but she knew which way they had gone. She stayed as close to the ceiling of the cavern as possible so she wouldn't get wet. In truth, she could be completely submerged in water and she would be fine, but travel would be much slower. In the interest of saving lives, Twiggy made a judgment call. The little orb made it all the way back to the fork in the river in good time. She took the path the others, unfortunately, found themselves on, and determined that it went sixty feet straight down. From her readings, the water was thirty meters deep. If anyone fell from that height all the way down to the bottom they would have been traveling at sixty miles an hour. Hitting the water at that speed could cause severe injuries or even death for a human.

Twiggy floated down past the giant spider that the other master, Laura, called CheeChee. The CheeChee had one of the women suspended from its web. Quickly surveying the rest of the surroundings, Twiggy noticed Kirk and the other male who was traveling with him, on the ground below. The fourth traveler was not in the immediate area. Logic dictated that Twiggy tend to the people that were present and accounted for, and then try to locate the missing one later. She scanned the two men lying on the cave floor. Kirk had pressure building within his cranium. If it wasn't relieved soon, he would certainly die. The smaller man, Gene, only had minor injuries. Twiggy positioned herself close to Kirk's head and let the nanobots out of their containment bin. The swarm of bots entered through his nose and mouth.

The woman called Penny reached the ground and immediately started flailing about. The CheeChee walked along the cave wall above them while the woman tried to free herself from the webs. Twiggy analyzed the situation and determined that the woman was terrified that the spider might consume her. It was a logical conclusion based on current events. All the humanoids present were covered in spider web. The woman had her mouth covered with a glob of web but that didn't stop her from trying to scream. Twiggy used a low yield laser on the webbing to free her.

Penny immediately went to Kirk and started shaking him back and forth. "Kirk! Kirk! Get up!" She started digging in his pockets. "Where is your stun gun?"

Twiggy flew in between Penny and Kirk. "Step back, please." Penny gave the orb the 'who the hell do you think you are?' look and disregarded it completely. Twiggy shot Penny with the low yield laser and it stung her skin. She jumped away as if she'd been bitten. Twiggy floated closer to her. "I said, step back. I do not want to hurt you."

Penny pointed a finger at Twiggy and shook it back and forth while she talked. "Bitch, I know you didn't just shoot me with no laser!"

"Penny?" Gene suddenly sat up and rubbed his head. "What happened?"

Twiggy scanned Kirk again and then sent a command to the bots to increase Kirk's adrenaline. She waited again. "Kirk, you need to wake up."

"Oh, nothing really, we fell over a waterfall and that big ass spider is trying to eat us for dinner, that's all." Penny looked up the cavern wall and saw CheeChee up there looking down at them.

While Gene tried to calm the woman, Twiggy kept a watchful eye on Kirk. Her most recent scan showed decreased pressure in his brain. Twiggy redirected air into his face. "Kirk, it is time to get up."

Kirk let out a moan and then rubbed his face and head. "Did someone run me over with a truck?"

"No, we fell over a waterfall, and then your spider friend tried to eat me." Penny put her hand on her hip and cocked her head to the side. She pointed at Twiggy. "And then that little bitch shot me with a laser."

"I have analyzed the situation, Kirk. I have come to the conclusion that CheeChee saved your lives." Twiggy moved backward as Kirk sat up.

Kirk looked around. "Where's everybody else?"

Gene shivered. "They didn't come down behind us."

"Where's Steven?" Kirk got to his feet and almost fell back down.

'The Dangerous One is gone. Laura is sad.'

Twiggy floated in front of Kirk. "Steven is not here. Laura sent me to check on you."

Kirk closed his eyes and shook his head. "Wait, what do you mean? Steven's gone? What does that mean?"

* * *

Steven crawled out of the water on his hands and knees, violently coughing water as it dripped out of his nose and mouth. He collapsed onto his stomach and then he rolled onto his back. He was exhausted. He lay there trying to catch his breath and thinking that he should have died. The cavern was lit by an eerie green light. He looked around while he took in huge gulps of air. He concentrated on breathing. In and out. He started coughing again so he turned onto his side. His heart was racing, but that was partially because he couldn't stop thinking about what might have happened to the rest of his party. Namely, Laura. He couldn't believe how quickly he had come full circle. He was alone, met someone, met more someones, and now... they are probably all dead, and again, he's alone. Lovely.

That's when he heard a soft growl that grew into a howl that echoed through the cave and ignited terror inside of him. It wasn't hard to figure out what was making the sound. He already knew. After all, he was underground in a cave. That was where they lived. He slowly turned onto his stomach and placed his palms down on the wet sand so he'd be ready. They were all around him in the water. The ugly, mutated dogs that glowed in the dark. And now he knew why. Whatever that green shit was in the water and all over the walls clung to their fur and made them glow. He knew as soon as he made a move they'd be on him. He was on his feet in an instant with his fists ready. It was the first moment that he became aware of an injury. His left ankle throbbed in pain so badly that he had to take the pressure off it. This concerned him because he was right-handed. He could kick or hit with either arm, but it was always his instinct to go with his right. If he had to put most of his weight on his right leg, it meant that he would be at a major disadvantage. If he did kick, he'd have to do it with his left leg and do it with the understanding that it would hurt like hell and cause further injury. There was no way he was letting those bastards make a meal out of him.

The thought of being eaten alive terrified him to his very core. His nightmares were about to be realized.

One of them always takes the lead. As soon as that one jumps, the others would follow. The biggest green one of the pack launched itself at Steven. As he hit the Alpha he felt his knuckles connect with the bones in its head. He spent years conditioning his knuckles so that when he punched or hit something it wouldn't hurt as much but...it still hurt. He didn't have time to think about the pain because several more were bounding towards him. It was as he feared, he had to use his feet several times to kick the evil critters away. Each time he involuntarily yelled out in pain. That very action seemed to stun them for a few seconds. It almost seemed like they were wondering where the noise had come from. Steven took advantage of their confusion and smacked a few of them so hard they hit the opposite wall. But the monsters were relentless. They had never given up in the past. Usually, he just barricaded himself inside his treehouse until morning. They always disappeared before daybreak. He didn't have that luxury anymore because he was deep in the heart of their territory. It would be a miracle if he survived and he knew it.

"STOP!" A female voice resonated through the cave. All of the howlers suddenly stopped and then ran behind a dark human figure in the cavern doorway. He stood there breathing heavily, trying to see the woman. The green goo only provided enough light to see things that were fairly close to him.

"Oh, it's you." The woman's voice broke the silence again. He still couldn't see her face, but she was short. In the shadow, he could tell that her hair was long and sticking up in places.

Her words confused him. Did she recognize him? Who was this woman? He leaned a little to the right as he tried to keep off his left foot. "Do I know you?"

"No. But I know you." She walked forward into the green light. She was in her fifties with long black, unkempt hair with gray streaks. She wore animal skins and was clearly in need of a shower. "You're the one who keeps killing my children."

His eyes grew wide. "What?"

He suddenly heard that familiar growling as some howlers bounced around her feet like excited puppies looking for a treat. He went into attack mode again and got ready to strike.

She held up her hand. "Don't. They won't attack you when I am around."

Steven wasn't about to relax. This was his personal nightmare. He scanned the area for any possible weapons or anything that would make the situation worse if he had to fight. That's when he saw Junior floating on a blanket of webbing. He was happy that the little guy was alive but very scared that the two of them would be gremlin meat very soon. The woman in front of him shook her head. She suddenly flipped her head and pointed behind her. The gremlins whined like sad dogs and bounded out of the cave.

197

"Follow me, if you want to live." He wasn't sure if she was joking or not, but under the circumstances, he didn't have very many choices. He had only three. Fight to the death. Fight until he succeeds. Or follow the gremlin whisperer. He didn't budge. He just stood there staring after the woman and listening. Thinking. He jumped slightly when she poked her head back in. "Are you coming?!"

Steven shook his head. It pissed him off that his life was a sci-fi horror flick in the making. Junior started climbing up his leg. He waited until the little guy made it up to his shoulder and then decided to follow the woman. He was a little uneasy on his feet, taking each step carefully, making sure his footing was sure. The strange thing was that his foot began to feel better. It still hurt, but not nearly as much as it had only a few short minutes before. He took a deep breath, "Junior, stay close to me. Don't wander off." He knew that his mother, CheeChee, didn't understand English, but that didn't mean that Junior wasn't learning. Maybe he was picking up bits and pieces. It's better to try than abandon all hope. He ran his hand along the wall of the cave as he passed. It was clear that it had been cut by the Newtonians. He hoped that meant that he was in an access tunnel close to where he needed to be. As he walked he saw one of the howlers clinging to the ceiling of the cave. He eyed it closely. It took every ounce of strength he had to walk past without attacking it. It was a tense moment. The howler watched him as closely as he watched it. He only turned away once he was past it. He smelled meat cooking and his stomach growled. At least he hoped that it was his stomach.

Steven watched the woman walk through an opening ahead of him and was surprised to find the cavern lit by a fire. Instead of smoke filling the cave and suffocating its inhabitants, it rose up and exited through a hole in the ceiling. The woman sat on a throne made of sticks and bone. The hair stood up on the back of his neck and he shivered. Dozens of mutant dogs watched him as he stood in front of her. He felt like he was about to be judged by a demon and the only thing standing between being flayed alive and living another hour was this strange woman and her opinion of him. Besides the meat cooking on a spit, he could smell a myriad of other odors, all unpleasant. She was the proverbial crazy cat lady. She sat upon her throne looking at him and leaning on her chin. Now that he could see her better, she was at least in her fifties and seemed to be of Indian descent.

She picked up a handful of cooked meat that had been cooling on a rock and held it up to him. "Eat." She had several missing teeth and the ones she did have were black and decaying.

Steven raised his eyebrows and put his hands up. "No thanks, I'm not hungry." In fact, he was starving. But looking at the meat in her dirty hands made his stomach turn.

The woman sighed and then tossed the meat to the howlers. "Suit yourself." Four of them growled at each other and fought for it. One with a white streak on its head jumped into her lap and she patted it. "Sit." She motioned to the large rock next to him. He looked at it. There was a brown stain on it that he tried not to dwell on. The wheels in his mind were working overtime.

Would his refusal upset her? He looked down at himself. His clothes were covered in mud and green goo. Not to mention the fact that he was still wet. He decided to sit down, stain be damned. All the howlers were looking at him. He wondered if they were thinking about how good he might taste. He looked at her and tried to smile. He knew he had to make nice and it had to be convincing. "My name is, Steven. What's yours?"

She looked past him, or maybe through him, trying to remember something, then pointed her finger around the room. "They call me, Momma."

All the howlers repeated, "Momma." When they said her name, it sounded like a cross between a purr and a growl. Another shiver ran up his spine. He looked at them. It was probably the only word they could say.

He winced and said, "I can't call you, Momma."

"No, I suppose you can't." She looked down at the howler in her lap and scratched its head.

Steven knew he had to handle things delicately, but he was getting impatient. He looked at his watch. It had been four hours since they started their underground journey. He was terribly worried about Laura but even if you removed her from the equation, they had a world to save. The world may have forgotten about Steven Foster, but he hasn't forgotten about it. He didn't want to see it end, not if he had anything to say about it.

He spoke softly. "I need to get back to my friends."

The woman smiled. "But you just got here. Stay, and visit with Momma for a while."

The howlers repeated, "Momma."

He swallowed hard and nervously started rubbing his palms on his knees. His heart raced in his chest because he knew he was in danger. Like him, this woman had probably been alone for quite some time. He tried to calm down. "You knew about me?"

Another howler jumped in her lap. "Yes. My babies told me about you." She tapped the side of her head, at her temple. "You are responsible for killing a number of them."

The conversation was taking a disturbing turn. He started to think he'd soon have to fight his way out. He needed to change the subject. "How long have you been here?"

She pulled a bug, or something, off of the howler in her lap and flicked it away. "That depends. What year is it?"

He looked at the ground. He found it hard not to relate to the woman, but at least she had her babies to keep her company. "It's 2017."

She stopped picking at the howler in her lap and stared off into space. "That can't be."

Steven looked down at his hands. He didn't know what to do or how to proceed. Perhaps he could just get up and walk away? 'Momma' was lost in her memories somewhere... or perhaps she had a stroke. Whatever the reason, she was staring off into space and no longer paying attention to him. He needed to get back to his friends. He needed to find Laura. He took a deep breath and immediately wished he hadn't. The stench of the place filled his nostrils, making him want to pull the neck of his shirt up over his nose. He looked at the howlers once again and did a mental count. He knew he could manage the thirteen that he could see in the room, but what about ones that might be lurking elsewhere? He looked at his watch. He couldn't wait for nightfall to come, he needed to get going.

"Look... Momma, I need to get going. My friends are in trouble."

"Human?"

Steven thought about the answer for a moment. It was best not to confuse her with words like 'Newtonians.' He nodded. "Yes."

She leaned forward. Her dark eyes focused in on him. "Why are they in trouble?"

He wondered how specific he should be. Technically speaking, her life was in as much danger as his. So were her precious babies. The woman before him was clearly off her rocker. He decided against telling her ridiculous stories about the Sun and the Moon, or the need to clear a photon cannon before it blows them all to smithereens. Instead, he thought he would be able to tug at her heartstrings. He told her about Laura and how much he loved her.

Momma shook her head. "How can you love a person like that in only two days?"

He fiddled with his fingernails, picking at them. "Magic." What else was he supposed to say?
She looked at him with hollow eyes. The corner of her lip moved slightly, like she wanted to smile. "Magic?"

"She and I touched this wand...thing. She saw my life, and I saw hers." He shrugged. "It was as if it was happening to me. I knew what she was feeling and why. Only, since I have my own thoughts and opinions, it wasn't the same experience."

Momma looked confused. He was losing her.

"One memory of hers was of her father slapping her hand away from a hot stove. It hurt her emotionally as much as it did physically. I experienced it the same way she did, except since I'm grown, I knew why her father did it."

She looked down at the howler in her lap and scratched its head. It turned its head toward her hand, encouraging her to do it harder. "So, you know everything there is to know about her?"

Steven smiled. "Right down to the things you never wanted to know about a person."

"And you still love her?"

"I know it sounds cliché, but more than life itself."

She suddenly inhaled loudly and let it out. "Well then, we need to go get her." She stood up.

Steven's eyes went wide. Did she just say WE? He got to his feet and waited for her to lead. He couldn't exactly tell her 'no thanks.' She had the upper hand. He didn't want to see what it would be like if she told her minions to 'sic em!' When she walked out of the cave, he waited a moment to see what would happen. He expected all the howlers to run after her. Instead, they just looked at him, tongues hanging from their mouths, panting. He raised his eyebrows and then quickly followed her out of the cave. The howlers bounded after them like excited basketballs looking for someone to play.

"Where were your friends headed?" She glanced over her shoulder as she made her way down the corridor.

'Shit,' he thought to himself. Now he had to explain a few things. One of the howlers latched onto his leg and started to hump it. Steven was in a state of disgust and horror. He instinctively launched the howler down the corridor and it hit the opposite wall. It fell to the floor and shook its head.

Momma instantly turned around and stuck her finger in his face. "You're lucky he's not hurt."

Steven stared daggers at the howlers at his feet and the ones that hung onto the walls. He knew that the woman in front of him was unstable and had been alone for a long time. But he also knew that for at least the last five years, it had been her choice. She knew about him and never sought him out or approached him. He would have loved the company. Given the circumstances, he probably really would have 'loved' the company. He liked to think that even he wouldn't 'go there' but he had been terribly lonely and depressed. It was a very real possibility. He silently thanked God that she didn't seek him out. If she had, it would have significantly changed his future. If everything turned out okay, he planned on living happily ever after with Laura as his beautiful bride. The howlers seemed to sense the woman's agitation. They bared their teeth at him and growled fiercely. Years of being terrorized by them flooded his emotions. He spoke through gritted teeth, "I would rather travel alone."

"It's like a maze down here. You'll never find your way around without me." She picked up the howler with a white streak on his head and cradled it. "You'll either wander around until you die or my babies will eat you. Probably both."

"These creatures have terrorized me for the last five years, I think I'll risk it." Steven walked past her and down the corridor.

"I could just let them eat you now." She said it as if she didn't care either way. She stroked the howler's head.

He glared at her. "I promise you, I'll take at least twenty of them with me."

She pointed to the cave behind them and made a few growling noises. The sounds she made managed to creep him out more than the howlers did. The animals whimpered and whined and all but one of them scurried down the corridor and into the cave. She looked back at Steven. "Spike stays with me."

Chapter Eight
Up, Up and Away

Kirk rubbed his eyes and looked around. The bioluminescent bacteria was everywhere. It lit up the area enough that he could see about six feet in every direction. They couldn't go back the way they came, so their only option was to follow the river and hope that it brought them to safety. They already knew that their journey would take a vertical turn in less than a mile. They traveled as fast as they could over the rough terrain. There wasn't a path, per se, there were only rocks and green goo. Twiggy and CheeChee had assured Kirk that his sister and the rest of the party were okay. He felt bad about Steven though. He hoped that he was alive so his sister wouldn't have to experience yet another loss. He helped Penny over some rocks and then grudgingly helped Gene over them too. They soon came to a sheer cliff face leading straight up. The river continued onward under the rocks. Twiggy scanned the area. "Captain Rogers, from the information available to me, I have extrapolated that your companion, Steven, most likely fell from the waterfall and plunged approximately twenty feet deep into the fast-moving water making it difficult for him to resurface."

"Twiggy, if you're about to tell me that Steven is dead, save it. I don't want to hear it." Kirk looked up the cliff.

Twiggy continued, "It is impossible for me to determine whether or not Steven is alive or dead. However, since there is no body, I have deduced that he must have traveled under this wall."

Kirk suddenly pictured poor Steven trying to resurface to breathe only to find he couldn't. It was a disturbing thought that he didn't want to pursue further. He knew he could climb the cliff with no problems whatsoever. But he also knew that both Penny and Gene wouldn't be able to do it quite so athletically. He was feeling much better and his head didn't hurt anymore. Twiggy had told him it was because he had nanobots inside of him, courtesy of Laura. It made him feel like a superhero. Invincible. All three of them started climbing the cliff. In more than a few places, CheeChee had to assist them. After they had climbed about five stories, the trio had to rest.

Kirk sat down on a ledge and looked at his friend. "What do you think, man? We gonna win the day?"

"Not a chance." Gene pulled on his shoelaces and then tied them.

Kirk turned his attention to Penny. "What about you, hot stuff?"

Penny wiped some sweat from her forehead and then smiled at him. "We have to. There are so many souls that depend on it."

He nodded. "Yeah, well, the clock's ticking. As soon as we catch our breath we have to get moving again. We have a cannon to clear." He stood and looked up. "I can see the top. Let's go." CheeChee secured webs for the three of them and Kirk brought up the rear so that he could make sure he was there to help Gene or Penny when they needed it. He hoped he wouldn't be spending the next few days trapped in that cavern instead of helping his sister save the world. It was all very surreal to him. How do you wrap your head around the fact that the fate of billions of people is literally in your hands? Every man, woman, and cute little baby. None of them know it. They are all living their lives, the same as they always do, not knowing that they have very little time left. People join the military for lots of different reasons, but the most popular answer that a person would give if asked, is that they wanted to help people and make a difference. Kirk just wanted to be an astronaut. It was all he ever wanted. He never wanted to be a hero. He never wanted to risk his life for others. He just wanted to go into space.

Well, he got his wish. He not only went into space, but he was now on a fantastical adventure. He had never been rock climbing on Earth, but now he was doing it inside the Moon. They were all racing against time to do the impossible and there he was, hanging from a spider's web, from a cliff. He needed to find his sister. Not just because he wanted to make sure she was okay, but because he wanted to be with her if they weren't successful. He watched as Penny and Gene reached the top and then disappeared over it. After a moment, Gene reached over the edge to grab him by the hand and help him up. They were finally at the top. Twiggy shined her light so everyone could see.

"It's a dead-end? Twiggy, what the hell?" Kirk was pissed. They just spent the last five hours climbing up a god damned cliff only to find a dead-end at the top. If he had known that from the start, they could have taken their chances in the underground river.

"You gotta be kidding me!" Gene put his hands on his head and paced back and forth.

Penny shook her head and wagged her finger back and forth. "I ain't climbing back down. You can forget that."

Twiggy floated next to Kirk. "I can assure you, this is the only way out." She shined a laser on the rocks. "You will have to focus your weapon here."

Kirk jammed his hands in his pockets looking for his gun but there was nothing there. He looked down and patted the outside of all his pockets. Nothing. "My gun must have fallen out when we fell."

"I think she means the one on your wrist." Penny pointed at his gauntlet.

Kirk rubbed his wrist. "But I can only fire it when I'm pissed off."

Gene raised an eyebrow. "What the hell does that mean?"

Twiggy turned her sensor to face Kirk. "That information
isn't entirely accurate, Captain Rogers."

"What are you talking about? Sheldor said that when the light is red I have to fire the gauntlet or it will explode. It's only red when I'm mad or..."

"Or what?" Penny asked.

"Scared." Kirk looked uneasy.

"That makes sense. If the thing senses your emotions, then fear and anger would signal that you might be in mortal danger." Gene smoothed his hair behind his ears.

"The weapon can be fired at any time. It *must* be fired when is in the red." Twiggy floated around Kirk.

He looked at his gauntlet. The last time he fired it, he nearly killed everyone. He had serious reservations about firing the weapon in such close quarters, but he didn't see that they had much of a choice. He surveyed the area. There were at least thirty feet of open space around them and nothing to take cover behind. He knew what had to be done. His friends would have to be secured by CheeChee's web just below the cliff's edge. He quickly put his doomed plan into action, watching as his friends lowered themselves over the side. CheeChee also secured a line to him, just in case he blew himself over the side. He positioned himself about ten feet from his target. His plan was to go small and work his way up, but he didn't even know where to start. He looked at his color indicator. It was yellow, which meant he was calm. He sighed and rolled his eyes. "This is never gonna work," he mumbled to himself.

"Will you just get on with it! My balls are halfway up my ass!" Gene yelled from the web he was dangling from.

Kirk clenched his fist and his teeth. He raised his arm to his target and tried to will it to fire. Nothing happened. "One of you might have to come back up here and kick me in the nuts or something."

Penny looked up from her rope at him. He could just barely see her angry face. She made a fist at him. "If you don't shoot a hole through that damn wall, so help me God, I will rip that little dick of yours off!"

Kirk was utterly shocked. "Little dick? That was just mean!"

"I'm sorry, baby! I was just trying to piss you off!"

"Well, it didn't work. It was hurtful." Kirk pouted.

"I know, I'm sorry, I didn't mean it. It's not true! Please forgive me!" Penny spun slowly around on the web as she looked up at him.

Gene was horrified. "Will you quit apologizing to him? Jesus, Kirk, what are you an infant? Just shoot the damn laser!"

Kirk rubbed his face. He definitely had performance anxiety. He knew how deadly the weapon was and he didn't want to hurt anyone. The fact that they were underground didn't escape him either. He could cause another cave in and they'd all be dead. Or worse, he would get the three of them free, but cause a cave-in where his sister and the others were.

Twiggy flew into his view. "I'm sorry for this abuse, Kirk."

"What? Twiggy, what are you talking about?"
Twiggy shot him with her low yield laser. It burned his left forearm. "Ow! Twiggy! What the hell are you doing?!"

Twiggy shot him again. This time stinging through his pants on his thigh.

"Watch it!" Kirk put up his hands. Twiggy fired at him again. This time he managed to duck out of the way, but she kept on shooting at him. Every time her laser hit him, it hurt a little more than the last. Instinct took over as he thrust his arm at the orb and made a fist. A powerful burst shot out of the gauntlet and it was aimed directly at Twiggy. The orb dropped out of the way just in time as the laser hit the rock just where she had intended it to. The blast was so intense that it blew Kirk right off the side of the cliff just as he feared. He tumbled over and slammed against the cliff face. Gene watched Kirk flail about as he swung toward him. He held onto the ledge next to him and then held out his arm for Kirk. They grabbed each other and both came to a stop. Kirk's heart was thumping against his chest and his ears were ringing. "Thanks, man." He climbed back up to the ledge and pulled himself over. There was still a cloud of dust hanging over the area that was making it tough to see. "Twiggy?" He waved some of the dust out of his face as he squinted in the low light. "Twiggy, where the hell are ya, girl?" A light suddenly emitted from the gauntlet allowing him to see. Kirk raised his eyebrows as fear started to well up inside of him. His indicator was still on yellow and the beam of light seemed to be slowly discharging the gauntlet's energy. He needed a light and evidently the gauntlet provided him one. He aimed the light where he had fired the weapon. The blast had penetrated the wall as planned. "I know you were only trying to help, Twiggy. Come out, come out, where ever you are."

Gene helped Penny up over the ledge and they dusted themselves off. "What now?" Gene asked, waving the dust out of his face and coughing.

Kirk looked around. He didn't like the fact that Twiggy wasn't answering him. Then a different but equally horrible thought occurred to him.

'Don't worry, Angry One, I am unharmed.'

He suddenly looked above him. CheeChee was on the ceiling of the cavern twisting something into a ball. When he looked closer he could see that it was Twiggy. CheeChee was wrapping her web around the orb over and over again making it look like a snowball. Kirk found it as funny as it was scary. The largest spider anyone has ever seen, who was his ally, defended him against another ally of his, who was a flying robot. He laughed uncomfortably, "Whatcha got there, CheeChee?"

'You missed. I didn't.'

Kirk nodded. "Yes, but Twiggy was only trying to help. Would you let her go, please? We need her to lead the way."

The spider's eyes stopped moving for a moment. She stopped twisting her web around Twiggy and seemed to be thinking. She suddenly dropped the web covered orb and Kirk caught it. He got the impression that the spider was angry. "Thanks, CheeChee. I appreciate your help. Really, I do."

He placed Twiggy on the ground and the three of them pulled the sticky webbing off of her. When the little orb began to float again, Kirk was elated. "Hey, Twig, you okay?"

"Yes, I am undamaged."

"Good," he leaned in close to her sensor, "NEVER shoot at me again!" He stepped through the gap he made in the
cave wall. "Let's go."

* * *

Laura and O'Neil stood in front of a row of machines that looked like hollow robots. A component was obviously missing and that was a person. Laura watched as O'Neil ogled the one in front of him. He looked like an excited child with a new big-wheel tricycle. She couldn't help smiling when she saw the look on his face, but then she watched it drain away into sadness. "What's wrong?"

O'Neil rubbed his eyes. "Nothing. I was just thinking about my grandkids. The boys would love these things."

Her eyes shot open. "Grandkids? I didn't know you had kids let alone grandkids! You never mentioned having a family."

He gave her a dumb look. "Maybe that's because you never asked." He pulled his phone out of his pocket. "It's a miracle this thing still works. Has to be those nanobots." He poked his phone a couple of times and then handed it to her. The phone had a picture of identical boys around the age of ten. "Twins."

Laura instantly smiled. She inspected the picture closely. The boys were definitely a bit darker than O'Neil and both had shoulder-length dark curly hair. "Oh, my god! They are so cute! How old are they?"

"I see that look on your face. My son is thirty-one. Plenty
old enough to have a couple of ten-year old's."

She shrugged. "It just seemed like you were always pretty lonely."

"I was. Till you two came along. Zander lives up in Seattle. I don't get to see him or his kids that much." He put his phone back in his pocket.

She looked at him curiously. She couldn't believe that she never knew that he had a family and she wondered if her brother, Kirk, knew about it. "So, you just have one kid?"

He shook his head. "Nope. I've got you two brats." He lightly poked her on the nose with his finger."

"Aww!" She hugged him. "That's sweet." When she let him go, she patted his chest. "There's still part of this story missing."

He nodded and sighed at the same time. "I'll give you the short version because you know I'm not the touchy-feely type." She frowned, but then nodded in agreement. He continued, "We met, fell in love, had a baby, risked my career, and was almost dishonorably discharged for fraternization... Yadda yadda yadda, And then one day she told me she was in love with someone else. The next thing I know she's nowhere to be found and I'm raising Zander on my own."

Laura knitted her brows together. "Did you ever find out
what happened to her?"

He shook his head. "No, but I guess it wasn't a coincidence that the man she was seeing disappeared too."

"Probably not." They held each other's gaze for a moment. She knew there was something big that he didn't want to talk about so she decided not to press the issue. They both turned back to the wearable robot things that O'Neil so desperately wanted to play with.

He leaned in close to the arm and examined it. "They're some kind of robotic suits used for assisted heavy duty lifting. Probably uses hydraulics. We already have something like these on Earth." He pointed at it. "But... these are so much more sophisticated."

Laura wondered if only Newtonian's could work the suits or if anyone could. She watched the colonel as he walked around the back of a suit and put his arms on each side. He carefully stepped up and then lowered each leg inside the suit's legs and then slid his arms in place. He had to crouch down to fit inside the headpiece. He looked woefully uncomfortable. He grimaced and shook his head then stepped out of it. She looked down the row of robot suits. They all looked the same size and she knew she had to be too small to operate one. By the look on O'Neil's face, he expected her to try. She walked around back of the suit and inspected it.

"I guess this isn't a good day for claustrophobia issues," Laura said looking at O'Neil. She half expected him to give her a 'get out of jail' free card but he didn't.

"Come on, kid. You can't say no to the universe." He put his hand on her shoulder and gently nudged her towards it.

She put one foot inside it. "I'm gonna get in this thing and then use those arms to crack your head open like a walnut."

As soon as her arms were in place something pierced the skin of her right hand. She flinched and tried to pull away, but it was too late. The suit began to adjust to her height. It made loud gasping sounds as it let out air and shrank until it fit her perfectly. Laura immediately tried to get back out, but she couldn't. She started to panic.

O'Neil saw the look of terror on her face. "Laura, you need to calm down. You're okay."

Steam from her heavy breathing fogged up the window in her helmet. She closed her eyes and tried to concentrate on a wide-open beach with a light breeze. She had to make a conscious effort to take deep breaths, in and out. When she opened her eyes, she could see a monitor reflected on the glass of her helmet. A red number flashed at her. Her heart rate was one hundred and twenty-three beats per minute.

"You good? Try to walk around." O'Neil encouraged her.

When she concentrated on his face and focused on the outside, she didn't feel as trapped as she did before. Taking a step was easier than she thought it would be. The exoskeleton responded immediately to her muscle movements almost as if it were instinctual. She suspected it had sensors that measured her muscle movement and mirrored it in the suit. She watched as O'Neil got his phone back out and held it up at her. She grimaced at him and then stuck her tongue out. He was obviously recording her.

"What?" He shrugged a half-apology. "It's for posterity."

She laughed and suddenly put one arm up and the other down, then bent her knees and shook her butt while moving her arms wildly.

O'Neil laughed so hard he had to grab his sides. "You look like one of those transmorpher things bustin' a move." Her feet made loud clopping noises that reverberated and echoed in the warehouse every time she stomped her foot down.

"I wonder, is this the best use of your time?"

Both the hybrid-human robot and the colonel turned to see Shelly and Ann standing behind them. At least one of them wore a smile, and it wasn't the android. Shelly taught her how to unlock the controls of two more suits so they all could work on clearing the cannon. Every time she thought about the task at hand, she likened it to a jammed shotgun with an old man squinting down the barrel. Only instead of doing something as ill-advised as that... they would be standing in the barrel trying to clear it by hand. Sure, that hand would be shoved squarely down a bionic robot arm with extraordinary power, but by hand nonetheless.

Standing in the massive cannon made her feel small. It was several stories high and equally as wide... and filled with rocks, boulders, and dirt. When they originally learned that the cave-in was only thirty-five feet, it didn't seem that bad and doable. A feeling of dread and deep sorrow filled her because she knew in all likelihood, they would fail. Thirty-five feet may not seem like all that much until you realize you have to factor in height and width too. She looked at O'Neil. He had the same look of dread on his face. Several of the larger maintenance bots flew over their heads. They watched as a red beam of light shot out from one as it tried to cut into the stones. Shelly explained that logic dictated that they would start on top and work their way down. After all, the cannon doesn't have to be completely clear in order to fire. It just has to be mostly clear. But as the bot demonstrated, every time they removed some rubble, more would fall in from above.

He explained that the maintenance bots were also having a hard time clearing the rubble because the bulk of the rock was made of a black quartz that resembled obsidian. The rock would reflect at least some of the laser lessening its cutting power. "The maintenance bots aren't made for this. The suits you are currently wearing, are." He pointed to one of the biggest boulders. "O'Neil, if you would, please point one of the arms at the boulder and concentrate."

"On what?"

"What would you like to see happen to the boulder?"

O'Neil pointed his right arm at the boulder. "That's easy." There was a sudden flash of light and the boulder exploded into tiny pieces that impacted their suits at high speed. It sounded much like a hailstorm on top of a car. One of the larger pieces of rock hit Shelly in the side of the head. A piece of his scalp, complete with hair, peeled off the side of his head and hung down to his shoulder. Shelly was an android so you might expect to see a metallic skull underneath his synthetic skin but that wasn't the case. It was as if any normal man had just been partially scalped. Laura's eyes grew wider than her head and she turned ghost white. She swallowed hard and pointed her robot arm at his head. He gave her a questioning look and cocked his head to the side, which only made it worse. O'Neil started giggling.

"You're gonna make me throw up in my helmet." Ann turned away.

Shelly whipped his head to the side and looked at Laura. The piece of scalp waved at her and then relaxed to the side. "What is she talking about?"

O'Neil laughed harder. He, and his whole robot suit, were hunched over with his hands on his knees. "Oh man, you've got to be doing that on purpose! There's no way you don't know about that."

Shelly's eyes suddenly rolled to the right of his face as he lightly tapped the side of his head, finally figuring out that something was amiss. He pushed the flap back and held it in place. "Oh, real mature."

As O'Neil tried to regain his composure, Ann picked up a large rock up over her head and threw it back down. Laura watched her curiously. "What are you doing?"

Ann pointed at the rock she threw down. "That must have weighed a couple hundred pounds." She looked up to the top of the cannon. "If we can pick up the rubble in these suits, maybe we can just throw it out of the hole." She started to climb up the mountain of rocks.

O'Neil looked at Laura and Shelly, a smile still on his face from his laughing fit, he nodded. "Seems like a plan."

Shelly seemed satisfied. "Then get to it. I don't need to remind you that time is running out." He walked towards the access hatch. "I'm going to the control room."

Laura watched him go and then looked up at Ann as she climbed. She yelled at her, "You know these things can fly, right?" She straightened her back and put her arms out. There was a burst of air at her feet and suddenly she was rising upward and past Ann.

"Show off."

Laura shook her head as she reached the top. Even though she seemed to be functioning normally there was a fear that lurked in the recesses of her mind. The fear that she'd never see Steven again. Her heart ached in a way that she had never experienced before. She had never been in emotional pain so bad, so intense, that she thought she might die or that the world was going to end. When she had lost her parents she was devastated, but she had Kirk to help her through it. And above all else, she knew that they wouldn't want her to be upset. It was different with Steven. The fear inside her was physically hurting her. So much that she felt like she couldn't breathe. She needed to know if he was okay. She forced herself to keep going even though something kept pestering her. She didn't know what it was until, finally, it hit her. Junior. She could feel him trying to contact her.

Chapter Nine
Getting to Know Momma

Steven followed the surefooted woman down the dark passageways wondering if she was leading him to Laura or his ultimate doom. He couldn't help wondering what her story was. How did she get there? Was it the same way he got there? How long has she been there? But he didn't know if opening that particular can of worms would be a good thing at the moment. He made the assumption that she must be Newtonian simply because she seems to be communicating with those damn howlers by way of telepathy. They listen to her and respond to her like any smart canine would. He could barely see. For all he knew, the howlers could be all around him. His heart was racing. He may be a fighter, but it doesn't matter how impressive you are if your opponents are smaller and faster than you are…and you are in a confined space. Those little monsters would make quick work of him and it would be all over in an instant.

He looked down the corridor ahead of her. It started to get wider and glowed with a dull green light. Soon they were standing in a vast cavern containing a lake of glowing green water. The green stuff was everywhere. It even grew along the walls and clung to stalagmites that hung from the top of the cavern like huge fangs from a long-forgotten monster. He suddenly remembered a beloved childhood film and wondered if maybe, just maybe, they were inside a huge space whale. He smiled to himself because it was such a ridiculous thought. He wished Laura was there because she would have laughed with him. He examined the green goo that clung to the cave wall next to him. He knew that he had been exposed to it before and suffered no ill effects, but that doesn't mean repeated exposure was a good idea. He felt Junior move from one of his shoulders to the other and it took every bit of self-control within him to keep still and not freak out. If he had been on Earth, exploring an underground river deep inside a cave would be something he would enjoy doing if it wasn't for the fact that the fate of the universe might rest on his shoulders.

Steven suddenly realized that the woman was staring at something he couldn't quite make out in the low light so he walked up and stood next to her. About six feet away, in all its splendor, was a human skeleton sitting between two stalagmites. If it once had clothing on, it had long since fallen off and rotted away. He looked at the crazy woman he knew only as 'Momma' and asked, "Who was that?"

At first, it seemed like she was ignoring him, but eventually, she took a deep breath and turned her attention to the path, or lack of one, in front of her. She waded into the water. "His name was Martin. I brought him here when he got sick. But even the healing powers of the green stuff couldn't save him."

Steven followed her into the water. It was so cold that he had to force himself to continue forward. He lifted his arms as the water got closer to his waist. He stared at the skeleton as he passed. It was dyed green by the goo and had what he thought were scratch marks all over the bone. When he realized that they weren't scratch marks at all, he swallowed hard. They were bite marks made by the teeth of the howlers. He watched as Momma crossed the green water as if the cold or the horror show didn't phase her at all. The howler she held looked over her shoulder at him. Its eyes reflected green making it look much more terrifying. "Who was he? Did you two come here together?"

She didn't answer and just kept moving forward eventually making it to the other side. He watched her climb out. "Momma, are you okay?"

The howler in her arms growled, "Momma."

He chewed his lip and considered his options. If he pressed the issue with this woman he could make a bad situation infinitely worse. This man, Martin, died of some illness and then the howlers ate him. At least he hoped it happened in that order. He didn't like thinking of the little bastards snacking on the poor man as he lay in the goo trying to get better. She started mumbling something incoherent that he couldn't quite hear so he concentrated on her words and listened. From what he could piece together Martin was her lover. She evidently broke her fiancé's heart to be with him and it was her belief that both of them were sent to hell for their actions. As he followed her out of the green cavern and back into the darkness, she whimpered softly and then asked, "What terrible thing did you do to end up here?"

Steven's heart sank. The poor woman believed that she was being punished for infidelity. It made him think of a particularly hard moment in his life when he found out his girlfriend had been cheating on him. He screamed at her and wished her to hell, but he knew that there was no way he would send even her to 'the hell' that he's experienced over the last five years. It dawned on him that his five years was probably a cakewalk compared to what Momma had been through.

He could hear her footsteps slow and come to a stop. He tried to see what she was doing, but it was too dark. He suddenly heard a loud metal on metal click that echoed down the passageway. A crack of light appeared in what he assumed was a door and as the woman pulled it open the corridor got brighter and brighter until he had to squint and shield his eyes. She walked through the door and into the light so he followed. He found himself in a wide-open space with floating ships that looked like the traditional 'flying saucers' that seemed to pop up every now and again in Earth's history. As happy as he was to be out of that dark corridor, he was fuming mad, and confused. If this woman had access to this hanger and knew this sort of thing was a possibility, why in god's name was she living in filth with gremlins? At the very least she could have been living in comfort with gremlins. He had to know why she chose to live the way she did. He had to know more. He quickened his pace to get in front of her.

"Hold on one second, if you had access to this place, why the hell do you live the way you do? No, in fact, why didn't you take one of these ships and fly back home?" Steven stared her in the eye.

Momma's hollow, lifeless eyes stared back at him for what seemed like an eternity. Finally, she looked down at the howler in her arm and then scratched at its head. She tilted her head to the side. "I already told you. Because I deserve this."

He shook his head and frowned. "No one deserves this. No one. You need to understand that."

Steven stared at one of the spaceships. He glanced over at Momma and her pet. Her mouth was agape as she slowly walked around it. He eyed her favorite monster. He hated the howlers but this one seemed pretty tame. He walked around the opposite side of the ship. It only looked like a saucer from the front. The body continued on to a rounded point.

"We need to get inside." Steven said as he ran his hand along the side. "Time is running out."

Momma walked underneath the ship and placed her hand on the bottom of it. "How do we get it open?"

When she said 'open' the ship obliged. A hatch in the bottom opened up. Steven smiled. "You did it!"

He climbed in and then helped her up. As soon as they were inside the lights came on and the controls lit up. Steven scratched the back of his head. He knew that Momma was the only one that could activate or fly the ship. But even so, what do they do? Where do they go? He still didn't know where Laura or any of his new friends were. Junior walked down his arm and onto the panel. Momma eyed the spider. Steven suddenly became afraid that she'd let her pet eat Junior.

"Someone is talking to your little friend." Momma squinted at Junior as if that made it easier for her to hear it.

Steven looked at Junior curiously. "Who? What are they saying? And how do you know?"

"He's projecting so I can hear. Someone named Laura is telling him that she's alive. And he's told her the same about you."

"Oh, thank God." Steven leaned on the panel and closed his eyes. It was a huge relief to hear that she was alive. "Will you tell him to tell her that I love her?" He watched Momma fall silent as she relayed the message to Junior.

"She tells him that time is running out. The cannon is still blocked." Momma reached over and picked up Junior and placed him on Steven's arm. "Also...he's terribly hungry."

Steven looked at the spider for a long moment and then nodded. "Just tell him to do it."

Junior moved to the inside of Steven's wrist and bit down, latching on. Steven breathed in quickly and held onto the control panel for support. He closed his eyes and took a few deep breaths. After a minute, he seemed to regain control. His breathing evened out and he opened his eyes. He tried to clear his head by shaking it. He felt almost euphoric. He raised his wrist and looked at Junior. "If I knew it felt like this, I would have let you do it sooner." With the smile still on his face, he looked past Junior to Momma. She had a serious look on her face. She raised her eyebrows at him. He suddenly realized that Junior and CheeChee had inadvertently given Momma information that he hadn't told her yet.

He turned his head and rolled his eyes. He wasn't sure how much she knew or where he should start. He put his hands up and about a foot apart. "Long story short? The sun is going to explode, killing everyone and we need to fix it."

Momma surprised Steven by not even missing a beat. "What do you have to do to fix it?"

He suddenly realized that his answer was going to sound crazy. But he figured since Momma was crazy, it might actually sound feasible. "Shoot it with a photon cannon."

"And the cannon is blocked?"

Steven nodded. "Now you're up to speed." He pointed at the monitor. "Can you tell this ship to take commands from me?"

She shrugged. "Ship, do what Steven wants you to do." She looked at him. "Will that do it?"

He walked over to the monitor. "Ship, can you show me the cannon and where we are in relation to it?" The screen showed them a schematic of the cannon and the cave in. According to the monitor, they were nearly twenty miles from where they needed to be. "Ship, I need you to bring us as close to the cannon as possible." It didn't feel like anything was happening, but the mileage on the monitor slowly ticked down until they were within a mile. Steven studied the map in front of him. "Ship, I need to know where my friends are." He rubbed the stubble on his chin. "I don't know what to do." He didn't really say it to her. He just said it out loud.

"Does this thing have weapons?"

They locked eyes. Somehow, he knew what she was thinking. He looked at the monitor again. His friends were represented by red dots. He raised his finger, pausing for a moment, and then poked one of the dots. A small box popped up with what he assumed was a live video feed. It showed Colonel O'Neil and Ann. They were wearing some kind of metal suits that made them look like robots. They were inside the cannon trying to clear it. The cannon was massive. At the rate they were going, it would take forever. He pressed the box. "O'Neil, this is Steven. Can you hear me?" He watched O'Neil's expression change as he looked around.

"I read you. Where the hell are you?" O'Neal looked at Ann.

"I'm in a spaceship." He looked at Momma. She was staring at the screen in shock. She had a tear rolling down her face. He watched her for a moment and then he shook off his confusion. He didn't have time to deal with her crazy at the moment. "I'm thinking about blowing a hole in the bottom of the cannon. Hopefully, all that debris and rock will just fall into the hanger below."

He watched O'Neil contemplating his idea. He didn't look too happy. "Honestly, Steven, I don't think we have much of a choice. Let me and Ann get clear and then do what you have to do."

Steven nodded. "Will do." He picked another dot and poked it. This time the video box showed Laura and Sheldor. He could barely contain himself. The two were in a small room with a lot of controls and panels with lights either flashing or lit up. He excitedly touched the box and spoke, "Laura! It's Steven. You have no idea how glad I am to see you!"

He watched Laura's face light up as she looked around, trying to locate his voice. "Steven?"

Sheldor looked around the room as well. He finally located the source and poked a screen. Suddenly they all could see each other. Laura looked at her monitor and smiled at Steven. Her eyes teared up and her face turned red. "Steven, we're too late. We're not going to make it."

"How long do we have?"

Sheldor looked into the screen at Steven and Momma. He clearly wanted to address the new member of the 'team' but he decided against it. "Two hours, at most. The Sun isn't going to adhere to an exact minute."

Steven relayed the plan to them and they both agreed that it may be their only option. He stared at the screen for a long moment, knowing it could be the last time he saw her. She looked tired and worn out. That wasn't surprising being that Junior was attached to him instead of her.

Laura rubbed her forehead. "Once you clear the cannon I have to turn it on. Kirk and the others still haven't made it here yet."

"I love you." He touched the screen. He knew that in all likelihood they were saying goodbye.

She held back tears. "I love you too."

He poked the video box again and then found three red dots that were together. He knew that it must be Kirk and the others. He moved to activate one of the red dots when Momma grabbed his hand. He looked at her. "What?"

"Who was the man in the first box?"

Steven studied her face. It told him that he couldn't escape the conversation. But they didn't have time. "I only know him as O'Neil." He took his hand away from her. "Look, whatever is going on with you, we don't have time for it."

He poked Kirk's dot and then the video box. The video showed Kirk, Gene, and Penny as they walked away from the camera. It was dark with the only light originating from whatever was recording them. Steven knew it must have been Twiggy. He watched them for a moment and wondered how exactly you tell someone he was about to shoot at his sister with a spaceship. Every salutation that he came up within his mind sounded stupid, but he couldn't just stand there watching Kirk forever. He had to say something to him and quickly. "Hey Kirk, how are you doing...brother?" He hoped the Captain would find it funny.

Just as the others did, Kirk immediately looked around trying to locate Steven. He finally decided the voice came from Twiggy. "Steven?" He squinted at a small screen sticking out of the top of the orb and grinned. "We didn't start off on a good note, but I'm really glad to hear from you."

Steven filled him in on what was going on as fast as he could and Kirk immediately started yelling. "I take it back. I'm not glad to hear from you anymore. Are you crazy?"

"It's our only option."

"Just wait, we're almost there!" Kirk turned around and started to run.

"I'm sorry, but there isn't time." Steven shut off the video and returned to studying the cave-in. He rubbed his chin again. "How hard can it be?"

* * *

Laura was afraid. Afraid that they were all going to die. Afraid that they wouldn't save the Earth. Afraid that she would never see Steven again. She knew that the most important thing was saving Earth, but she couldn't help feeling the way she did. It didn't help that she felt very bad. Shelly assured her that she was doing much better after being exposed to the green goo. Even so, she felt like crap warmed over and then put through a wood chipper.

'Laura! Whatever you're doing, don't! Just wait for me, please!'

It was Kirk's voice and he was literally screaming inside her head. "Kirk? How are you talking to me?"

Shelly looked up. "Not to point out the obvious, but you're both Newtonians. It's literally in your blood."

'Please tell Steven not to do this!'

"We have no choice!"

Suddenly the floor EXPLODED causing shrapnel and blinding light to shoot across the room at them. Shelly reacted quickly and grabbed her. He put his arms around her and shielded her. She buried her face into his chest and closed her eyes tight. For those few moments, she was so scared she couldn't even breathe. She felt the floor move and vibrate as she heard an avalanche of rock and debris moving. She finally pulled her head away from his chest and allowed herself to breathe which proved to be a mistake. She immediately started coughing. She waved the dust out of her face and tried to look down through the hole in the floor. There was so much dust floating around she couldn't see whether or not the cannon was clear.

Shelly walked to the control panel behind him and pushed a few buttons. "The cannon is clear. I'll need a minute to re-direct the maintenance bots. They will use their shields to seal the open areas of the cannon. That should bring the risk of radiation exposure down to a minimum." Laura had blood dripping down the side of her face. Shelly wiped some of it away with his bare hand. "The maintenance bots won't be able to get in here." He touched her shoulder. "You know what that means, right?"

'I heard that! Do not fire that cannon! I'm coming!'

* * *

Kirk ran ahead with Twiggy, never giving a second thought to Gene or Penny. He ran as fast as he could, hoping that he would make it in time. It was a small corridor cut out of rock with rough edges that kept nicking him as he ran by. He ran up to a door and tried to open it. When it wouldn't open, he found the sensor pad and placed his hand on it. He barely waited for the door to slide open before he started running down metal scaffolding over a wide-open space. Occasionally he looked down and saw what looked like mining equipment. His feet clanked with every step.

"Twiggy, how much further?" He puffed as he ran. All he wanted was to get to her before she did something stupid.

Twiggy floated ahead of him. "If you maintain your current speed you will meet up with her in approximately two minutes."

Kirk pushed harder and ran faster. It seemed like a million things were going through his head all at once. He couldn't stop thinking about the little girl that used to look up to him and counted on him to protect her. He followed Twiggy up a set of stairs and then into the cannon's command center. Laura and Sheldor were inside. There was a glass door between him and them. He walked up to the glass while he tried to catch his breath. Sheldor looked like he was in a trance and Laura was standing next to the control panel. She held the key in her hand. His heart skipped a beat as he watched her slip the key into place and then moved to place her hand on the sensor to activate the cannon.

He placed his hand on the door. "Laura, stop!" She flinched and turned to look at him. The glass door slid open and Kirk rushed in and grabbed her. Before she could do anything, he pulled her over to the door and shoved her out. "Twiggy, shut the door and keep it shut."

"Kirk, what are you doing?" Laura tried to go back in before the door shut, but Kirk held her out. He let go just as the door slid shut.

Sheldor suddenly snapped out of his trance. He took a moment to update himself on the current situation, first looking at Laura on the other side of the glass door, and then at Kirk. "It's time. You must activate the cannon now."

Kirk's sad eyes focused on Laura. "Love you, sis."

She put her hands on the glass door as tears streamed down her face. She could barely speak, "I love you too."

Kirk placed his hand on the sensor. The cannon fired filling the room with a blinding light. When the light faded away Kirk took his hand off the sensor and stumbled to the glass door. Laura looked up at him and he tried to smile at her. He turned to Sheldor. "Did it work?"

Sheldor's eyes darted back and forth as information flowed through his brain. "The data I'm receiving is certainly promising."

Laura sobbed, "Why?"

Kirk was obviously suffering from radiation poisoning and getting weaker by the moment. He looked her in the face and cracked a smile. "Don't expect some bullshit about the needs of the many. This was about the needs of the you." Breathing was getting difficult for him. "Live long and... you know the rest." He was struggling to take shallow breaths as he leaned against the glass door and slowly slid down to the floor.

She kneeled down in front of him and pressed her hands against the glass. "Kirk?" He slumped over onto the floor. "No!" She stared at his chest for any movement, any hint that he was still breathing. There was none.

Sheldor walked over to the door. "I'm sorry, Laura. But you're going to have to leave. This whole area will be decontaminated shortly and none of you should be here when that happens." She involuntarily emitted a sorrow filled moan. She looked from him back to Kirk's unmoving form. Sheldor followed her stare. "Don't worry. I won't leave him here. I promise." She stood up and blinked heavy tears out of her eyes. Sheldor watched as they rolled down her cheeks and then dripped off her chin. He looked her in the eye. "You have my word. I won't leave him here."

Laura turned and left the command center with Twiggy in tow. She needed to find Steven because all she wanted to do at the moment was curl up into a little ball and cry. Her brother had sacrificed his life for her and the entire solar system. He was a hero times infinity, but it certainly didn't take away the profound sadness that she felt. She couldn't bring herself to walk fast. It was as if she was sloshing through the swamp of eternal sadness. A thick mud was trying to pull her down and threatened to drown her. She didn't know how it happened, but she suddenly found herself standing in front of O'Neil, Ann, Penny, and Gene. They all looked at her and intuitively knew that someone had been lost. They all must have exchanged stories before she arrived so it wasn't hard for them to figure out that it was Kirk.

"Aw, kid." O'Neil shook his head and then hugged her to him. "I'm so sorry."

Gene looked at the ground and turned away. He was trying to hide his tears, but not doing a good job of it. Penny consoled him even though tears were running down her face too. As O'Neil rubbed Laura's back, he looked at Ann. Her focus was on the cannon. He followed her gaze to find a spaceship, just like the one they used to get to the moon, silently hovering out of the damaged cannon and landing on the warehouse floor. He watched as two people got out. He squinted to see better. "Who's that?"

Laura turned around. They saw each other at the same time. Steven and Laura ran into each other's arms. Steven held her tight.

O'Neil was completely fixated on the other person. His mouth suddenly dropped open. "Con?" He took a few steps toward the woman. "Con!" He yelled and started running to her. He stopped dead in front of her. His face showed a combination of shock and fear. He whispered, "Connie?" He touched her face to see if she was real.

She dropped Spike on the ground. "Andy." She fell into his arms.

"All these years, you've been here?" He held her tight and leaned his head on hers. "I thought I'd never see you again."

Sheldor's voice came out of Twiggy, "I'm sorry to break up the reunion, but you people have to leave. Go back to Atlantis. Fly the ship down the cannon. It will land in the hanger. I'll be there as soon as I can."

The sad group headed toward the spaceship while Spike ran after his momma. No one noticed or cared that the Twiggy wasn't following them to the ship. The little orb flew up a set of stairs and into a room just in time to witness Sheldor roll Kirk onto his back. He looked Kirk in the face and was surprised to see him looking back at him. "You're alive. I thought you were dead."

"I wish I was." It was barely a whisper.

Sheldor tipped his head slightly. "I'm confused. Do you wish to live or not?"

"Yes."

"Yes, you wish to live?"

"Yes."

Sheldor smiled broadly with a twinkle in his eye. "Good, because I have an idea." He was all too pleased with himself.

He grabbed him under the arms like a parent would a small child and picked him up. Kirk's head flopped awkwardly to the side and bounced as Sheldor walked. He placed him in a vertical coffin-like cylinder that was against the far wall of the room. Just as he was about to close the door, Kirks gauntlet fell to the floor with a clank. Sheldor knew that wasn't a good sign and that he had to hurry. He pressed a few buttons on the side of the pod and a clear door slid shut. Crystals immediately started to form against the glass as Kirk was instantly frozen. Sheldor leaned close to the glass and looked at him. "Twiggy, I need you to do something on behalf of Kirk."

Chapter Ten
Bye Bye Love

The spaceship floated into the cannon and then gained speed. To the extremely bummed out passengers, the ship felt like it wasn't moving at all. O'Neil watched the monitor. It showed the ship breaching the end of the cannon and the edge of the Moon into space. He looked at Laura. She was crying softly into Steven's shoulder. He felt useless. "Kirk spent most of his adult life trying to get to space. Now here we are." Everyone turned to him. Laura had an involuntary spasm where she sucked in air. An unfortunate byproduct of sobbing. "How 'bout we take her for a spin around the sun? You know, to honor Captain Kirk?" He cracked a grin, but when he saw that no one else thought it was even a little funny, the grin drained away into a sigh. He looked at Connie. She was standing next to him with that filthy animal in her arms. He was glad that she was looking down at it and not at him. Otherwise, she would have seen the disgusted look on his face. He looked at Gene.

"I don't think that would be a good idea," Gene said and then rubbed his eyes.

That answer annoyed him. "Why?"

Gene shrugged dramatically. "The moon is a spaceship. Those two fell in love by touching a glowing stick. We've met robots and giant freakin' spiders... The sun will probably turn out to be a giant colossal captive demon that needs to be put back in its place every once in a while, by shooting it with a goddamn laser." He put his hair behind his ears and looked at the floor.

O'Neil raised his eyebrows. "Okay then," he dismissed Gene's words and looked at the couple, "Steven? What do you say? Laura?" He desperately wanted someone to agree with him. Kirk was a good kid with a good heart and he wanted to give him a proper send-off. He was almost sorry he couldn't shoot his body into the sun as they went by.

Penny chimed in. "Well, no one asked my opinion, but I think we should do it. We already saved the world so if we die in a fiery ball of doom," she shrugged, "who really cares? Let's go for it."

O'Neil walked over to Laura and grabbed both her hands in his. "Come on, you do the honors." He led her over to the monitor on the wall. Steven moved to be next to her.

"Be careful. You don't want to slingshot us around the sun. We'll end up in 1986 talking to whales," Gene chuckled.

O'Neil narrowed his eyes at him in his silent way of telling him to shut the hell up and then turned back to Laura. "Just tell the ship what you want it to do."

The monitor was already showing a picture of the sun. She stared at it with her bloodshot eyes and sighed. She looked up at Steven who nodded at her. He took her hand gently and placed it on the sensor. It lit up with a soft blue color as soon as her hand touched it. A tear rolled down her cheek. She stared at her hand for a moment and then looked Steven in the face. "Technically, we could go anywhere. We could go home."

Steven rubbed her shoulder and looked at O'Neil. He made eye contact with Steven and then looked at everyone. "I have no authority over you all but we have to go back for Kirk. I'm not leaving him inside the moon with an android that looks like a TV nerd. But let's do this first."

Laura nodded. "Okay. Ship, we'd like to take a trip around the sun and then return to Atlantis."

There was an audible soft tone and then a female voice came from the ship. It sounded exactly like Laura. "A trip around the sun would take approximately three Earth hours."

Laura and Steven looked each other in the eyes and then suddenly smiled. She shook her head. "That's just weird."

O'Neil watched as Steven placed his hand on the side of her face and then kissed her gently on the lips. He smiled, knowing that she'd be okay with him and that they'd be happy together. Steven would take care of her and be there for her. Kirk was her older brother and protector, but now that he was gone, at least there was someone that could fill that role. He turned around and looked at Ann. She was leaning against the wall talking to Gene but staring at Connie. After a couple of seconds, she must have realized someone was looking at her and they locked eyes. Her cheeks turned red, but she didn't look away. He smiled and walked up to her. "Is there any particular reason you're giving Connie the stink-eye?" He laughed and she smiled.

She looked at the ground briefly and then glanced Connie's way again. "It's nothing. I guess I kinda thought that you and I would end up together."

He exaggerated disappointment and shock. He put his hand on his chest. "Wait...you mean, we're not?" He cocked his head and then put his hand on her forearm and let it slip down to her hand. He squeezed it and then held it. The pink was still in her cheeks as she laughed. He was certain there was a bit of pink in his own cheeks. He hadn't asked anyone out in years. "Listen, when all of this is over, what do you say about some coffee?"

Ann glanced over to Connie once more. He could tell that she was very concerned with the situation. "What about her?"

He ran his thumb along the back of her hand. He shrugged. "Yeah, I got baggage. She's my son's mother." He didn't want to get too much into it so he paused to think. "She and I were done a long time ago. Is she gonna be in my life? Yeah, she is. For a long time. Are we going to be together? No, definitely not."

Across the room, Penny shifted her weight and looked at Gene. She made sure everyone could hear her when she spoke. "So... what? Are we expected to just stand around for three hours?" She spread her arms to her sides. "What
kind of spaceship has no place to sit down?"

O'Neil shook his head. No matter what, there would always be one person stirring up trouble. If Penny didn't have something to sit on, they were bound to hear about it the entire trip. He looked at Ann briefly and then turned to Laura. He waited to see what she would do. She was staring at Penny. She seemed more surprised

than angry. Her eyes were asking Penny if she was serious. Instead of arguing and possibly making the situation worse, Laura turned to the ship's computer. "Ship, I guess we are in need of comfortable seating."
"As you wish," her own voice replied to her.

The floor suddenly seemed to be made of rubber. Large square blocks pressed upward through the floor as if a child's building block was coming out of a dark gray balloon. The squares slowly morphed into two couches and two chairs with no seams that matched the floor exactly. Penny shook her head and twisted her face in a look of disgust. "I'm not sittin on that."

Steven took Laura's hand and led her to the couch. "Suit yourself." He sat down on the couch and pulled his love down onto his lap and then cuddled her close. She let her head rest on his shoulder.

O'Neil looked at Ann and then motioned to the other couch. "Shall we?" They made themselves comfortable on the couch and began to chat between each other. Both Gene and Connie sat in the chairs, leaving only one free spot large enough to accommodate Penny. The spot next to the cuddling lovers. She made another face, but eventually walked over and sat down on the couch.

A little over an hour later they all stood in front of the giant wall monitor. "Yep, looks like a great big ball of fire," O'Neil watched orange oceans of fire dancing about, "but who doesn't like staring into the fire?"

* * *

CheeChee hung from the ceiling of the warehouse. From her vantage point, she could see almost every corner. She didn't know where any of her new human friends were, they had all disappeared on her. If they went somewhere, they certainly didn't tell her where they were going and she couldn't reach Laura or Junior telepathically. It was a fact that worried her greatly. Her keen senses felt minor vibrations. Over the last few days, she had come to realize those vibrations were made when a human was talking. She walked along the ceiling toward the humming she heard and eventually saw a fading trace of heat. She walked across a clear wall that let her look at the people inside the room. She immediately became concerned when she watched the android called Sheldor pick up the Angry One and put him in some sort of box. She watched curiously as Sheldor pushed a few glowing lights on the box and then leaned down and lifted the bottom. The box seemed to levitate as he pulled it along and out the door. That was when he noticed her. He cocked his head to the side and cracked a grin. "Well, hello there!"

CheeChee knew that he said something to her, but she didn't know what. His dark eyes lost some of their light as he seemed to look off into the distance. He ceased to move and was frozen in time. She extended one of her legs and tapped it on the top of his head. It was a very awkward extended pause. She began to wonder what the protocol would be in the situation she was facing. The android wasn't moving anymore and one of her friends was now in a floating box. What comes next? Sheldor suddenly looked directly at her and started emitting clicking and shushing noises that CheeChee understood perfectly. He informed her that he read everything there was to know about her species from Atlantis' database which allowed him to absorb her language. He told her that the Angry One was very close to death and that his body was eventually going to die. Admittedly, she didn't really understand what he meant by that. If your body dies, you die. That is the way things worked. Maybe he learned her language but didn't have a good enough grasp on it to communicate effectively. He led the floating box down a set of stairs and then explained to her that he needed to take him back to Atlantis and that she was welcome to accompany him. This was when she decided to see if he could understand her too. *'Where is Laura? And what of my offspring, Junior?'*

Sheldor told her that Laura and the rest of the group were headed back to Atlantis. Unfortunately, he had no news about her male offspring, but he was confident that he was fine. She decided that her best option was to go back with the android. He led the floating box into a large hole that fed into a tunnel. Perhaps it was the cannon everyone kept talking about, she wasn't sure. She walked after him, wondering how exactly he planned to travel the many miles back. There was light shining from a large opening in the top of the tunnel. Sheldor and the box stopped underneath it. They both watched as the box floated up and out of the hole. Then two of the larger maintenance bots floated in and down to the bottom of the tunnel and hovered next to them. Sheldor climbed on top of one of the discs and motioned for her to do the same on the other. She looked at the disc and back at Sheldor. It wasn't the first time she'd found herself on top of one of those things, but she didn't really want to repeat the experience. She quickly reasoned that if she wanted to know what became of her male offspring, she would have to ride on one of the discs again. When she got on the disc it lifted her straight up and out of the cannon into the beautiful lush surroundings of the terrarium. The light was fading and she knew night would be coming soon. She looked around and watched as Sheldor loaded the Angry One's box into a large orb-like the one she once rode with Laura. She stepped off her disc and happily followed him on board.

They sat in silence for a very long time. Maybe the android was just trying to be cordial or perhaps he was just bored, but he finally spoke. "I can see them moving around." At first, she had no idea what he was referring to until he leaned forward and inspected her back. She concluded that he must be looking into her egg sacs. "Do they communicate with you?"

CheeChee explained that when her children experienced strong emotions she felt them too. Like Sheldor, her offspring could see through the egg sac, but not very clearly. An object would have to be pretty close in order for them to get a good look at it. Unfortunately, at their stage of growth, the emotions that are exchanged between her and her children was almost always related to fear. This is somewhat beneficial because when they emerge from their sacs, they will have already been taught what to fear and what not to fear. It is a very valuable lesson that they will need in order to survive at such a small and vulnerable stage.

From her vantage point, she could see right into Kirk's box. His face had white frost on it and he was very still. She remembered a time long ago when she found an animal frozen in the snow. She had tried to feed on it but it was as hard as a rock and very cold. She found the correlation very unpleasant. All things considered, she liked the Angry One. He was a brave human who was more than just the Angry One. He was also a leader who cared very deeply for his sister and the other humans. She found herself hoping that his body didn't die like Sheldor said it would because she wanted to form a more lasting relationship with him. She started thinking about how much Laura cared for Junior and suddenly came to the conclusion that you can't have too many friends. Especially ones that look out for the safety and welfare of your young. Before the humans came along she was all alone but she didn't know the difference. She didn't know friendship. The humans didn't belong there and that they would probably eventually go back to where they came from. The thought upset her more than she was prepared to admit. As the orb landed, she was grateful there would be something to distract her from her thoughts.

She let Sheldor exit with the floating box first. She followed him as he led it out of the orb. The main door of the structure opened for him as soon as he approached it. "You can come in if you wish. But if you'd rather stay out here, I've programmed the doors to open for you. All you have to do is stand in front of them and you can come and go as you please."

CheeChee considered staying outside because she was hungry, but she was also eager to see Junior. She needed to make sure he was alright. Without him, her species would go extinct. But beyond that, she felt a knot of fear inside her that wouldn't go away. It made her feel like she couldn't breathe. It was a feeling she wasn't accustomed to. Since he was cast out into the world, she only had a few short hours to bond with him. But that time she spent with him had been enough to make her realize she didn't want to experience life without him. She followed Sheldor down a long hallway and into a room with many colorful, tiny lights alongside of a flat platform. The floating box settled down on the platform and the android plugged something into the back of it and then started poking some of the colorful lights. She didn't know what he was doing, but she hoped that it was something that would save her friend. She watched as he ran his hand along the smooth surface of the box. He leaned down and looked inside. CheeChee understood that Sheldor was an android and a machine, but he clearly had feelings. She believed the emotion on his face was that of sadness.

The little orb that the Angry One referred to as Twiggy floated in and hovered next to Sheldor. He suddenly looked at CheeChee and said, "Let me show you something." He turned and walked over to a nearby wall and stood in front of what appeared to be a window and looked inside. She walked up to him and peered inside the window. There was a small, fat, and hairless animal submerged in some sort of fluid. It was pale and almost see through. It took her a few moments to realize what she was seeing. It was a tiny human. Her eyes danced about as she examined at it. It looked delicious, but she knew he wasn't showing her food. She waited for him to explain.

"When we were at the Chancellor's manor, Kirk touched a Genesis Orb that was primarily used to assist infertile Newtonians. The orbs could use the DNA of up to three different people to create life." He looked at one of the monitors and hit a couple of buttons. "In Kirk's case, it used just his DNA, which effectively makes what we are looking at, an exact clone of him. A copy, if you will." He turned and looked at CheeChee. "I have an ethical conundrum that I need you to help me with. You see, the captain was exposed to a lethal dose of radiation when he activated the cannon. His body will die, but I can transfer his memories into his clone."

'Then you should do it.'

"Agreed, but the humans might argue that such a thing is wrong because the child you see before you would grow into his own person. Instead of growing his body to adulthood, I could take him out right now. Someone could raise him as their own." He tilted his head and looked at the child. "I could raise him as my own."

She understood his ethical dilemma, but at the same time
she cared for Laura and knew that she would want her sibling back. *'Then do it and do not tell them.'*

"Agreed. But they would still find out. Kirk's body has scars. Not to mention a missing kidney." He pressed a large red button and the infant was slowly lifted out of the fluid and the glass door slid open. Sheldor turned around and focused his attention back on the Angry One's box. He poked a few of the glowing lights and then the box slid open with a hiss. She watched the Angry One's chest carefully to see if there were any signs of life. Within moments his chest started to rise and fall. Sheldor quickly reached into the box and grabbed the captain's arm and pulled it out and to the side. He held his hand out to the floating orb. "Twiggy, if you would." The orb floated over to him. A small hatch in its side opened up and a rod slid out. Sheldor turned again and lifted the tiny clone out of his enclosure and held it next to Kirk. He quickly grabbed the rod from Twiggy and placed in the baby's palm, which triggered the child's hand to close and the rod began to glow. Sheldor grabbed Kirk's hand and held it close to the rod. He paused only for a moment to think about the ramifications once again and then folded Kirk's hand around the rod. Even though the man was unconscious, Kirk's body flinched and tensed up. The clone's eyelids rapidly fluttered and his breathing increased.

'Is it working?'

"I think so." When the infant's eyes stopped moving and the rod stopped glowing, he released his grip on Kirk's hand. He returned the clone to his bed of fluids and watched as the door slid shut and the child's body was slowly lowered back into the water. "I guess we won't know for sure until his body is done growing." He turned his attention back to Kirk. "He's still alive but it won't be long now." Kirk started to groan in pain causing Sheldor to grimace. He walked over to a cabinet and rummaged through it for a moment. He grabbed a small object that she couldn't make out and then he walked back over to the Angry One and pressed it to his neck. "This should alleviate the pain." He leaned in close to Kirk. CheeChee could tell the android was struggling to find the right thing to say to him. She didn't understand the words that he spoke to Kirk, but she felt that she understood the sentiment. "It's okay, Kirk. I will keep an eye on her. I promise."

She watched his chest stop moving and knew that he was gone. She suddenly became aware of a loud sorrow-filled screeching noise. At first, she thought it was the android, but she was soon surprised to learn that the noise was coming from her. It was involuntary and she couldn't stop. Never before had she experienced such pain and sadness. She turned to look at the clone. He was resting peacefully. She watched as his eyes moved back and forth under his eyelids and then he grinned slightly. The little Angry One was dreaming of something pleasant. It eased her pain enough that the noise subsided.

'I find that I don't like death.'

Sheldor nodded. "I find that I don't like it either."

* * *

The would-be heroes returned from their trip around the sun. As they walked by the dining hall Sheldor called to them, "Well, hello." O'Neil looked at Sheldor through the doorway and then the rest of the crew behind him. He stepped into the room and the others followed. The table was filled with a colorful array of fruits and vegetables. Sheldor glared at them. "Come in, sit down."

O'Neil looked at the spread on the table and then back to the door. Then he looked at everyone's tired faces. "Actually, we're kinda beat. I think everyone just wants to crash."

Sheldor crossed his arms and looked him in the eye. "Did I give the impression that I was asking?" Without breaking eye contact, he bent forward slightly. "I said SIT down."

O'Neil furrowed his brow and looked at Laura and Steven. They were already taking their seats so he did as well. Sheldor waited for everyone to sit down. He was obviously angry. "I hope you people are happy."

"I'm gonna go out on a limb and say...you seem upset." O'Neil picked up a round, purple vegetable the size of an apple and sniffed it.

"What's wrong, Shelly?" Laura looked up at him. He made eye contact with her and then briefly put his hand on her shoulder before walking around the table to properly glare at everyone.

254

O'Neil chuckled. "Shelly?"

The wall behind them glowed softly and then images started to appear. It was soon clear that it was a news broadcast from Earth. A blonde woman dressed in a blue blouse was addressing her viewers about a mysterious message in the sky over Pasadena, California. The next image was that of a blue sky with the white cloud-like words 'be good, or else' seemingly written in the sky. The screen then showed thousands of people on their knees praying. "The message has been in the sky for almost three days without fading or dissipating. No one knows for certain where the message came from or who is responsible for it." The next scene showed tents and RV's set up anywhere and everywhere. "People are showing up in record numbers to see the message for themselves."

Sheldor pressed his lips together. "Between Gene's message in the sky and your joyride around the sun, Earth is now aware aliens, and perhaps God, actually do exist." He pointed at the monitor. It featured a man in a suit with an information box that read NASA next to him. The box widened to fill the screen. It showed an out of focus dot they claimed was a spaceship. "I suppose I should be grateful that there is nothing to suggest that they know anything about the Moon's origins." He clasped his hands behind his back. "You do realize this complicates things, right?"

O'Neil nodded and sighed at the same time. He looked across the table at Ann. She had a confused look on her face. "He means we can't go home just yet."

"What? Why?" Penny and Ann looked at each other with their mouths hanging open.

Sheldor explained that there was never a reason to have cloaking devices on the ships. There was no need to be invisible or to spy on other civilizations because there weren't any. At least none that they had ever encountered. Otherwise, why would they have traveled for hundreds of years to get to Earth? Of course, Gene argued that if that were so, then why were they inside a spaceship that was disguised as a moon? Apparently, that was never the intention. After traveling for hundreds upon hundreds of years through space, the ship accumulated debris. He told them that it shouldn't take him long to figure out how to mask the ship and bring them all home. Until then, they would be his guests.

Ann crossed her arms. "Why can't you use the teleporting system? I mean, that is how we got here in the first place."

"That will take some calculations and further testing as well. The system is calibrated for Newtonians, not humans." Sheldor noticed Laura shaking her head. "Miss Rogers here has more Newtonian DNA than any of you, and she ended up dangling from the side of a cliff when she was teleported here. Do you really want to take that risk?"

Ann slapped her hand down on the table and made eye contact with Penny as she stood. "I guess I'll just turn in then." Penny got up too, and both the women left the room.

O'Neil suddenly did a double-take and looked around the table. "I guess I should go find Connie. I have no idea where she is." He quickly left.

Sheldor stared at Gene until he became uncomfortable.

"I'm not using the teleporter," Gene said matter-of-factly. "You can't make me." He got up slowly and walked out of the room.

Sheldor turned back to the remaining two, Laura and Steven. "I have some information I think you'd be interested in." Sheldor sat down in front of them and then noticed Junior attached to Steven's wrist. He tapped the table with the tip of his finger and then starting emitting a series of clicks and shushing sounds. Steven and Laura looked at each other confused. Junior suddenly disengaged from Steven's wrist and then walked along the table. He continued off the side and crawled down the leg.

Laura raised her brows at Sheldor. "That's amazing. Where did you learn that?"

Sheldor looked slightly annoyed for a moment. "Listen, don't let Junior feed on you guys anymore. His mother and I had a talk and we feel that it's time he learns to hunt on his own."

Steven laughed. "So, you and CheeChee are co-parenting Junior now?"

Laura couldn't help smiling. "Is that what you wanted to talk to us about?"

"No," he looked at her smile and couldn't help smiling back, "how are you feeling?" His eyes looked lazy for a moment as he put his chin in his palm and leaned on his elbow.

"I'm fine. A little tired, but other than that, I feel okay." She narrowed her eyes at him. "How are you feeling?"

He seemed surprised. "Fine. Why do you ask?"

Steven put his hand in hers and held it on top of the table so that Sheldor could see it. "Because you're making eyes at my woman."

"Don't be ridiculous. Although it's true that I'm rather fond of her, it's not in a romantic way." He weaved the fingers of his hands together and laid them on the table. "Steven, I know that you've been concerned about what might have happened to your grandmother." Steven looked at Laura, asking her without words if she was the one that told him that. She nodded at him. Sheldor pointed to the monitor which showed a cafeteria. It was filled with a lot of people with gray and white hair eating. It didn't take Steven long to recognize someone in the crowd. He quickly got out of his chair and walked to the monitor. "What is this, an old folks home?"

"An assisted living facility, to be more precise." Shelly stood behind Steven with Laura. "The Latin gentleman sitting next to her is her new husband, Edwardo." He went on to explain that the two shared an apartment together, but that they were provided three meals a day and transportation where ever they wanted to go. "From what the director told me, she has a lot of friends and seems to be very happy."

Steven turned around to face him. "You spoke to him? What did you say?"

"I merely told him that I was an investigator seeking information on the whereabouts of Steven Foster. He already knew of your disappearance. Your grandmother told him. I asked him if anyone that fit your description has ever visited before. That sort of thing."

Laura wrapped her arm around Steven's and hugged it to her. He watched as Edwardo smiled and then kissed his grandmother on the cheek.

"You can call her if you want." Sheldor looked at him out of the corner of his eye.

"What would I even say to her? What could I tell her that would make any sense?" Steven shook his head.

Laura rubbed his back. "At least you know she's okay. She didn't die alone and afraid like you thought she did."

"The way I see it, you have a few choices. You can tell her
you were abducted by a South American cartel and held captive for five years, or you could tell her that you were in an accident and a woman convinced you that you were her husband and you've been living with her all this time." Sheldor smiled. "Or...you could tell her the truth." He shrugged. "Realistically, Steven, even if she told people, who would believe her?" He asked Laura for her phone so she gave it to him. He spent a minute fiddling with it and then handed it back. "I programmed it so that you can call Earth. I also put her number in your contacts." He walked to the door. "Laura, come see

me in the infirmary in the morning. You need a checkup."

Steven waited for Sheldor to leave. "Someone wants to play doctor with you." He smiled down at her and pulled her into a hug.

Laura laughed. "Shut up." They both looked back to the monitor and at his grandmother. She and Edwardo were getting up to leave. "What are you going to do?"

He shook his head. "I have no idea."

Chapter Eleven
Limbo

He woke up groggy. It was warm and it felt like he was floating. 'Is this death?' He opened his eyes, but he couldn't see clearly. There was light far off into the distance. 'The light at the end of the tunnel?' He wondered if he should try to go towards the light but when he tried, he found he couldn't move. The great floating nothing. Somehow, he ended up in purgatory. He tried to laugh, but that didn't happen either. That's when it registered within him that he wasn't breathing. He found himself praying that these were just the last seconds of consciousness between death and brain death and it just *seemed* to be lasting forever. He couldn't imagine spending the rest of eternity alone with his thoughts. Especially since he couldn't reach his joystick. The last thing he could remember was telling the android that he wished he was dead. He meant it at the time. He was in so much pain and he just wanted it to end. If that meant death, he was okay with it. He was still so very tired. He wasn't in any pain and he was grateful for that. He could vaguely remember something about the sun and saving the Earth and he wondered how all that went. He thought he heard voices. 'Was that Laura?' He was so proud of her. He spent much of his life trying to protect her and take care of her. How is it that he didn't notice that she was a strong woman with the will of a warrior running through her veins? Yes, he was remembering more now. She was going to do it. She was willing to sacrifice herself for everyone. How did he not notice that his sister was fucking amazing? He found himself very thankful for the time he was somehow granted to come to this conclusion. Laura would be just fine without him. He closed his eyes and listened to the soft mumbling sounds that resonated through around him. It was like a lullaby that helped him drift off to sleep.

Little did he know, just a few short feet away, Sheldor was examining Laura. She was lying on the exam table as she was being scanned. He looked at the data on the monitor and nodded. "Your new kidneys are almost fully grown and working at maximum capacity." He grabbed her hand and helped her sit up. "You should live to a ripe old age."

She cracked a small smile but looked sad. "Where is Kirk's body? You said you wouldn't leave him."

Sheldor's eyes flicked over to the clone's enclosure. The once see-through window was now opaque. Since he no longer had a need for Kirk's original body, he put it in the adjoining room. He didn't know what to do. The clone wasn't fully grown yet. Moreover, he wasn't one hundred percent sure the memory transfer worked. When he takes the clone out of the growth chamber they may end up with a fully-grown man with the brains of an infant. He looked at the door to the adjoining room and then back to the clone's enclosure. He has been conscious for several thousand years, but nothing flummoxed him more than that moment.

"Are you alright?"

He sighed. "Not really."

"What's wrong?"

Sheldor folded his arms. "I like you, Laura. I prefer not to lie to you."

Her face quickly changed from one of curiosity to utter disappointment. "You didn't bring him back here with you?"

"No, I brought him back here. And I may have done something a bit...unethical, to save him."

Laura breathed in quickly as a big smile ran across her face and tears came to her eyes. He put his hands up at her before she could say anything. "I'm not sure if it worked yet. I need time."

She kept looking from one of his eyes to the other. A tear ran down her face. She jumped down from the table and suddenly hugged him tight. It surprised him so much that he was momentarily stunned. He slowly let his arms enclose around her as he hugged her back and let his chin rest on the top of her head. "But you don't even know what I did."

"I don't care."

There it was. Just like that, he was relieved of his ethical quandary with those three little words. He wouldn't have to tell her that her brother's dead body was in a stasis chamber in the next room. He wouldn't have to tell her about the clone. As she said, she didn't care. She stepped back, wiped her eyes, and then cleared her throat. "You'll come get me when you know?"

"I will." He watched her walk out of the room a little bit happier than when she came in and he shook his head. "I just had to add emotions to my programming. I may currently be the most intelligent being in this universe but in reality, I'm really, really stupid."

* * *

Laura laid in bed next to Steven happily watching him sleep. His black hair was all mussed up and in his face. The light from the artificial sun outside made his skin glow softly. He looked perfectly at peace. She wanted to memorize every detail down to the shape of his lips. He hadn't shaved in at least a day so he had an evening shadow that she was surprised to find sexy. A dark blue sheet covered most of his body. It was her favorite color and it looked good on him, but it was preventing her from seeing his wonderful body. She looked at the little bit of chest hair that peeked above the sheet and grinned. Then she gently pinched the sheet between her finger and thumb and slowly pulled downward while looking him in the face to see if he was waking up. She stopped when she could see his bellybutton. She smiled as she looked at his muscular chest. She wanted to watch him sleep but she also wanted to lean over and gently kiss him awake so that they could make love. She wanted so badly to play with the hair on his chest and it took every ounce of restraint that she had to keep her hands to herself.

He suddenly breathed in and then hummed softly. It made her heart skip a beat. His eyes opened slightly and he realized she had been watching him. He grinned. "Creep."

"What's creepy about watching the man I love sleep?" She nuzzled up next to him and kissed his neck.

He was clearly still very sleepy but he reached out and grabbed her and pulled her closed to him. He covered them both with the sheet. "Why do you have clothes on?"

"Don't you remember? Shelly wanted to play doctor with me this morning."
"Oh, yeah. How'd that go?"

She wanted to tell him about her morning, but he had already fallen back to sleep. She wondered if it was because of Junior. He was much bigger than she was so Junior's bite shouldn't have had the same effect on him. Junior was only attached to him for a few hours. Maybe Steven's withdrawal wouldn't be as bad as hers. She decided to just let him sleep and wriggled out of his embrace. She kissed him on the cheek as softly as she could and left the bedroom. As she walked down the hall, she thought about the last few days and the ways in which her life will be forever changed. She had thought her life was over but she now had two functioning kidneys and a man that she wanted to be with forever. Maybe she was still in the hospital. Maybe she was in a coma and her adventure was nothing but a hallucination or a dream. If it was a dream she hoped that she would never wake up from it.

She thought about Steven and knew she never wanted to be without him. This posed a tiny problem in her mind because he wanted to go back to Earth and she wanted to stay. She knew Steven like the back of her hand. She knew how he felt about the time he spent there. Of course, it was possible that he changed his mind, but she doubted it. There was no way she would ever leave him. Not by choice and definitely not willingly. She always thought it was stupid when she heard someone say that they'd die if they ever lost someone. It seemed childish and unreal. She made fun of them within the confines of her own mind because needing someone so much that your life would be over without them was utterly pathetic. She was officially inducted into the Pathetic Hall of Fame. Because she knew she wouldn't be able to live without Steven. The mere thought gave her physical pain in the pit of her stomach. If Steven went home to Earth, she would have to go with him. She would have to.

Laura eventually found herself outside enjoying the feel of the simulated sun on her face. She took in a deep breath of fresh air and smiled broadly. She could feel her arachnid friends nearby. She walked into the forest to meet them.

'You seem well, Laura.' CheeChee was hanging from a web above her.

"I am well." She scanned the trees above her looking for Junior. Her eyes finally fell on the tyke as he spun a small animal into a prison made of webbing. "Did he catch it himself?"

'Mostly'

"Then I'm mostly proud of him."

* * *

Sheldor hadn't left the infirmary for days. He was concerned that Kirk would wake up inside the incubation chamber and panic. He looked inside at Kirk's body, which was fully grown and ready to be removed from the gel. Sheldor lifted him out of the liquid and put his slippery body on the examination table and then pushed him onto his side. He grabbed the blanket that was resting on the side table and plopped it over Kirk's nakedness and then placed a towel under his head. He knew what was coming and it wouldn't be pretty. Sheldor patiently waited. Kirk suddenly convulsed. It was minor at first and then grew to be more violent. Clear gel began to spew from his mouth and nose with each convulsion. His eyes shot open as he quickly sucked in air and then started coughing until he threw up some more.

Sheldor held him on his side so he wouldn't topple off the table. "That's it, just a bit more." He attempted to give him a reassuring pat on the arm. "You're going to be fine. That's it."

Sheldor still wasn't sure if the memory transfer worked. He hoped it did because it definitely wasn't going to happen again. The original Kirk was dead and the information in his brain was now incapable of being replicated again. When Kirk finally stopped coughing, Sheldor realized he was unconscious again. He could see his chest rising and falling with each breath, which was a very good sign. He looked at the diagnostic panel and nodded to himself. His body was perfectly healthy. He wiped Kirk's face with another towel and then laid him on his back. He vigorously started to dry his body with towels. The android was nervous and perhaps a little bit afraid. It worried him that he wanted Kirk to survive so much. It worried him even more that he didn't want to disappoint Laura. He wasn't accustomed to being so emotional.

After Sheldor managed to get a shirt and pants on the clone he looked him in the face with great concern. He took his knuckles and rubbed them back and forth below Kirk's collarbone. "Kirk. Kirk, wake up." The clone's eyes opened slowly and then focused on him. Sheldor smiled briefly. "Help me out here, buddy, say something."

The clone grimaced and then groaned loudly that ended in a squeak. He rubbed his face and eyes. "What do you want me to say?"

Sheldor let out a huge sigh of relief. The mere fact that the clone spoke meant that the memory transfer worked. Otherwise, he wouldn't be able to speak at all. "We thought we lost you." Kirk tried to sit up so he offered him a hand and pulled him up."

"I had the weirdest damn dream." Kirk was stuck in thought for a moment. "Wait, the last thing I remember..."

"We have to talk." Sheldor confessed to him. "Kirk, the only way I could save you was to clone you." From the look on Kirk's face, he was very confused. Sheldor explained what he had done and how he had told no one. He didn't know how he would react or what he would do, but he hoped he wouldn't be angry. Kirk just sat there with his legs dangling over the side of the exam table and stared at the floor. Sheldor put a hand on his shoulder. "Should I be apologizing?"

"Nah, man, it's just...weird." He slapped Sheldor on the arm and then patted his shoulder. He got up and tested out his new legs. He was unsteady at first, but eventually he took his first steps. Sheldor supported him as he made his way into the adjoining room so he could look at his body. Kirk looked through the window of the pod at his own lifeless face.

Sheldor watched him curiously. "I considered not telling you, but I knew you would find out eventually."

Kirk couldn't take his eyes off his dead body. "You mean my surgery scars?"

Sheldor smirked. "I could have just told you that I took the liberty to fix them while you were healing."
Kirk turned around and leaned up against the stasis chamber. "Then I'm confused."

He tipped his head to the side. "From birth to death, on average, humans live between eighty to a hundred years."

Kirk nodded. "Yeah."

"You were born yesterday."

He grimaced. "Oh." He suddenly made a weird face and audibly crunched down on something with his teeth. He spit it out in his hand. It was a small ball of metal. "What the hell?"

"A dentabot. Your new body grew from a baby all the way to adulthood. The dentabots made sure your baby teeth were removed and your adult teeth were straightened."

Kirk poked at the little circular robot in his hand. "I think I swallowed one."

Sheldor waved it off. "No matter." He walked over to the stasis pod. "What do you plan to do?"

"Sheldor..."

C. J. Boyle

"Please, call me Shelly."

Kirk raised his eyebrows and then gripped the android's shoulder. "Shelly, I woke up fifteen minutes ago. Do you think I could have a little more time to think about it?"

"Certainly," he reconsidered, "how long is 'a little time'?"

"Are we in a hurry?"
"Everyone thinks you're dead."

Kirk looked at his dead body again. "I am dead."

Sheldor set down a thermos of water next to him. "You need to hydrate. I'll be in the next room."

Kirk watched Shelly leave and turned back to look at his own face. It was a lot to wake up to. He needed to decide whether or not to tell his friends and family that he was a clone. The truth was that he was grateful to be alive. Mostly he was grateful that someone else made the decision for him. He doesn't have to feel guilty about the life that Kirk Rogers' clone might have had. Or about the individual person he may have been. He wasn't asked about whether or not he had an opinion. He felt like himself but somehow, he also felt like a fake. He didn't want Laura to feel that way about him too. But could he live the rest of his life a lie?

He leaned in close to the pod so that he could look himself in the face. "It wasn't your fault, you know? You were just a kid. Too young to be responsible for a three-year-old. I know. I know. You wanted her to get into trouble. You resented all the attention she got. That's why you didn't tell mom and dad that she was messing around under the kitchen sink." He laughed. "She sure got all the attention after that, didn't she? Even yours. You did everything you could have possibly done." He put a hand on his side. "You wore that scar like it was a goddamn badge. But that badge is gone now." He put his hand on the glass over the face of his predecessor. "It's time to put that all behind us. You're forgiven." He suddenly scoffed. "I don't know what happens with clones. Did I take over your soul? Did I get a new soul? Do you go off to heaven or do you wait for me to die?" He closed his eyes and prayed. "Jesus, please take care of this part of me until I join him."

Kirk sat with his namesake and predecessor for hours trying to decide whether or not to tell the people he cared about that he was a clone and not the original. These weren't your normal set of problems or mundane lies. He may have said goodbye to the guilt he felt regarding Laura but he would be replacing it with a new guilt. The guilt that he was keeping something major from her. But in reality, he'd be sparing her the knowledge that he might be an abomination, or at the very least, a fake. He rubbed his wrist. It felt odd to him because he was almost always wearing his watch and he wanted it back. He turned his head towards the door and yelled, "Hey Shelly!"

Shelly walked into the room with a worried look on his face. "Is everything alright?"

"No. I'm dead. Everything's not alright."

"Have you decided what you are going to do?" Shelly was fiddling with one of the stun guns.

Kirk eyed it. "Why do you have that?"

"I thought you would be in need of it."

Kirk's mouth dropped in shock. "Why the hell would I have need of that?"

Shelly walked over to the stasis pod and looked inside. "Newtonians did not bury their dead because of the limited space they had here."

"That literally explains nothing."

"If you shoot someone with one of these just once, it knocks them out and causes minor brain damage." He held it out and gave it to Kirk. "If you shoot that same someone again within a span of a few minutes, it will kill them."

Kirk found himself drawing conclusions, but he still wanted to hear the android say it. "And if you shoot someone with it three times?"

"Every nucleus in every cell of their body begins to superheat like microscopic supernovas and…"

"I get it. Body go bye-bye." Kirk looked at the gun in his hand and then back to his predecessor.

"Not exactly the way I would have phrased it, but yes. Body go bye-bye." Shelly sighed and motioned to the pod while nodding his agreement. He walked over to the pod and pressed a few of the buttons until it eventually popped open with a loud hiss of air. There were small ice crystals here and there on the body but otherwise, it looked like he could wake at any moment. Kirk felt anxious like he wanted to run away and the more he fought against it the worse it was. He was instantly that little kid with a rifle in his hands and his father behind him pointing at a deer. Only this time, he was about to shoot himself, not a deer. Granted, the 'self' he was about to shoot was already dead. Kirk walked over to the pod and looked down at himself. He reached down and took the watch off his body and fastened it to his wrist. "I'm gonna take care of this for you," he said under his breath. He looked at Shelly. "Our dad gave this to us." He didn't know how else to phrase it.

"Would you like me to do it?" Shelly asked quietly.

"No." Kirk held up the gun, pointed at his predecessor, and fired. Nothing happened. He didn't know what he expected. The body wasn't going to suddenly sit up and shout curse words at him. "Well, that wasn't so hard. Two more." He held up the gun and did it again. He held the gun in place, pointing it at his own dead body, stuck in a mental battle. He chided himself for having a problem at all. He was Kirk Rodgers. He had all of Kirk's memories. He still felt the same way about pizza and puppies as he did before. He closed his eyes, swallowed hard, and then fired. There was a bright flash and then ALARMS immediately went off scaring the hell out of him.

"Perhaps, I may have neglected to mention that this is always done outside," Shelly said matter-of-factly as he turned to a panel and hit a few buttons, turning the alarm off.

"Ya think?" He yelled as she coughed. "Smells like pork." He turned a shade of green and retched.

O'Neil ran into the room, followed closely by Steven. He stopped suddenly when he realized who he was looking at. "Holy shit!" His mouth dropped open, "of all the things I thought I'd find in here..." His eyes narrowed at Shelly and then moved to Kirk with the same look. "Are you a robot?"

Kirk shook his head. "No."

O'Neil glanced at Steven and raised an eyebrow. "You sure?"

"Yeah." Kirk turned to Shelly for confirmation.

"He's not a robot. But if he were artificial in nature, he'd be an android, not a robot."

O'Neil scrutinized him carefully, up and down, but his dark eyes smiled even though he didn't. He turned to Steven. "Maybe we should bleed him."

Steven shrugged. "I don't know, remember The Thirteen Colonies? The cybernetic people appeared to bleed."

Kirk threw his arms out. "Bro! Come on!"

Steven smiled and pointed at Kirk. "He called me bro. That's definitely not him!" He laughed and the others joined in.

O'Neil grabbed Kirk's hand and shook it, but then pulled him into a man hug. They patted each other on the back.

"Kirk," Steven was suddenly serious, "does Laura know you are alive?"

Kirk shook his head. He didn't know how he was going to handle that. He didn't want her to wait any longer than necessary, but he knew it was going to be hard.

Steven leaned his head toward the door and waved to him. "Let's go find her." They walked out of the infirmary and O'Neil turned to follow them.

"O'Neil, we have things to discuss." Sheldor clasped his hand together and watched O'Neil walk back into the room with a look of confusion on his face.

"I've been in here racking my brain trying to figure out how to get you folks home in one piece when it finally hit me." He walked over to a table and picked up a large hypodermic needle gun. "It would be infinitely easier to make the computers recognize you people as Newtonians rather than reprogram them for humans."

O'Neil's mouth dropped open as he pointed to the large needle. "What do you plan on doing with that?"

Whatever the android wanted to do with it, he sure wasn't going to cooperate. Sheldor put it back down on the table and explained his plan. He created a small chip that could be inserted via the needle gun just under the skin. It would make anyone appear to be Newtonian. It seemed like a good plan to O'Neil, in theory, but he still didn't want anyone to stick him with that needle. Then Sheldor pointed out something to him that he had not considered. What if he needed O'Neil's help once again? At least with the chip permanently embedded inside his body, Sheldor could locate him anywhere at any time, and use the teleporter to bring him safely back to Atlantis.

O'Neil finally agreed, so Sheldor once again approached him with the needle. "You'll feel a little pinch." He walked behind him and held the unit to his neck. "Take a deep breath." Sheldor squeezed the trigger and it was done.

"This place...it's kind of large for just one...person to run. Wouldn't you say? Shelly?"

"O'Neil, I'm not a moron. I know what you want. Even if I suggested an international joint venture, no matter how well the candidates were vetted, there would always be one person that either had their own agenda or succumbed to bribery or threats. There is just too much at stake." He put the needle gun down. "And what about you? Do you believe you should be able to go back and forth at will?"

O'Neil's eyes drifted to the side for a moment as he fished for the right words. "I helped save the universe."

Sheldor smirked. "Steven and Kirk saved the universe. The rest of you were inconsequential."

"That was hurtful. Hurtful and inaccurate." He rubbed the back of his neck. "What now?"

Shelly gave O'Neil a huge creepy grin. "Now...You're the guinea pig."

Chapter Twelve
Let The Chips Fall Where They May

Laura enjoyed spending time in the forest with CheeChee. It was warm with a cool breeze. It was hard to believe that the place she was enjoying so much was actually very dangerous. She knew enough not to touch the giant yellow, thorny caterpillar she was watching because it was likely poisonous. But it was also very beautiful. Beautiful all the way up to the point that Junior pounced on it and bit its little head off.

"Well, that was pleasant." She twisted her face up in disgust and then swallowed hard as she turned away. She suddenly felt a combination of sadness and shame from the young arachnid which instantly filled her with guilt. "Junior, I didn't mean to make you feel bad. I'm so sorry." The little guy was standing over his kill looking at her. "I'm so proud of you. Don't be ashamed of who you are. Not for any reason." Junior resumed feeding on his catch. She paused to see if any other feelings were projected her way. She felt terrible for making him feel bad about himself.

'Do not worry, Laura. He will be okay.'

Laura suddenly laughed and had silently hoped that nothing ever happened to CheeChee because she didn't think she'd be able to teach her children to hunt. Her friend must have picked up on what she was thinking because she felt happiness coming from her.

'You may have great difficulty raising them but I know you would try. That means a lot to me.'

That's when Laura noticed Connie moving between some trees some distance away. She obviously didn't know Laura was there, but it still looked like she was trying to sneak away. She couldn't imagine what was going through the woman's head. When Steven spoke of her he clearly thought she was crazy but she still couldn't believe that the woman wouldn't want to go home after living the way she did for several decades. She had to run in order to catch up to her. "Connie! Connie! Wait!" The woman stopped in some tall brush and looked Laura's way. As she got closer, she realized that Connie at least had the forethought to change her clothes and take some supplies. When Laura caught up to her, she stood in front of her trying to catch her breath. She silently chastised herself for being woefully out of shape and not being able to sprint fifty yards without being out of breath. She promised herself that now that she was completely healthy, she would start exercising regularly.

"What do you want?" Connie, the woman that the gremlins apparently referred to as 'Momma' looked at Laura with a child's confusion.

She really didn't have any experience with the woman and suddenly regretted her decision to follow her. She opted for the obvious. "Where are you going?"

"Home."

Laura knew she didn't mean Earth. "That's impossible. That's hundreds of miles away."

"I'll get there."

Laura hoped that her expression didn't convey what she was thinking. Because she was thinking 'this chick is

279

nuts.' She wanted to say anything that would make her come back inside long enough for O'Neil to reason with her. "If you wait, I'm sure Shelly would take you."

The woman turned away and began to walk again. "As I said, I will get there."

Laura followed her. She couldn't just let her leave. "Don't you want to see your son?"

"What would you know of my son?"

"O'Neil is my..."

Connie suddenly spun around. "Is your what?"

The woman was practically nose to nose with her. Laura's eyes went wide. "My surrogate father?" She said it like a question because she wasn't sure the woman would believe it. "Me and my brother, Kirk."

O'Neil suddenly appeared next to them, but he was facing the opposite way. He immediately turned around. At first, he looked amused but when he saw them his face changed to confusion. "What's going on?"

Laura and Connie looked at each other out of the corner of their eyes and then back to O'Neil. He was waiting for one of them to respond, but just as suddenly as he arrived, he disappeared. Laura waved her hand where O'Neil used to be but nothing was there. She didn't know why O'Neil just magically appeared before them, but she knew it must have something to do with Shelly and the teleporter. She decided that it wasn't important at the moment. "Look, I can't pretend I know anything about you or your situation. But don't you at least want to come back and...I don't know, record something for your son? I'm sure he's wondered about you all his life."

"Hey, Laura!"

She turned around to see Steven and Kirk a few yards behind her. She screamed with joy and ran towards them. She suddenly stopped when she remembered Connie. When she turned back, the woman was gone. Her disappointment was soon overtaken by joy. She ran into her brother's arms and they hugged each other tight. "I'm so sorry," she said through sobs.

Kirk let his head rest on the top of hers and a tear fell into her hair. "For what?"

"Being a brat."

He chuckled softly. "I'm the one that's sorry." He stepped back and looked down at her. He touched her chin briefly and took a deep breath. The weight of what he had done had finally dawned on her. He was willing to sacrifice his life for her. She thought that she had watched him die and he was only concerned about the needs of the one. Her. She burst into tears and Kirk hugged her again. He rubbed her back. "Ohhh, come on. It's okay!"

She talked through her tears with her voice a whiney octave or two higher than normal. "Don't ever do that again, Kirk!"

Kirk laughed as he squeezed her and released her. "Okay, I'll never save your life again, I promise."

O'Neil materialized in front of them. It was an odd and amazing thing to witness. The air in front of them got warmer and wavy like the heat rolling off of boiling water and suddenly...he stood before them. He held up some sort of gun with a needle on the end of it. All three of them just stared at him blankly. He nodded at Laura. "Where is she?"

"I don't know." She shrugged. "I tried to stop her."

"No worries. I'll find her." And he was gone again.

Laura took Steven's hand with one arm and hooked her other around Kirk's and they all walked back to Atlantis together. She couldn't help but wonder how the next few days would play out. She felt like she needed a few minutes to talk privately with all the important men in her life. She was beginning to realize that just because she merged with Steven days ago and knew who he was and what he wanted then, doesn't mean she knew what he wanted now. Even if they had been exactly the same after merging they started having different thoughts and experiences afterward. She needed to ask him what he wanted to do. She knew their lives would include his grandmother, Kirk, and probably O'Neil but when she thought about life on Earth, she didn't know what that meant anymore. Before she found herself on this fantastic adventure, she was a self-absorbed woman who never made any plans for the future. Why plan for the future when you were sure you weren't going to have one?

After they went inside, Kirk went off to find Sheldor so Laura pushed Steven down the hall and into their room. As soon as they were inside she pulled him over to the couch and pushed him down. He raised his hands and laughed. "Why are you being so violent?"

She climbed on his lap and kissed him. "You haven't seen violence from me."

He put his arms around her. "True. But you didn't bring me in here to jump me, did you?"

Laura smiled wickedly. "Yes, I did." She kissed him passionately and then scooted as close to him as humanly possible. "But maybe we could talk first?"

He shook his head and looked deeply into her eyes. He slipped one hand under her shirt and ran it up her bareback. He gave her a sly smile. "Just for future reference, you can't expect a man to chat while sitting on his..." He looked down, "Lap."

Her smile matched his as she raised her eyebrows at him. "No?"

He frowned and pondered for a moment. "Well, you can talk...but he won't be able to listen." He pulled her in close and kissed her then paused briefly to slip her shirt up and over her head. He suddenly grabbed her and stood up. She locked her legs around him and he walked her into the bedroom and gently put her down on the bed. As he climbed on top of her he whispered, "We can talk later."

It was an hour before 'later' finally came. Laura cuddled at Steven's side, happy and exhausted. She lightly traced hearts on his chest with the tip of her fingernail. She was beginning to realize that she didn't need Junior to make her feel high, Steven could do it easily. He was amazing.

He was softly moving his thumb back and forth on her arm while he stared up at the ceiling. She wondered what he was thinking. He breathed in suddenly and turned toward her, laying onto his side to look her in the eyes. She marveled at the fact that all he had to do was look at her and her heart would literally skip a beat. Just like the moon controlled the oceans of Earth, he controlled her heart. She was so happy that her eyes began to tear up. A tear rolled out of her eye and dripped off the side of her face onto the pillow.

His face was suddenly full of concern. He wiped a tear from beneath her other eye. "What's wrong?"

"Nothing," she smiled, "I'm just happy. I love you so much, Steven."

"I love you too." He kissed her lightly on the lips, but let them linger for a moment. He put his forehead against hers. "You want to stay here, don't you?"

"How did you know that? I didn't know it when we merged."

He smiled at her. "No, but you're as much of a sci-fi nut as your father was. You have so many questions that you want answers to."

Laura shook her head. "I know, but that doesn't mean..." She sat up and tried to reassure him.

He shushed her. "It's okay. It's okay."

"But your grandmother!"

"I already talked to Sheldor. He said we could go and then come back."

"But you hate this place," she said softly. She couldn't believe what she was hearing.

"But I love you." He kissed her again. "Besides, now that I know I can leave whenever I want, it doesn't seem so bad."

A giant smile ran across her face as she pounced on him. She pushed him back on the bed and climbed on top of him again. "I think I want to show you how violent I can be."

He feigned shock. "What?!"

* * *

O'Neil was on a mission. He spent the last thirty years wondering where Connie was, what she was doing, or if she was even alive. He knew that she had misgivings about being a wife and a mother, but he never believed that she would disappear the way she did. When he finally found out that her leaving wasn't voluntary, he was relieved. It meant that she wasn't the terrible, awful person that he thought she might be. What was her excuse that day? She took off without a word. No explanation. The two of them barely had the chance to talk at all. He showed her a few photos of Zander and his family but didn't go into too much detail about their lives or how hard it was to raise him alone as a single father in the Air Force. He wasn't going to take any chances. This time, he was going to know where she was at all times and he didn't care if she liked it or not.

Shelly was getting better with his pinpoint accuracy. O'Neil appeared right behind Connie. He had intended to sneak up behind her and shoot the chip into the back of her neck, but her time in the wild taught her a thing or two. She knew he was there almost before he did. She dropped Spike and then turned around swiftly and hit him in the stomach with a walking stick. O'Neil fell backwards onto the ground and held his stomach. The howler was a foot away from and growling fiercely. He knew he was in trouble. "Connie! It's me!"

Her demeanor instantly changed when she realized who she hit. "Andy! I'm so sorry!" She kneeled down next to him. "What are you doing here?"

O'Neil sat up and dropped his mouth open. "What are you doing here?"

Connie opened her arms. "Look at me, Andy. What would Zander think?"

He looked her over and grimaced. He nodded, agreeing with her. Her mouth alone would disgust anyone. "Shelly can fix all of that in two days." He shrugged. "Take a shower and run a comb through your hair..."

She sat down next to him. "And then what? How do I face him? What would I say?" He quickly picked up the device and popped her in the back of the neck with it. Her hand went to the back of her neck. "What was that? What did you do?"

"Look, Connie. We may not be together, but I'm not letting you go again. And if Zander wants to meet you, I intend to make that happen. So, you can either let Shelly do some work on you or you can meet him like this.

Either way, you can no longer disappear again." He got to his feet and held out his hand to her. "Are you going to come back with me, or not?"

"I guess I don't have much of a choice, do I?" She grabbed his hand and he pulled her to her feet.
"No, you don't." He pulled his phone out of his pants pocket and pressed a few buttons. He held it below his mouth. "Shelly, we're ready."

"Acknowledged."

For O'Neil, it was like he was the one staying in place and
the scenery around him changed. The forest around them disappeared and they reappeared on a platform in the command center inside Atlantis. Sheldor was standing behind a console and Kirk was standing next to him. He walked up to them smiling. "Welcome back. Looks like you still have all your parts." He nodded at the woman and held out his hand to her. "Hi, Connie. We haven't met. My name is Kirk."

She looked at his hand for a moment but eventually shook it. "Hi."

O'Neil smirked at Kirk. "Did you get your chip?"

"Yeah, I didn't think I needed one because I'm staying here...but Shelly clued me in on the benefits."

"You're staying here?"

Kirk played with some buttons on the console. "Yeah, for now."

287

"I am too," Connie chimed in.

O'Neil glanced at her. "That remains to be seen." He turned to the android. "Shelly, my friend here needs a checkup...and some teeth. If you don't mind."

Sheldor looked at the woman. "Certainly. Come with me,
please." Connie looked at Shelly as if he had two heads. He walked to the doorway and then turned around to wait for her. He motioned to the doorway. "Please," he said again.

Connie glanced at O'Neil for guidance. He nodded at her. "It's okay, Connie. He won't hurt you."

Connie and Sheldor left the room, leaving Kirk and O'Neil alone. The colonel put his hands in his pockets and exhaled loudly. "Are you sure about this?"

Kirk pointed to the console that he stood behind. "Let me show you something." Kirk put his hand on a small monitor and then lifted his hand at arm's length. He flipped his fingers away from him and a hologram appeared before them. It was a fierce hurricane. Kirk lifted his hand again and flicked it towards a monitor on the opposite wall. It came to life and showed a news broadcast of a category five hurricane that was closing in on the coast of Florida. The projected path would take it across the peninsula into the Gulf of Mexico, where it was expected to gain strength again before hitting New Orleans. It was estimated that it would cause billions of dollars in damage, not to mention, many lives.

"Jesus." O'Neil watched the monitor with growing concern reflecting in his dark eyes.

Kirk looked back down at his console. He didn't seem concerned at all. His fingers danced across the console. "Most of the time, what's everyone do? Batten down the hatches and get outta dodge... let the chips fall where they may." His hand suddenly hovered above the console and he smiled. "But now..." He placed his hand on the console and looked at the hologram of the hurricane. The spiral became unstable, wobbled, and then fell away into nothing. Kirk looked infinitely proud of himself. He folded his arms across his chest and smiled. "Now, we can stop it with a sonic wave just by pressing a few buttons."

"Aren't you afraid people will think the aliens did it?" O'Neil said, remembering how angry the android was at them for accidentally revealing themselves.

Kirk shrugged. "Hopefully, they'll think they just got lucky and thank their lucky stars that they aren't dead."

Barely two hours later, Penny and Ann stood on the platform waiting for them to flip the switch to send them back home. Kirk walked up to Penny and gave her his best smile. Her beautiful caramel cheeks glowed when she smiled back. He took her hand and brought it up to his lips and kissed it. "It's been fun, hot stuff." He winked at her.

She looked him up and down and a sly smile crept across her face. "Yeah, baby, it certainly has."

O'Neil stepped up to Ann to say his good-bye's. "I'll call you soon."

Her eyes lit up when he spoke to her. She grinned. "You better."

He looked back at the people in the room. They all pretended to do something else. He leaned in slowly to Ann, testing to see if she was receptive. When she smiled and tilted her head back slightly, he knew he had the green light. He kissed her softly on the lips. "Don't do anything I wouldn't do."
"I won't."

Kirk walked behind the console and poked at it. "Okay, as requested, I'm sending you guys to Ann's apartment because no one's in it." Without moving his head, he rolled his eyes upward to grin at them. "Happy trails to you." He hit the button and the two women shimmered and then faded away.

"I'm starting to feel a little bit like my namesake," Kirk said deadpan.

O'Neil laughed. "You don't say?"

* * *

Steven was nervous as hell. He stood in the entryway of his grandmother's duplex at the assisted living facility, wondering what the hell he was doing. It was a warm day, which he was grateful for because he had been standing there at least ten minutes. He was seriously regretting the fact that he asked Laura to stay behind. He looked down at himself and wondered if he looked okay. He wasn't sure about the status of his grandmother's house or any of his belongings so O'Neil offered to get him some clothes. Apparently, the only clothes the man owned that weren't Air Force uniforms were jeans and t-shirts. Steven wanted to look nice but he'd have to live with stonewashed jeans and a navy-blue t-shirt. They were a little baggy but he thought he looked pretty good. He stared at the door trying to decide what to tell his grandmother. He entertained several stories that were more plausible than the truth. He could tell her he was in jail, captured by terrorists, in a coma, or stranded on a deserted island. The last one was the closest to the truth, but not believable. He was relatively confident that his grandmother would know in her heart that he wouldn't disappear without a trace on purpose. Telling her the truth seemed like the best option. He suddenly became aware that someone was walking by the duplex. It was an elderly man and his dog.

The old man looked hard at Steven. "Can I help you, Sir?"

Steven looked back at the man and tried to smile. "No, thanks."

But the man didn't move on. He stood and watched Steven as if he was a thug hanging around the wrong neighborhood. He knew he no longer had the choice. He closed his eyes briefly and then knocked on the door. He jammed his hand in his pocket and held the device that would send him back to Atlantis once activated. He never wanted to press a button more in his entire life. The only thing the device actually did was send a signal to Sheldor notifying him that he would like to return. He heard someone approach the door and then he heard it unlock. He held his breath. The door opened slowly as a short gray-haired lady peered out at him. Suddenly the door swung open and there was his excited grandmother standing there with her hands pressed together as if in prayer.

She somehow seemed younger than she did five years ago. Her face was fuller and she had a little pink in her cheeks. Her eyes smiled and twinkled just as much as her mouth did. "Steven!" His dread turned into instant joy when he saw her smile. She opened her arms and he hugged her tight. "I knew it! I knew you'd come back one day!" She grabbed him by the arm and pulled him inside. "Come in! Tell me where you've been."

With those words the dread he was feeling crept back inside his mind. She took his hand and walked him into the living room. She insisted that he sit down and tell her where he'd been the last five years. The spotlight was on him. He felt as if he had a million eyes and ears on him. The ultimate stage fright. His head felt hot and he started to sweat. This was the woman who raised him as her own. If she disowned him, he'd be crushed. He hadn't said a word to her yet. He was mute again. The smile fell away from her face and was replaced with one of concern. "Steven? Are you alright?"

He looked at his hands. He could feel his eyes stinging. As soon as a tear formed at the corner of his eye, he wiped it away. "Grams, I'm so sorry."

"It's okay, Steven. Whatever it was that took you away from me...I'm just glad to have you back now."

Her words managed to relax him a little. He took a deep breath and exhaled. He needed to just stick with the truth. He told her how he left that day to go pick up her medication, but somehow ended up in a forest in the middle of nowhere. He didn't know how he got there and no matter which direction he walked in, he never found any signs of civilization. He told her that every night he was stalked by a pack of wild dogs that wanted to eat him and that he had to sleep in a tree. She listened quietly. He couldn't tell if the look on her face was doubt or concern, but he hoped that she believed at least part of what he was telling her. It was incredibly difficult for him but he explained in great detail how he learned to survive in the wilderness. "Believe it or not, I can catch a fish with my bare hands," he said holding his hands up. Her eyes began to shine with tears. He took a deep breath and continued. "I didn't talk to anyone in so long...I just stopped talking altogether."

Tears ran down her face. She dabbed them with a tissue. "How did you finally get out?"

It was time to talk about Laura and how she saved him even though he was a hairy caveman that never spoke. He was very careful not to mention things like big terrifying spiders or spaceships, but everything that he did tell her was one hundred percent true. "When she found me, I was a little messed up. She took care of me, Grams."

"It sounds like I owe her a debt of gratitude," she said smiling.

"I was afraid you wouldn't believe me."

She tilted her head to the side and smiled softly. "Steven, you know I could always tell when you're lying. Which means, I could always tell when you're telling the truth."

He leaned over and hugged her tight. "Grams, I missed you so much. I was so worried about you."

The two talked non-stop for the better part of an hour until Edwardo came home. At first, he questioned Steven's whereabouts for the last five years, but when he saw that his explanation was okay with his wife, Edwardo seemed fine with it too. The only time that his grandmother expressed concern was when Steven told her that he was in love with Laura and wanted to marry her.

"But Steven," she said, "you just met her a few days ago."

He nodded and then smiled so wide he thought his face would break. "I know. But it feels like I've known her all my life."

She looked genuinely excited. "Well, then...I can't wait to meet her!"

* * *

Shelly sat across from Kirk watching him select a fruit. He chose a large orange and immediately started to peel it. He glanced at O'Neil and then back to the android. Things seemed a little tense between them. He briefly shared a look with Laura, who was keeping herself busy while Steven was visiting his grandmother. She slowly shook her head and then rolled her eyes. He smiled.

"All I'm trying to say is that the United States military already knows about aliens and spaceships. We flew one up here, for crying out loud," O'Neil said throwing his hands up.

Shelly rolled an apple back and forth on the table.

Catching it with one hand and rolling it back to the other, back and forth. "Yes, but even your government isn't prepared to admit to its own citizens that aliens exist."

O'Neil fidgeted in his seat. "Look, you saw what Kirk did with the hurricane. He probably saved hundreds of lives. We could do so much good. Help so many people." He looked at Kirk silently expecting him to help.

"Don't look at me," Kirk shook his head. "I think maybe the tech should be leaked slowly over the next fifty years. Otherwise, you'll have nations fighting over the moon. There will literally be a war, O'Neil. World War III, and you know it."
O'Neil raised an eyebrow and nodded slightly. "Maybe you're right. So, how do we proceed?"

Shelly exaggerated a frown. "Carefully."

Kirk bit into an onion, crinkled his nose, and then nodded in appreciation. He talked with his mouth full. "Where the hell is Gene?" Both O'Neil and Kirk looked at Shelly.

"I have no idea."

"What do you mean, you have no idea?" Kirk dropped his mouth open, showing everyone a chunk of unchewed onion. "What about the little red dots?"

Laura laughed. "Little red dots?"

Shelly pointed at him. "If you're going to stay here, you

are going to have to stop saying things like that." He started tossing the apple from hand to hand. "He somehow managed to mask himself. I'm confident he is still here, somewhere." He suddenly stopped tossing the apple back and forth. A lightbulb obviously went off in his head. "Let's take a walk." All the men stood up to leave.

"Wait!" Laura bolted out of her chair. "What about Steven? What if he wants to come back?"

Kirk pointed at the flying orb as they left. "Twiggy will help you, won't you, Twiggy?"

"Yes, of course, Captain Rogers."

Sheldor knew there was only one place that would be able to shield Gene from the sensors, and that was aboard one of the ships. He led Kirk and O'Neil to the transport and they all got inside. They were soon in the hanger that the men landed in. They could tell right away which ship Gene must have been in because the ramp still protruded from the bottom. O'Neil and Kirk looked at each other and shrugged. They climbed aboard the spaceship and found Gene sitting at the console pressing some of the buttons. He got out of the chair so fast he almost fell down. "I'm not letting you teleport me!" Gene squeaked.

O'Neil put his hands up. "Relax, son. No one is gonna make you do anything you don't want to do."

Shelly felt annoyance bubbling up inside him. He wondered if his programming was malfunctioning or if it was perfectly normal. "While it is true that no one will force you to use the transporter, you will not be using this ship."

Gene quickly turned to the console and hit a few buttons. When Shelly realized what he was doing he lunged at him but Gene leaned over and hit one last button. O'Neil and Kirk grabbed Gene and pulled him away from the console, but it was too late. The ship lurched forward so quickly all four of them were thrown to the floor. The disturbance only lasted a minute. They all got up and looked around wondering what just happened. Kirk looked at the monitor behind Shelly and pointed. "Is that what I think it is?"

Shelly was instantly horrified. "Wormhole!" He again dove towards the console too late. The ship was sucked through the wormhole. The ship shook and the passengers were thrown about as if weight were a mere illusion. The sound of metal threatening to give way resounded through the ship. The shaking finally stopped and they stood up slowly. Shelly glared at Gene. "Well, that was unfortunate."

Kirk looked at the console. "Dude, for a few seconds I could see right through you. What the hell happened?"

Shelly turned to the monitor and looked at the readings. There was no sign of the wormhole. "Congratulations, Gene. We're now seventy-five hundred lightyears away from Earth."

"What?" All of them said it at once, but Kirk appeared more upset than the others. Shelly looked him in the eye. He knew Kirk was smart enough to figure it out. He rubbed his face with both of his hands. "Oh my god!"

He suddenly slapped Gene upside the head. "Do you realize what you've done?"

Gene ducked and covered for a moment and then stood back up. "I didn't mean to!"

"Will someone please clue me in?" O'Neil was utterly confused.

Shelly took a deep breath and let it out again and then clasped his hands together. "Thanks to Gene, the ship was sucked into an unstable wormhole and now that it's gone, it will take approximately one year for us to get back home at top speed."

Gene blinked a few times. It was obvious by the look on his face that he was questioning the validity of the android's words. "It took us only three hours to fly around the sun from the moon."

Shelly barely heard the boy. He was too busy trying to figure out if the spaceship had enough supplies to keep the three of them alive for one whole year. The ships were not meant for long distance travel. He quickly set the ship on the best course. "You assume travel would be in a straight line without obstacles. If you travel through a mountain by way of a tunnel, it significantly reduces travel time." He put his palm on the console and then lifted a hologram of space in front of them. He pointed to one spot and a tiny ship appeared. Looking through the hologram to the other side there were asteroid fields, black holes, supernovas, and dark spots with nothing in them. He pointed to the big blue marble in front of Gene. "As you can see, we have several formidable obstacles in our way."

Kirk examined a large blob of darkness in front of him. He pointed at it. "This doesn't look so bad."

"That, is the equivalent of a tar pit with little hope of escape. It is comprised of microscopic organisms that will breakdown and consume any object that comes in contact with it." Shelly looked from Gene to the others to gauge their reactions. All of them were somber. O'Neil pointed to Gene and then Kirk as he whispered to himself.

Kirk's eyes floated to the left when he noticed. "Whatcha doin' there, chief?"

"Just trying to figure out who is murder and who is suicide." O'Neil pointed to each of them again and then himself.

Shelly looked down at his console and pressed a few buttons. On his display was the colonel's current physical readings. His heart rate was regular and his breathing was steady so he dismissed what he said as a joke. "There is only enough food and water for two of you to survive the trip."

Both Kirk and O'Neil turn to Gene and then back. Shelly shook his head. He explained that there was one stasis unit on the ship and to make it fair each one of them would have to spend four months in stasis.

Kirk shook his head. "Forget about fair. I'm not going into stasis."

* * *

Laura couldn't wait to see Steven again. The more time that went by, the more she was afraid he would choose to stay on Earth. Each time those thoughts crept in she would remind herself that she knew where she could find him. There was no way she was going to let him get away. She smiled to herself as she leaned back in her chair. She was bored. Suddenly there was a jolt like a small earthquake. She sat up quickly with her eyes wide and her arms seeking balance. It stopped as soon as it started. She immediately turned to Twiggy. "What the hell was that?"

Twiggy's sensor turned until it faced her. "One of the ships exited the hanger at a dangerously high speed."

Her thoughts quickly went to Kirk. She tried to reach him telepathically but she couldn't sense him at all. She was angry and hurt all at the same time. Why would he just leave like that? Without a word? No nothing? She suddenly remembered Gene's refusal to use the teleporter. She had to assume that Kirk was taking his friend home in the spaceship and got a little carried away. "Was there any damage to Atlantis?"

The orb was silent for a few moments before answering. "The hanger suffered significant damage. The maintenance bots have already sealed off the area and have begun repairs."

"How many humans are left aboard the station?"

"One, besides you. The master, Connie," Twiggy said floating over to a monitor. A map appeared showing Atlantis and then Connie. She was over two hundred miles away.

"I guess she figured out how to get back to her children," Laura said with a grimace. She looked at all the equipment in the command center. She didn't understand any of it. "Twiggy, do whatever you can to find out what happened and where they went, okay?"

"As you wish," Twiggy agreed.

There was a soft tone so she turned toward the sound. It was the console for the teleporter. A light was flashing. An excited smile ran across her face. She got up and practically flew the four steps to the panel and placed her palm on the sensor while she looked at the teleporter pads. She watched him slowly appear as if he was nothing more than a multicolored fog. His form gained depth until he was fully formed and standing before her with a smile on his face. They ran into each other arms and held each other tight. She touched the side of his face and looked into his eyes and knew that his mind was finally at peace. She kissed him softly on the lips and then grabbed him by the hand. She smiled at him over her shoulder as she pulled him towards the door. "We're all alone." She winked at him.

"Well, then..." He rushed at her and swatted her on the ass. "We better take advantage of that."

She didn't think about her brother much that evening. She just enjoyed spending time with Steven. She was sleeping peacefully in his arms. Even in sleep, she had a happy smile on her face.

"Laura, we need to speak."

A female voice registered in the back of Laura's mind but she didn't know if she heard it with her ears or with her brain.

"Master Laura, I must give you my findings."

Laura breathed in sharply and sighed. She knew it was Twiggy without opening her eyes. She didn't want to move. She just wanted to stay exactly where she was. She suddenly remembered that she asked the floating orb to find out where her brother went. She opened her eyes and turned over to look at her. Instead of seeing a floating orb over her bed, there was a woman standing there. Fear shot through her as she sat up, grabbing the sheet to cover herself. "Who the hell are you!" she screamed.

The commotion woke Steven out of his slumber. He sat up and looked at Laura wondering what the problem was and then saw the woman standing next to their bed. "What's going on?"

"It is I, Twiggy." The woman was by all accounts, an amazon. She was at least six feet tall with an hourglass figure and long red hair. Her eyes managed to stand out the most. They were bright green and clashed superbly with the red of her hair.
Laura's eyes widened and her eyebrows shot up as she looked at Steven and then back to the woman. She thrust her arm out to her. "Twiggy...what the hell?"

The woman that claimed she was Twiggy held Laura's stare and then suddenly looked down at herself. She smoothed the fabric of her green dress downward. "This is the likeness of my original master's wife. I honor her. You don't like it?"

Laura tried hard not to show how confused she was. She knew that Sheldor seemed to have free will but she didn't think Twiggy was the same. "How?" She paused trying to think. "Why? What's going on?"

"You told me to do whatever I could to find out what happened to the master, Kirk." She cocked her head to the side and looked at Steven's chest.

Laura looked at Steven and then back to Twiggy. She snapped her fingers at her. "Twiggy!" When the woman looked at her, she continued, "and you for some reason needed a body?"

Twiggy nodded and smiled. "Yes. It is easier to fly a ship with a body." The new android explained that in order to find out what happened to Kirk and the others, she needed to fly one of the ships several lightyears past the sun to take some readings. What Twiggy said next was very upsetting. "The master, Kirk, and the others flew their ship through a wormhole that is no longer accessible. There is no way of knowing where they ended up."

It wasn't until days later when she finally came to terms with the fact that Kirk wasn't coming home. At least not anytime soon. She hoped that he and the others were okay, but there was no way of knowing for certain. She was worried sick about him. Steven had to almost constantly reassure her that if he was out there and alive, that he was trying to get home. Several weeks went by and CheeChee's daughters finally emerged from their egg sacs. Steven and Laura were sure to be present for the event. Just outside Atlantis in the forest, CheeChee made a large nursery for her young. It was as large as a house and made of her sticky white webbing. Laura watched Steven carefully choose his footsteps and she mimicked them exactly. She watched her friend settle in the middle of the nest and decided to position herself so she could see the large spider's back. CheeChee's daughters struggled to emerge from their sacs but eventually they broke free of it and crawled around on their mother's back. One of them in particular seemed to have more difficulty than the others and Laura wanted to help free it but CheeChee wouldn't allow it. She said that her young had to accomplish this task on their own. Seeing all of them explore their surroundings was fascinating to Laura. They didn't know whether to play with prey or eat it, but she was certain they would figure it out. The hardest part was going to be coming up with different and unique names for twelve girls. As she looked at them, she wondered exactly when she crossed from thinking the spiders were scary and disgusting to thinking they were cute and cuddly. Steven stood beside her, rubbing her back and watching the spiders play.

He leaned in close and spoke low. "Someday we're going to wake up and they're going to be eating us." He grinned down at her.

She hugged his arm close to her and laughed. "Yeah, I know."

* * *

Somewhere, in a nebula far, far away, Kirk stared through the glass of the cryogenic pod at Gene's face. He had been in there for weeks but Kirk still wanted to pull him out of there and beat the living daylights out of him. It was Gene's fault they were lightyears away from home. Kirk knew that he was afraid of using the transporter but the excuse wasn't good enough for him.

"Quit staring at Rottenbury and come eat," O'Neil called to him.

Kirk begrudgingly turned around and walked over to the couch and took a bowl out of O'Neil's hand and sat next to him. He shoveled a spoonful into his mouth. "I can't believe we have to eat cornmeal for a year."

"It's quite possible we could find a planet to harvest food from," Sheldor chimed in from behind them. "We will come to a promising one within three days."

Kirk smiled and then frowned. "It will be good to get out
and stretch my legs but...won't we be adding time to our journey?"

Sheldor had a disapproving look on his face. "Kirk, you're an Air Force captain, an engineer, and an astronaut wanna-be. Do you expect me to believe that you would rather pass up the opportunity to study something because you'd like to get home in one year instead of one year and ten days?"

Kirk knew the android was right. If they passed any interesting things along the way, he knew he would have to stop and investigate. He looked at O'Neil. He was looking at his cellphone. It displayed a picture of Ann on it. "I'm sure Laura told her..."
"Yeah, but how long do you think she'd wait?" He jammed his phone back into his pocket. "Shelly, how many movies did you say you had?"

"All of them."

O'Neil looked skeptical. "What do you want to watch?"

Kirk slapped his spoon down into his bowl and then put it on the table. "As long as it doesn't have 'star' or 'trek' in the title, I don't care."

O'Neil raised an eyebrow. "What about gate? Is gate okay?"

"As long as it isn't proceeded by 'star' sure."

"What about galaxy? Is galaxy okay?" O'Neil chuckled.

"Does it have 'star' or 'trek' in the title?"

"No, it does not." O'Neil shook his head.

"Then we're good."

The End

Ready to find out what happened to our heroes?

The Adventures of Kirk Rogers
The Kirk Rogers Series; Book Two – The continuing series finds Kirk and his friends stranded on an alien planet and tasked with rescuing a woman in stasis before a prince kills her and takes the crown. Rated PG13 for Language and Sexual Situations

Look for my other titles at:
Amazon.com, Createspace.com, & barnesandnoble.com.

The Link Between Us - After a mummified cavewoman was found deep in the permafrost of Siberia, an ancient virus was released that soon evolved half of mankind into vicious monsters that fed on anything that moved. When her son turned into a Link, it caused Kera to lose all hope but that didn't stop people from looking to her for direction and leadership. Taking refuge in a prison, she became The Warden. She found it very hard to adjust to the new normal and went on many dangerous missions hoping that she'd eventually be killed. As time went by and more was learned about the Links, Kera finally realized that losing her son didn't mean her life was over. Rated R for Adult Content/Violence/Sexual Situations.

Sarisart - When Laura Newman woke up in the morning that day, she had no plans to be kidnapped by a bunch of mercenaries, or being transported to another planet via wormhole...but that's what happened. Being the only woman amongst a dozen men, Laura finds herself drawn to one while trying to keep the others away. With very little hope of getting home, they must learn to get along and survive in a harsh environment. Rated R for Adult Content/Violence/Sexual Situations.

Melody's Penny - When Ian Murphy quit his job at the FBI to take care of his niece fulltime, he certainly didn't have any desire to meet someone new or fall in love. After his online gal pal disappears without a trace he is compelled to find her. (PG13)

Hollywood Games - After breaking up with a girlfriend who was only using him, the last thing on Orlando Baldwin's mind is finding new love. After all, being a big-time movie star isn't easy. His life takes an unexpected turn when he gets trapped in an elevator with a newbie screenwriter, Laura Jenkins. When they get caught in a compromising position their agents advise them to pretend to be in a relationship. They reluctantly do it to further their careers but things – of course – get complicated. PG13

C. J. Boyle
(985)248-9655 (text only)
https://twitter.com/C_J_Boyle

Printed in Great Britain
by Amazon